DURING THE 1920S AND 1930S, AROUND THE TIME OF THE Harlem Renaissance, more than a quarter of a million African-Americans settled in Harlem, creating what was described at the time as "a cosmopolitan Negro capital which exert[ed] an influence over Negroes everywhere."

Nowhere was this more evident than on West 138th and 139th Streets between what are now Adam Clayton Powell, Jr., and Frederick Douglass Boulevards, two blocks that came to be known as Strivers Row. These blocks attracted many of Harlem's African-American doctors, lawyers, and entertainers, among them Eubie Blake, Noble Sissle, and W. C. Handy, who were themselves striving to achieve America's middle-class dream.

With its mission of publishing quality African-American literature, Strivers Row emulates those "strivers," capturing that same spirit of hope, creativity, and promise.

ALSO BY **Y. BLAK MOORE**

Triple Take

the Apostles

Y. BLAK MOORE

STRIVERS ROW / ONE WORLD
Ballantine Books New York

the Apostles

Strivers Row
An imprint of One World
Published by The Random House Publishing Group

www.striversrowbooks.com

Library of Congress Cataloging-in-Publication Data

Moore, Y. Blak (Yanier Blak)
    The Apostles : their only religion was money, women, and power / by Y. Blak Moore.—1st trade pbk. ed.
        p. cm.
    ISBN 0-345-47570-4
    1. African American men—Fiction.   2. Adult child abuse victims—Fiction.   3. Ex-convicts—Fiction.   4. Gangs—Fiction. I. Title.

PS3613.O569A88 2004
813'.6—dc22   2004050093

Manufactured in the United States of America

First Edition: October 2004

9 8 7 6 5 4 3 2 1

Book design by Shubhani Sarkar

Dedicated to
my resurrection, Yanier Franklin Michael Moore.

To my flowers,
Cacharel and Ciara.

To my father and mother,
Franklin and Betty Moore,
both of you have shaped my life forever.

To my brothers,
Black Jamie and Lil Bryan,
I hope you have both found peace.

To all warriors who have lost their lives or freedom
in their quest for a rightful place in this society.

I don't glorify violence; I just don't pretend that it doesn't exist.

—Y. BLAK MOORE

the **Apostles**

"Turn on your stomach."

Silently the boy refused. His trembling brown frame was covered only by a pair of white briefs.

"Boy, you better turn yo motherfucking ass over now!"

Still the boy refused to obey. He knew that his submission was needed for his stepfather to attain the level of power over him that he craved, but he couldn't submit to the man's will.

His stepfather tried a different tack. "C'mon, boy. Take this shit like a man. You want to be man, don't you? Men take what's coming to them. So gone 'head and turn on over so that we can get this shit over with."

The boy shook his eight-year-old head.

His stepfather ran his hand over his straightened hair.

"Now that's what I'm talking about. That shit right there. I'm sick of this little no-talking role you be trying to play. I done heard you talk plenty when you be with them little niggers down there in the alley. You little slick bastards is always scheming up on something to get into. Now you want to sit here and act like you can't talk. That's some bullshit! Your mother wants me to make a man out of you, and I'll be damned if I don't!"

The boy already knew this beast couldn't make him into a man. He knew that a man wouldn't roll over and take a whupping. Not that he was scared of being beaten. That was nothing new. Before he died, his father had administered his fair share of those, but they were always tempered with love and understanding. This man had none of that in him. He wasn't trying to make him a better person as he claimed—he simply reveled in beating on someone who was powerless against him. More than anything in the world, Shawn missed his father. That quiet, strong man with the receding hairline and thick glasses was gone forever. He managed to make the newspapers on his way out though. An out-of-work construction worker who tried to rob a currency exchange and ended up on a slab in the morgue. Where was the justice in that?

Swack!

The first blow from the belt landed on his shoulder.

"You know you stole that two dollars out your teacher's desk drawer! Now you might as well turn over and take your whupping! You not opening your mouth is the same as lying. The only thing worse than a liar is a thief and you both."

Where was the justice in this? Shawn knew that he didn't steal the money. He knew who took it, but he would never tell; it just wasn't in him to snitch. And there was no way that he could make his teacher or this buffoon understand that after his father was killed trying to rob that place, he made a vow that he would never steal anything in his life.

Whap!

The boy writhed in pain from the lick, but he still refused to turn onto his belly.

"Boy, I said turn yo black ass over! I ain't gone tell you that shit no more!"

As his stepfather hollered these words six inches from his face, he could smell the potent mixture of malt liquor and cheap wine on his breath. He looked at his stepfather with disdain. This was the man whom his mother had chosen to love in his dead father's place. An unemployed cardboard box maker to replace an unemployed, dead construction worker. A man whose big dream was to buy a Cadillac with the money he was waiting to get from a settlement from the cardboard factory for a fraudulent back injury. This man who spent most *of his day sleeping in the bed that his father had bought. The sick bastard even dared to wear some of his father's old clothes.*

Whack!

The blow landed across his naked thighs. Its force made him scoot backward on the bed a bit and rub his thighs, but he didn't turn onto his stomach. Tears jumped into his eyes, but he willed himself not to release them.

Thwack!

The belt slapped across his arms and curled itself around to his bare back. Two large tears dropped from his eyes. A large welt rose instantly on his back and his small brown arms. The boy could hear the Commodores' "Zoom" playing in the living room. He knew it was his mother's favorite song. He liked the lyrics too. Some shit about "flying away." He also knew that his mother had turned the record player volume up so loud because she didn't want to hear him getting beaten. She would be sitting in the window seat with her favorite cup full of Thunderbird wine, listening to her favorite song while her husband beat the shit out of her only son. Later, much later, she would sneak into his room and tend to his wounds. She would rub his head, kiss him on the forehead, and beg him to try and get along with his stepfather. She would tell him how much she loved him and how one day soon she was going to take him and his younger twin sisters and leave this man.

"Little nigger, you better lay on your motherfucking stomach or I'm gone beat your ass just like that! That's yo damn problem now, you can't do what I tell you to do! You act like you slow or something! You little motherfucker, you just like yo punk ass daddy—a fucking thief. That's how he got his dumb ass killed, trying to steal somebody else's shit!"

Whack! Whack!

Two licks in quick succession. One landed on his shoulder, the other on his neck. This time he had to groan in pain. He closed his tear-filled eyes, balled his hands into fists, and pounded them into his thighs. He was angry with himself for allowing that groan to slip out.

"So you ain't gone lay down, huh? Well, that's okay, you little fucker. I'll beat yo ass just like that!"

"You,"

Whack!

"little,"

Whack!

"ungrateful,"

Whack!

"son of a bitch."

Whack!

"I,"

Whack!

"hate yo,"

Whack!

"black,"

Thwack!

"non-talking,"

Whack!

"ass!"

Inside Shawn screamed. He screamed for his dead father. He screamed for his mother to protect him. And he screamed for himself. But not a sound would he allow to cross his lips.

2

THE FIVE MEN WALKED INTO THE REAR ROOM OF THE CANDY store and video game parlor. They all took seats around the wooden table. The surface of the table was scarred with cigarette burns and the ancient carvings of men's and boys' names. There were no formalities among the old friends as they made themselves comfortable. There was plenty of trash talking and playful chiding in the group. Well, all of them except one.

Though Shawn "Solemn Shawn" Terson laughed lightly at some of the jokes, for the most part he preferred to nurse his Dr Pepper. He was dressed plainly, as was his custom—blue jeans, a black Mecca sweatshirt, and a pair of soft-bottom Kenneth Cole shoes.

Fresh from working out at Bally's gym, Dante "Tay" Thompson was attired in a black Ultrasuede Sean John jogging suit with a pair of all-white Air Force Ones on his feet. His average height was belied by his great physical strength, which was a huge source of pride for him. When it came to bench-pressing, Dante could hold his own with Big Ant, who was a hulking six-foot-three, two-hundred-ninety-pound chunk of darkness. The large round belly that Anthony "Big Ant" Hamilton sported often fooled men into thinking that he was weak, but in the end they found out that his arms and chest were as firm as his belly. Murderman and Mumps though, between the two of them, had never lifted a weight. Thomas "Mumps" Murphy believed that any kind of physical activity would mess up his perfect manicure. Sweating was against his religion, he would often say. Though he was proficient in most of the areas of ghetto vice, gambling was his passion—high-stakes gambling. Today he wore a milk white Coogi sweater with the matching hat. Coogi jeans and a pair of white Coogi tennis shoes completed his outfit. His top teeth were all platinum and a platinum link necklace with a diamond frosted crucifix hung around his neck.

As always, Michael "Murderman" Moore resembled a coiled, poisonous viper ready to strike at any moment. The man actually felt naked if he didn't have a gun on his person or at least close enough to get to at all times. He wore a black Adidas hooded sweatshirt with a pair of black Levi's 550 jeans. His feet were kicked up on the table and on them was a pair of white-and-black Adidas shell toes. His shoulder-length hair was braided into an intricate pattern. A pair of black Adidas baseball batting gloves hung out of the back pocket of his Levi's. Between the laughing and joking his head swiveled back and forth; he never truly let down his guard even among his friends.

On the other hand Big Ant was totally relaxed. The big man wore a coverall suit lacquered with oily stains and a well-worn pair of Timberland boots. His hair was in direct contrast to his unkempt clothes. It was neatly shaped into a short Afro with a chiseled goatee complementing his dark facial features. Laughter danced in his dark gray eyes as he joked with his friends. He looked over at Solemn Shawn and noticed him glance at his Kenneth Cole wristwatch.

"All right, c'mon, y'all, let's get on with this," Big Ant remarked, taking the hint from his friend. "I got to finish putting these tie-rods on this deuce and a quarter so I can get it to the pipe shop tomorrow."

Mumps commented, "Man, you bought another one of those raggedy old cars. Nigga, you need to stop being cheap and buy you some new shit."

"Mumbo, I can't fit in most of that new shit. Plus that computerized shit is built to self-destruct two to three years after you get it. The injectors go bad, them fucking computer sensors fry, and they all made of fiberglass. Now take my '74 Chevy or my '76 Bonneville. All steel, big engines, Holley carbs, Flomaster pipes, enough room for a big man and a bucket of chicken."

All of the men laughed, even Solemn Shawn. Rubbing his freshly faded head, Solemn Shawn silently agreed with Big Ant, but that was another matter for a different time.

"Settle down," Solemn Shawn said.

The group's eyes focused on their leader.

"Sorry about the tie-rods, Ant. This is pretty important. First order of business is your new phones. I got Tay to splurge and get the ones with the color screens and you can add cameras and stuff. Go pick them up from Drisell's shop. Everything's paid for so don't let that old dude try to slick a few bucks out of you."

Solemn Shawn continued. "We been doing this thing for close to twenty years. I'm thirty-three years old. I guess that I've come to a point in my life where I realize that this good run that we've had has got to come to an end one day. Police aren't getting any dumber, cats are snitching like never before, and they're making new laws every day to get rid of us. The odds are more and more in their favor. I've given it plenty of thought and I realize that one day soon I'm gone have to give this shit up."

"SS, you sound like you finta die or something," Mumps teased.

"It's nothing like that, Mumbo, I'm just tired. We haven't struggled like we have all these years to end up some has-beens. Our generation is dead. Locked up, doped up, cracked up, or dead. The young cats coming up behind us don't have any respect or understanding for the game. It's getting redundant."

"You right about that shit," Big Ant growled. "These fucking shorties ain't got no respect for shit. All they want to do is kick shit off, then do a drive-by. Then when they get caught, these little motherfuckers tell on everybody."

Murderman interjected, "All these young punks think that they killers. They want to air out the block and they want everybody to know that they did the shit. No-shooting niggas be hitting innocent kids and shit."

"That's that fucking rap music," Dante said. "Ever since niggas started all that killing on them fucking records, all of a sudden these fucking kids think it's a game to take somebody life. All they want to do is shoot guns, rock ice, and ride on dubs. But that's all they been seeing from every angle. They hearing it and seeing it in them damn videos. They ain't got no positive images."

Solemn Shawn contended, "I'm not going to get up on the pulpit, but I think it's up to us to show them some positive images. If we don't start trying to help the kids, they are going to keep heading down the wrong paths. We don't need another drug dealer, we need some pharmacists; we don't need another thug, we need an orthodontist, a stockbroker, a school counselor, a coach, a yacht captain, a world-class chef, a chess champion."

Murderman asked, "All the shorties want to be is the next Allen Iverson or the next Jigga. They don't see no glamour in that shit that you named. So how is you gone change they thinking?"

"I don't know if we can. But recently I was contacted by State Representative Coleman Washington. He dropped a little something in my ear about trying to build a community center."

"But we already got a community center, SS. That little joint on 71st Street," Mumps countered.

"That's true, Mumbo. But that one is small potatoes. It isn't accessible to anyone outside of that neighborhood. They have next to no funding and limited activities. It's stuck in the middle of rival gangs. Basically the place is ancient and off the beaten track. If you were a traveler and you were wounded, do you think that you would get help on a back-country road, or on a main thoroughfare? I would take my chances on that main street. The way this guy was talking it would be the mother of all community centers. All of the things that I've mentioned and more will be taught there."

The group was silent after Solemn Shawn's speech.

Murderman vocalized the group's fears. "SS, what you finta do? Disband the Apostles?"

"No, nothing like that, M1. This isn't some movie plot. I know the family won't be completely legal in five years."

Solemn Shawn's reference to Michael Corleone's line from *The Godfather* drew brief laughs from his crew. "No, it's just like I said. I'm tired of this shit. I not asking anyone else to be. That's just how I feel. This is kind of the last thing I want to do before I retire. I don't have the exact detail on just how much this thing is going to cost, but me and Dante will find that out when we meet with Washington. I know this type of thing isn't cheap, so we're going to need all the help that we can get. Any questions?"

"Yeah, SS, I got a question."

"Go ahead, Mumbo."

"Just why did the state rep come to you?"

"Money. It's that simple. Whereas he would have to wait on grants forever, he knows that we can get our hands on a couple hundred thousand in way less time. Question, Ant?"

"Yeah. It sound like we talking 'bout some crucial shit. Who gone run this joint? I know you don't think they gone give us jobs."

Solemn Shawn stood to his feet. "Well, from what I'm guessing and I may be wrong, it'll have a board of directors like any other major corporation. The board will be composed of a chairman that will probably be Washington, and whoever else he decides to hire. I might sound like an idealist, but I want to be a part of something like this. This is maybe the biggest thing that we'll do in our lifetimes. It won't make up for the wrongs that we've done, but I think that this place will make a difference in somebody's life. Now, I don't want to try and undertake something as great as this without all of you. If you're not all for this I'll leave it alone. But I've got to admit that I really want to do this."

Dante said, "Well, personally I know that most of us got kids and we want them to do better than we did in this shit. This sounds like the kind of place that can help make that shit a reality. Am I wrong, y'all?"

"I'm on board, y'all. I hope they got a gambling class," Mumps said.

"It's cool with me," Murderman announced.

"I got four shorties. Shid. You know my answer," Big Ant remarked.

Shawn was all smiles as he looked around the table at the coleaders of the Apostles. All along he knew that they would support any decision that he made to move the organization forward, but what he had in mind was on such a grand scale he didn't want to go ahead without all of their backing. These men had been with him during many of the Apostles' battles to survive, but this was outside of the usual sphere of ghetto survival. This was a conscious effort to make a future for the children. The future was something that no one who lived like they did cared to contemplate or discuss. The majority of the time life for Black men in the ghetto ended badly—bullets, selling and becoming addicted to illegal narcotics, and incarceration ended the dreams of many a young Black man. Maybe, just maybe, if this thing worked, it might save a new generation from that bleak future.

3

ODELL WALKER CROSSED THE STREET. HE WALKED SWIFTLY with his hands in his pants pockets. He kept his kinky head down as he scanned the sidewalk and street. In the six blocks that he traveled, the only thing he spotted of any interest was a Newport 100s box, which proved to be empty upon inspection. Though the March wind in Chicago was biting, Odell didn't notice. The twenty-dollar bill in his pants pocket clenched in his right fist created a shield around him that fought off the baby hawk of the Chicago spring. It had taken him most of the morning to earn that twenty bucks.

"Cheap bitch," he said to himself. He had to laugh at Mrs. Freeman, one of his mother's church cronies. Mrs. Freeman was a wily old bird. The crafty old gal had gotten a full day's work out of him by midmorning and only paid him a measly double sawbuck for all his labor. Plus she kept such a tight grip on her natty little coin purse that he never had an opportunity to maybe snake another twenty out of it. Somehow, she managed to keep him busy at all times—emptying garbage, sealing leaks in the garage roof, nailing banisters, sweeping the sidewalk and steps, and picking up the litter that gathered along the back gate in the alley. Only now did he notice just how much work she had managed to get out of him for a measly twenty singles. Yeah, he had to give it to Mrs. Freeman, she was good.

He knew the few odd jobs she gave him made her feel like she was doing her part to help stem the small crime wave that he'd become to feed his habit. No heavy stuff like armed robbery or home invasions, Odell preferred to stick to the small-time stuff. A little breaking and entering and some shoplifting, mostly petty thefts. It didn't take a genius to cipher that when you moved into the arena of peeling cars and stickups your life was easily forfeit. Any one of the young, vicious cats these days would leave you stinking with no hesitation, to stop you from making off with his whip. It was tempting, but Odell was no fool. He felt his life was worth more than a couple of sun-visor TVs or some twenty-inch rims. One day he was about to break the window of some young cat's Monte Carlo for a cell phone that was on the seat; just as he was looking around for something to bust the window, the owner of the car ran and jumped into the car with a chrome-plated Mossberg shotgun and peeled off. Boy, was he glad that he hadn't broken that window.

Odell skeeted a thin line of spit through the gap in his teeth as he crossed another street. The gap in his teeth was due to the absence of his right front tooth. He used his tongue to lick the breach in his smile. His gums had healed perfectly—almost like there was never a tooth there. As long as he lived, the space in his mouth would serve as a reminder never to steal from one of those little mom-and-pop stores. Especially not a mom and pop that had an ex–Golden Glove winner for a son and security guard. The son had snuck up on him while he was stuffing toothpaste and tooth-brushes into the waistband of his jogging pants. Without warning the guy rattled off a series of punches to Odell's face that made him lose control of his bladder. He tried to run, but he was already out on his feet. Spinning around he tried to grab onto one of the store's shelves for support, but his equilibrium was off and he missed the shelf by a mile, landing face-first in his own urine. After he suffered the indignity of losing a tooth and urinating on himself, the own-ers still had the nerve to summon the police.

The thought of the three months he had to spend in the county jail made him shudder, though he had to admit that he did gain some of his weight back. When he first got out, people said that he looked like his old self. His old self. He looked down at his dirty khakis. It wasn't so long ago that he used to wear nice clothes—back when he was a clerk for the Social Security Administration. That was only six years ago. Six long years of crack addiction. It had taken a little under two years for him to lose everything—typical substance abuser cliché. Smoke crack, lose job; smoke crack, lose apartment; smoke crack, stop paying car notes.

Odell looked up. He was nearing his destination; only a few more blocks. As he crossed a side street, he noticed a familiar insignia on the wall of an abandoned building. Someone had painted a six-foot-tall green *A*, adorned with a halo, on the crumbling edifice. That emblem meant different things to different people. To Odell it meant that he was on his way to satisfying the itch in his throat that indicated he needed a hit of some good crack. And some sex. He knew his girlfriend would be mad that he had been gone all morning, but when he came through the door with one of the Apostles' half-sixteenths she wouldn't trip too hard. He could have bought a couple of bags from the young dudes who hung out on the block—it would have been more convenient, but convenience is where the advantages of copping from them ran out. They couldn't fuck with the Apostles when it came to selling drugs. Those dudes were selling match heads of straight garbage and acting like they were doing you a favor by serving it to you. And if you complained, you could get your ass whupped. Those young cats loved treating the customers like they weren't shit. And then they always wondered why their profit margin was so low.

The Apostles didn't do business like that. They knew how to treat the customers. You didn't have to worry about being attacked without provocation. Things like selling dummy bags and sticking up customers were strictly prohibited on Apostle land.

Running his fingers over the double sawbuck in his pocket made Odell feel good. Fifteen, twenty minutes tops he would be back at his girlfriend's apartment with a twenty of that good yam. Her kids were at school so they would have the whole place to themselves. He would strip down to his boxers and make Monique do the same. It was always better like that. There was nothing in the world like some freaky sex while you were smoking some good crack.

That thought made him walk a little quicker, though he never stopped scanning the ground. Not once did he look behind him—only down and side to side. If he would have looked back he could have easily spotted the two detectives in the cream-colored Crown Victoria shadowing him. There was nothing discreet about the tail they had on Odell.

Gang Crimes Unit Detective Spenser "Grove" Hargrove was the driver. In the seat beside him sat Anthony "Bull" Thensen. The hefty detective wore a bored expression. Bull always looked bored. When his wife of seven years left him she attributed it to his jaded attitude about everything but police work. The only time that Grove had ever seen his partner animated was during one of the many "jump-outs" they performed during their stint in the Gang Crimes Unit. At those times Bull's eyes would take on an evil glint and he would even smile as they kicked in doors, conducted field interviews of suspected gang members, or gave chase to the "rabbits" who thought they could outrun a car and radios. Both of them loved being assigned to the GCU. Not only did it mean a pay raise, but it garnered a certain amount of notoriety in the department.

The GCU was assembled in the late '80s to try to stem the tide of crack cocaine, and slim the profit margins of the street gangs that were growing rich off the distribution of the controlled substance. The federal government allotted the city's government unheard-of sums to fund its private war on drugs—thus, the GCU was born. They were better equipped than the regular city cops, had a bigger budget, and had free rein to operate just within the laws of the land. Initially the unit was comprised of all white cops. They were sent into the heart of Chicago's ghettos with the mission of being the frontline warriors in the administration-sponsored war on drugs. Big mistake. Some of the good ole boys thought that they were down in the land of cotton the way they took to busting heads. Lack of direct supervision and the close-knit ties of the GCU made them as similar to a street gang as they could come without crossing over into blatant lawlessness. Under the advisement of the city's lawyers, the first Black mayor of Chicago decided to get a tighter rein on the Gang Crimes Unit. First he had to integrate the squad. Several high-profile wrongful-death lawsuits against the municipality involving members of the GCU gave the mayor the ammunition he needed. They would no longer be allowed to operate with impunity. The first Black and Hispanic officers who were assigned to the GCU were handpicked by a commission made up of civilians, politicians, and police officials. Bull and Grove were in the first batch of officers slated to join the GCU. They met all of the qualifications—hard-nosed, with questionable ethics, and Black.

Hargrove and Thensen took to their GCU assignments heartily and even turned out to be quite adept at working the streets. They could go where their white counterparts couldn't, plus neither of them was a stranger to the slums of Chicago.

It was Grove's idea to follow Odell. He didn't know the man personally, but he recognized him. He was just another one of the countless cluckers in the city. Since the beginning of their shift, they had been shaking down crackheads and dope fiends. Something big was brewing in Chicago's gangland and something big meant big money. Not that they were dirty cops, but hey, everybody took a little cream off the top of the bucket. It was considered one of the fringe benefits of being in the GCU. Payoffs were a thing of the past. Whenever you bumped into a large amount of illegal money you could take some, if you made sure that enough was logged in to evidence so that the case would stick. There were members of the GCU who grossed their yearly salary in a couple of drug house raids. Lucky bastards. The higher-ups turned their heads, knowing that the more money that was at stake, the harder the troops would work.

Grove and Bull were looking for a big payday today. Lately they had only had slim pickings. What they needed was a big bust. Some stash house apartment filled with money and drugs was the only thing that could satiate their appetites right now. They knew there was money to be had; they just had to find out where it was. Grove was confident they would be able to score. After all, the streets were full of people who were willing to tell on anybody, just so they wouldn't have to go jail.

Bull said, "Grove, slow this motherfucker down. You right on this nigga's ass. He gone fuck around and spot us."

Grove laughed. "This crackhead motherfucker wouldn't notice us if we was following him in a 747. He ain't looked up but one time since we been following him. He so busy looking on the damn ground, we could walk down the street behind him and he wouldn't notice us. Shit, he too busy doing the 'cop walk.' "

"The cop walk?"

"Yeah, when crackheads is about to cop some shit they got this walk. Hands jammed in the pocket, holding on to the money. Making sure they don't lose that shit. Shoulders all tense and shit. The look on they face be like, I hope these niggas is working. Walking all fast and shit. Hold up, this nigga is stopping."

Odell walked up to a youth leaning on a fence in the middle of the block. The Black youth was sporting a black Avirex jacket. On his head was a white do-rag covered with a black fitted baseball cap. A large *A* was emblazoned on his hat. Black baggy jeans and black Timberland boots completed the young gangster's outfit. Nonchalantly he leaned against the fence smoking a blunt.

"Is y'all working?" Odell asked the youth.

"Nall we ain't, but they is," the youth answered, blowing smoke past Odell. "Them fucking twisters in that Ford is working."

Odell looked down the block and spied the Crown Victoria for the first time.

"Fuck, where did they come from?"

"I don't know, homie, why don't you ask them. I'm outta here."

Calmly the young Apostle stepped inside the gate and walked down the concrete stairs leading into the gangway. Once he made it to the gangway, he grabbed the back of his pants to hold them up and broke out running.

"Fifty-one's, fifty-one's on the block!" he shouted as he disappeared into the alley between two garages.

"Damn, that fucking lookout peeped us," Bull said. "That's yo no-driving ass."

Not sure what to do, Odell stood in the middle of the block. As the youth dipped in the gangway he had felt his hopes dashed to the ground. There would be no half-sixteenth, not with the people sitting on the block. He decided to walk it off. He walked to the corner and looked for a stoop that he could chill on until the police left and the Apostles opened up shop again.

The detective car swooped down the block and came to a screeching halt in the street next to Odell. Almost before the car came to a complete stop, Bull was out of it and running toward the crackhead with his pistol brandished.

"Get yo fucking hands out of yo goddamn pockets!" Bull yelled.

Odell complied quickly.

Grove took his time joining his partner after seeing that he had the situation under complete control. He left the Crown Victoria in the middle of the street with its lights flashing. Walking straight up to Odell, Grove grabbed him by the collar, spun him around, and slammed him into the brick wall behind him. With the speed born of constant practice, he searched the trembling man. He took Odell's twenty-dollar bill and stuck it in his own pocket, then spun Odell around to face him.

"What's your name, shithead?" Grove inquired.

"Odell Walker, sir."

"What are you doing around here?"

"Nothing, sir. I was just out for a walk. I got into an argument with my girlfriend and I needed to take a long walk to cool down, sir."

Grove couldn't help but laugh. "That's a good one, ain't it, Bull?"

Bull's bored look had returned to his face. "It's all right. I've heard better. Really it sounds like this asshole is trying to be funny."

Grove grabbed Odell by the collar again. "Motherfucker, you ain't trying to be a comedian, is you?"

"No, sir."

"Bull, this motherfucker think he the next goddamn Chris Tucker, I think."

"No, sir. I wasn't trying to be funny, sir."

Grove pulled Odell in close. "Motherfucker, we know that you was finta cop a bag from that little bastard that ran. I've got your money."

Odell was unperturbed. "That's not true at all, sir. I just stopped to ask that guy for a cigarette. All of a sudden he just ran off. That's all it was."

With a wicked smile on his face, Grove released Odell's jacket. He smoothed out the wrinkled fabric with his hand. "Bull, you know what? I like this dude. Odell. It is Odell, right?"

Fearfully, Odell nodded.

"Odell, you seem like a smart enough dude. We can use a dude like you on the streets. Nothing big, just some extra eyes and ears for us. If not... Show him, Bull."

Bull reached into the pocket of his jacket and pulled out a sandwich bag full of dime bags of crack.

Grove never took his eyes off Odell. "That's about a fifty pack. Not a lot of shit, but if we put it on you and write in our report that we picked you up on school grounds, shit, that's six to forty-five easy if you've got any priors in your background. All we need you to do is tell us a few things."

"I don't know nothing," Odell pleaded. "Man, that type of shit could get me killed."

"C'mon now, Odell, nobody would know. Plus we could make it worth your while. Bull, throw me that bundle."

Bull tossed Grove the bag of crack. Grove untied the knot in the bag and pulled out ten dime bags. He tied the bag up and threw it back to Bull.

"See, Odell, I've been worried about the gangs around here. It's been too gotdamn quiet lately. We ain't really be having no chance to lock motherfuckers up. We want to know just what the hell these motherfuckers is up to. If it's something off the meter we'll make sure that we tighten you up for helping us out. Plus I'll consider it a personal favor and maybe one day I can return that favor. You know, if you get busted snatching purses or something I can be your get-out-of-jail-free card. Now if you decide not to help us . . ."

With a lightning-fast sucker punch to the midriff, Grove folded Odell up. The unlucky crack consumer fell to the ground holding his stomach. As he tried to suck some air back into his lungs, Grove stooped down beside him.

"Look, man. Don't think of it as being a snitch. It's more like you're doing your civil duty by cooperating with the police."

Grove rose. He laughed at Odell, as he removed a business card and the twenty-dollar bill from his pocket. He dropped the card and the bill by Odell's face on the concrete.

"Give us a call. Don't try and be cute neither, because if we don't hear from you, next time we kicking yo ass and locking you up." The detective laughed as he sprinkled the ten dime bags onto Odell. "Consider this a down payment."

Odell lay there as the gang crimes dicks pulled off. More than anything he was thankful that he didn't piss his pants when Grove hit him. That would have made the walk home a long, wet one. He rose up to a sitting position and collected his money, the business card, and the crack bags. By his foot was a half-smoked Kool cigarette. He reeled it in and scooted over so that his back was against the brick wall behind him. He lit the cigarette and it wasn't too stale, so he inhaled deeply. The card the GCU detectives had given him just might come in handy, he thought. It wouldn't hurt to keep his eyes and ears open. In the ghetto, information was a commodity.

Or maybe I just might sell them chumps a few dead ends, he thought.

Odell laughed as he pictured the two detectives kicking in the door of Mrs. Freeman's house because he'd sold them a bullshit lead. It would serve her right for being so goddamn cheap.

4

THIRTY-FOUR GANG MEMBERS STOOD SHOULDER TO SHOULDER in the small residential garage. The limited space was packed. Different aromas blended to make a collage of smells. There was the scent of motor oil, rubber, cigarette tobacco, the musty smell of rank armpits, and the stink of Wayne's sweat.

Of all the men and boys waiting for the proceedings to begin, Wayne was easily the most discomfited. Jokes were being cracked, cigarettes were being smoked, but Wayne just stood there, sweating. It wouldn't have taken a particularly astute observer to notice that he was terrified. The moment that he feared was at hand.

Wayne was a twenty-four-year-old member of the Governors, a street gang that forever lived in the shadow of the more organized Apostles. He had been a member for about five years. It all started as a way for him to sell his work and not be taxed by the wild young gangsters who ran his neighborhood. If you were a small-timer and not plugged with the gang from your set, you would never be able to make much money, plus you were vulnerable to robberies. If the gang that controlled your neighborhood didn't particularly care for you, they would let you work for a while to get things moving. Then they would push you out of your spot and take over. Your clientele would become their customers. The Governors were especially good at these hostile takeovers; they were parasitic by nature and cruel by design.

So far, Wayne had managed to stay one step ahead of them. He would participate in gang activities, but only enough so that he could squeak by without them noticing his lackluster performance. Or so he thought. Some of the higher-ranking members had noticed his lack of enthusiasm when it came to dealing with the gang he had claimed, but there was never enough evidence for them to pursue him. Wayne knew something had gone wrong though, when he was ordered to be at a special meeting. The young Governor named Cave who delivered the message was obviously strapped and he never let him out of his sight until they reached the garage.

Wayne knew by the way that the other members looked at him that some bullshit was about to jump off. That and the way Cave planted himself by the door and never moved again. Wayne hoped that this was some minor bullshit. He was used to them trying to get to him. The older cats were always trying to press charges against one of the younger brothers for breaking "Government Law." For small infractions you could pay a fine or get hit in the eye. Being punched in the eye was almost a badge of honor for the lower-grade Governors. To wear "Governor's glasses" meant that you were grimy enough to accept physical punishment over a monetary penalty. More serious violations of Government Law required stiffer penalties such as "crushing," which meant being beaten and stomped by your fellow gang members until the Head Governor halted it. The most serious penalty by far was the "Cold War." If Cold War was decreed upon you, no one in the gang could talk to you or have anything to do with you for an indefinite amount of time. Any property that you owned could be seized by another Governor and even if you were "brought in out of the cold," the members didn't have to return any property they'd taken from you. Cold War was something that all Governors feared. Being excommunicated meant social and perhaps even physical death. It was also extremely hard to get back into the Head Governor's good graces. Usually it took something as extreme as killing one of the Governors' enemies. You had to be able to prove that you had done the deed though, and that was where things could get hairy. The "State Department" still had to vote you back in and they were notorious for being hard on any member who wasn't part of their inner circle.

The inner circle was comprised of members who had been down since day one. The Governors were the brainchild of Vaton "Vee" Dawson, though it was patterned after the Apostles. In his teens while he was locked away in the St. Charles Boys Reformatory, Vee was a member of the Apostles; those days were responsible for the creation of the Governors. Vee considered himself in "God's grace," meaning he was a totally dedicated member of the Apostles, but no matter what he did, Solemn Shawn never gave him any real power in the gang. For some strange reason the quiet youth never trusted him as much as he trusted Dante or Murderman. Try as he might, Vee could never impress Solemn Shawn with his daring deeds and ruthless acts, and in fact Solemn Shawn would always tell him that he was needlessly cruel. Though he was a part of them, Vee secretly hated the Apostles, but he had made so many enemies trying to impress Solemn Shawn and his counsel, he knew that it meant certain death for him to disassociate himself from them while he was incarcerated.

Vee felt that Solemn Shawn was too soft. The way that the (then small) group of boys adored Solemn Shawn made him sick to his stomach. They wouldn't make a move without his approval and careful planning.

Upon his release from the juvenile prison, Vee hit the streets determined to take over the flourishing Apostles, but he soon found because of the revolving door of the juvenile jail system that Solemn Shawn's influence reached beyond the walls of St. Charles and was just as strong on the city streets. His task was a delicate one in the beginning: to try to usurp the throne of the Apostles without showing his hand. Try as he might, Vee couldn't shake the resolve of the members to wait for Solemn Shawn's release so that he could take his rightful place at the helm of the Apostles as a free man. Fearing the repercussions of his treasonous acts, Vee left the Apostles to start his own organization before Solemn Shawn's release. Though he made the offer of money, drugs, and positions of power in his newly formed organization as attractive as possible, he managed to convince only seven of the swelling membership of the Apostles to join him. He was disappointed at the dismal result of trying to split the Apostles, but he vowed to become a force that they would have to deal with someday. Over the years his gang had grown to roughly one thousand members, but the Apostles had surged to a couple of thousand members. They were all over the Windy City and had even branched out to surrounding midwestern and southern states.

Vee could only hope that one day the Governors would represent as much muscle on the street as the Apostles.

Vee rubbed his forehead and caused his white Cleveland Indians baseball cap to tilt backward, revealing his nappy braids. He straightened his cap and elbowed his way to the front of the circle. He stood directly across the circle from Wayne and smirked. Lately his members had been toeing the line, so there hadn't been much of a chance to pass down any punishment, physical or otherwise. But now the opportunity presented itself in the form of the terrified man standing across the circle from him.

Vee shook his head slightly as he grinned. He knew beforehand that it was going to go badly for Wayne. Of the eight men that made up the State Department of the Governors, the majority of them never cared too much for Wayne. As Head of State, Vee could have vetoed any decision that the State Department made, but there wasn't any danger of that happening, not when Wayne had one of the finest girls in the neighborhood as his woman.

Unconsciously Vee licked his lips as his mind brushed up against Wayne's girl's skin for the millionth time. Even her name was magic: Sakawa. Damn, that girl was bad. She had to be at least six feet tall, thick as a ghetto burger on white bread, and her skin was a reddish-brown hue. Her hair was black as a crow's feather and hung to the middle of her back. To top it all off, she was bow-legged as a cowboy, giving her the most carnal walk that Vee had ever had the pleasure of witnessing. He had an opportunity with her, but he managed to blow it by lying to her about staying home for the night, then getting caught in a dollar party hugged up with a hoodrat. He thought the little chickenhead that he was grinding would be some sure action, but out of nowhere Sakawa materialized in front of him. She only stayed long enough to let him know that she had seen him, then she left. No fussing or fighting. After that night she refused to hear anything that he had to say. He'd tried begging, buying her gifts, even threatening her, but nothing worked. Somehow, Wayne managed to come up with her and she'd been with him ever since.

"All right, everybody shut the fuck up and put out them squares!" Vee ordered.

The dull roar in the garage faded.

"Governors, we are gathered here to decide the fate of one Governor. First we got to display the charges against him. Governor Wayne, step to the middle."

Hoping that his knees wouldn't buckle and betray his fear, Wayne, stepped from among the ranks of his fellow Governors. In the middle of the circle he stood looking down at the oil stains on the concrete floor. At that exact moment, he wished that he could be like that oil and slide down the floor drain—anything to get the hell out of here in one piece.

Stay strong, he told himself. *They ain't got nothing on you. Ain't no way they could know what you did. Damn that Bull and Grove. Them two dicks could make a nigga's life straight hell.*

Vee announced, "Governor Wayne, the State Department has brought charges of treason against you. The same as all Governors you got the right to face yo accuser and his witnesses against you. Governor Bing, Governor Tonto, and Governor Toobie, step forward."

Three Governors stepped to the circle.

"Governor Bing, tell the Governors in this room the same shit that you told the State Department."

Bing cleared his throat. He was a tall boy, about six foot six. His slender frame moved with the grace of a ballet dancer and he walked on his toes. At his height and age of eighteen he should have been in somebody's school playing basketball, but he actually hated hooping. As a child his family forced him to play basketball because of his height. Under the advice of her friends, his mother dragged him to basketball camps, made him run drills and join any team that she could get him on. Never once did she ask him if he liked the game—that was irrelevant. Ironically he was good— real good. He had a post game and outside shot; he could run the floor with or without the ball, jump, rebound, and pass. The total package. The only problem was that he detested the game. Maybe not so much the game, but what it represented to his mother. To her, he wasn't James Bingham her son, he was a commodity. Despite her good-paying job in the mayor's office, his entire family dreamed of climbing out of the ghetto on his back as a superstar basketball player. They anticipated him going to the NBA after two years of college. They had everything planned for him, but Bing would prove them wrong. He decided to pay them back for all the things they wouldn't allow him to do as a child, because his mother feared that he might get injured and lose his basketball future. It was impossible to forgive his mother for all the time she made him spend running wind sprints, when all he really wanted to do was be at home playing with his Erector set. If his family would have taken the time to ask him, they would have found out that he really wanted to be an engineer. Two years ago in his junior year of high school, he grew tired of living for their dream and left home. Somehow he managed to graduate from high school. He decided not to play basketball in his senior year but even without a senior-year performance he was still of interest to several college basketball programs and they devoted a major portion of their recruiting efforts in his direction—to no avail.

Bing had grown up around the Governors so it was a natural thing for him to join them. He started off trying to serve a little crack here and there, but that proved to be too hectic for him. Maximum risk, often minimal payoffs. The girl he was dating at the time would always have some bomb-ass weed to smoke, so one day he cut into her and asked her where she got it from. She was the receptionist for a large construction company and the owner was her supplier. It took some fast talking, but Bing finally got his girl to agree to talk to her boss about making a purchase. Using his girl as a go-between, Bing soon scored his first pound of weed.

The weed was off the chain. The connection was friendly and reliable and made sure that everything flowed quickly and smoothly for him. Competition in the neighborhood was basically nonexistent on the weed side—everyone else sold crack or heroin. In a stroke of marketing genius, Bing packed the weed into little glass bottles instead of the customary coin bags or small Ziploc bags. Money came in hand over fist. Shit, everybody smoked weed. Dudes sold other drugs just to make money to buy that green shit. They were bringing him all the money and they would have kept right on bringing it, if it hadn't been for Wayne.

Bing shielded his eyes from the harsh light of the solitary, bare lightbulb. He was so tall that it was at eye level. "Governor Vee," Bing said, and jerked his thumb at Wayne, "this stud is a trick. He sent them gang crimes dicks Bull and Grove to my tip."

"No, I didn't," Wayne protested. "That's some bullshit. This nigga up in here lying and shit."

"Nigga, shut yo ass up," Vee ordered. "Don't interrupt these fucking proceedings again or Governor Tango gone hit you in yo eye."

Tango, a short, squat bulldog of a man, stepped forward. Wayne noticeably shifted around so that he could keep his eye on Tango. He did well to do so. Tango was a notorious eye shot artist.

Vee directed, "Go ahead, Bing." This was going exactly as Vee hoped it would. Again he licked his lips, already tasting Sakawa's secret delights.

"I was at my girl's crib breaking down the twenty pounds of weed I had just copped. I usually don't grab that much, but my connect told me that it would be dry for a minute, so I scraped together as much cabbage as I could and my man let me owe him some. Me and my girl was laying back bagging that shit up in quarter pounds, just smoking and chilling. I ain't know that Wayne had got bumped by Grove and Bull trying to serve some clucker a quarter onion."

Wayne wanted to protest, but a look at Tango's clenched fist made him hold his peace.

Vee asked, "How did Wayne know that you had that much shit? Do y'all do business or something?"

"Nall, I don't fuck with this stud like that. We was at the record store on 75th at the same time. That's where I get my weed bottles. He was copping some CDs and I was making a big order for weed bottles. When I asked for five thousand bottles that goofy-ass nigga behind the counter blurted that shit out loud and this nigga heard him. I had came up there in a livery cab so Wayne told me to let the cab go and he would drop me at the crib. He kept asking me what I needed with all them bottles. I played that shit off, but the nigga asked me to sell him an ounce of weed. I didn't want to, so I said I wanted two fifty for the shit and this nigga was like, 'cool.' I still didn't want to sell him shit, but I had just used all of my paper to pay for the weed and the bottles, so I was like, fuck it, I'll sell this nigga a onion. Wayne took me to the crib, I went and got the nigga a ounce, he hit me with the ends and bounced. The next day Bull and Grove was kicking in my girl's door. I had to jump out the second-floor window, but them studs put all that weed on my girl and locked her up. Now I need seventy-five hundred to reach for her before she start running her damn mouth. Now I ain't got shit because of this snitching-ass nigga. I should beat yo..."

Bing took a step toward Wayne, but Vee stopped him.

"Hold on, Governor, we'll get to all of that if this nigga is guilty. Governor Toobie and Tonto, what y'all got to say about this shit?"

The twin Governors took their places under the lightbulb. The identical twins could be told apart by their hair and Toobie's various body piercings and tattoos. Toobie wore his hair long, hot-combed straight and parted down the middle. Tonto, older by forty-six minutes, chose to wear bald fades. Caramel-colored skin drawn tightly over their thin, muscular frames completed their appearance. Both men were respected for their loyalty to the Governors, but their fellow gang members knew that loyalty was overshadowed by their love for each other.

As usual Tonto spoke first. "Me and Toobie was serving on the block when Wayne came out there. We had been copping some work from this nigga lately, so he be coming out there hollering at us. A clucker pulled up with some dude car she had beat for and she—"

Toobie jumped in, "Was talking about she just hit a lick on a pappy for his Lincoln and some ends. The broad was finta buy twenty dimes from us, but Wayne overheard her and snatched her up. He talked her out of buying the twenty sawbucks. He told her that he would give her two eightballs of yam for the two hundred. Wayne dipped and came back with the shit, then he got in the car with the bitch to serve her. Grove and Bull was pulling down the street and he didn't see them. Me and my brother got little through the gangway. The dicks hopped out on Wayne and the bitch. We ran through the gangway and up into the abandoned building right there on the block. Tell 'em, Tonto."

"We was in the building and up on the second floor; we could see the whole shit from the window. The dicks found that quarter onion on Wayne when they put him on the curb and made him take off his shoes. They cuffed this nigga and let the bitch go. When they was finta put him in the back of they car, Wayne was like, wait a minute let me holla at y'all. First they was acting like they didn't want to hear him, then they walked him into the gangway on the side of the building that we was up in. We couldn't hear everything, but we did hear Wayne telling them that he knew where a lot of weed was and who had the shit."

Toobie cut in, "Yeah, we even heard the twisters tell this nigga that he bet not be lying. They said that they was gone keep the yayo that they got off of him. And if they ran up in that crib and there wadn't no gang of weed up in there, they was gone be back to get him. We heard some sounds like they was whupping his ass and he was screaming like a bitch. Then the dicks came out the gangway and got in they car and left. This nigga came out a few minutes later and he was all dirty and shit and his jacket was ripped. We didn't know that they was talking about Bing or we would have wired him to the business. The next thing that we know the twisters was hitting his girl's tip."

Leaving Bing and Wayne in the middle of the hostile circle, the twins stepped back into the ranks.

Head down, with his hand cupping his chin, Vee asked, "So what happened, Wayne?"

"These niggas is lying," Wayne countered. Out of the corner of his eye he caught a blur of movement, but he wasn't quick enough to avoid Bing's right hand before it crashed into his jaw.

Quickly Bing followed the right to Wayne's jaw with an overhand left that landed on the bridge of his nose. Wayne melted to the concrete floor. Bing pounced on him and began slamming the defenseless man's head against the unyielding floor of the garage. The sickening thuds of skull meeting concrete could be heard distinctly in the garage as the Governors watched Bing beat Wayne unconscious.

Vee allowed Bing to have his way with Wayne for a few moments, then he motioned to Tango to restrain Bing. Tango needed the aid of several Governors to pull Bing off Wayne.

Wayne was in pretty bad shape. When he finally managed to get to his feet he seemed to be having a bitch of a time trying to stand in one spot. Blood flowed freely from a cut on the bridge of his nose and his right eye was swollen shut. An egg-sized lump could be seen on the back of his head.

Vee was pleased. "Wayne, Wayne, over here," Vee called, as he snapped his fingers. "Wayne, the case against you is fucked up, man. Do you have anything to say before I cast judgment on the charge of treason?"

Wayne protested, "But I didn't get a chance to say shit." He held his head back to try to stem the tide of blood from trickling onto his leather Phat Farm jacket.

"That shit is irrelevant. You been found guilty of treason. Does any Governor feel that the decision is wrong?"

Silence followed, which meant that none of the Governors present disputed Vee's decision.

"Wayne, you are now considered an enemy of the state for your treasonous acts. Treason against another Governor carries a maximum penalty of Cold War."

Wayne shuddered at the verdict.

"You gone pay for Governor Bing to get his lady out the County. Nigga, that new Buick Regal of yours, you can hand over the keys and the title. Any money or product you got, hand that shit over too. If you don't we gone fuck you up and if you try and go to the twisters on us, we gone snuff yo pussy ass."

Dazed at the quick verdict and still feeling the effects of the ass whupping that Bing gave him, Wayne stumbled backward. Vee nodded to Tango and the short Governor struck out. His blow landed with startling accuracy on Wayne's jaw. Wayne's jaw flapped loosely as he tried to talk, then he slumped to his knees—passed out from the pain.

Vee directed, "Bing, take Tango, Itchy, and the Twins. Grab this nigga and take him to his tip. Take everything. If his bitch home and she get in the way, then whup her ass too."

This was working out better than he could have ever planned it. If his Governors beat up Sakawa, who would she have to talk to but him. Sweet. It wouldn't be long now before she came running to him.

Watching his Governors dragging Wayne out of the garage door, he said, "After y'all take his shit, dump this nigga in the dog-shit basement where we be fighting the pits at. Make sure y'all piss on his trick ass, too."

The intensive care unit at the Cook County hospital was ancient, but clean. The ward had been sectioned off into dual bedrooms so its inhabitants could have a bit of privacy. Dr. Peterson directed his brown, beat-up Rockports to the third cubicle of the ward. He was followed closely by several new nurses and two interning doctors. The interning doctors were a blond-haired golden boy, top-of-his-class type and a young, red-haired, pinch-faced woman hiding her wandering eye behind a pair of almost masculine-looking eye-glasses.

With the nurses in their wake, the trio of doctors stopped out-side the third cubicle. Ceremoniously Dr. Peterson pulled a clip-board from the wall outside of the cubicle and flipped through the chart. With an air of arrogance he turned to the interns, seemingly ignoring the nurses.

In clipped tones he said, "This patient was brought in several days ago. A Wayne Maxwell. He was severely beaten. He suffered a badly broken jaw and severe brain trauma. He slipped into a coma, which is a normal finding when we are dealing with brain injuries. It's kind of like the brain shuts itself down for repairs. As of this morning his CAT shows his brain activity seems to have returned to near normal. Any questions so far?"

The redheaded woman doctor spoke up.

"Uh, Dr. Peterson, in your professional opinion what is the per-centage of patients who return to normal after these types of brain injuries?"

Dr. Peterson looked up from the chart and ran his eyes over the intern. She was a little homely with her compressed countenance, but her scarlet mane was definitely an eye-catcher. *I wonder if her pubes are fire red too,* he thought before answering. "You never can tell with injuries of this nature. Sometimes the patient experiences deficiencies in his motor skills, some memory loss, especially centered around the incident in which the trauma occurred. Other times they simply wake up as if from a deep sleep. Then still, we've had some who don't wake up at all. All we can do is hope for the best. There is still a lot that we don't know about the brain and its intricacies. Is everyone ready to have a look at the patient?"

"Yes, sir," the blond intern chirped. He was mad at himself that he hadn't asked such a question.

"All right then, let's have a look-see," Dr. Peterson said as he pulled back the curtain to enter the cubicle.

Wayne's bed was empty.

"That's funny," Dr. Peterson said as he peered at the chart in his hand. "It seems our illustrious friend is out and about. I didn't schedule him for any tests so he should be here. One of you please get the ward nurse."

The blond intern bolted before the pinch-faced intern could move. In his hurry he bumped into one of the new nurses, who made a kissing sound. The other nurses smothered their giggles as Dr. Peterson rejoined them in the ward hallway. A few seconds later the blond intern returned with a bored-looking, shapely Black nurse a few steps behind him.

The seasoned nurse gave the new nurses a knowing look as she brushed one of her long, brown-tipped dreadlocks from her face. "How can I help you, Doctor?" she asked with a note of impatience in her voice. "I'm shorthanded for the day and I have patients to attend to."

Dr. Peterson looked down his nose at her. "Nurse, I need to know what happened to my patient."

"What patient?"

"Wayne Maxwell. His chart doesn't have him listed to be anywhere else, but he isn't in his bed."

The nurse shoved past the doctor and walked into the cubicle. It was official—Wayne's bed was empty. She turned back to Dr. Peterson. "He was in here when my shift started this morning. I only had a moment to peek in on him, to check his vitals and everything, but he was here. He was awake and mumbling to himself when I checked his drip and took his vitals. He didn't even seem to notice me, just kept on mumbling to himself like I wasn't there. Everything was fine so I left. We don't have a lot of hands around here so I had to keep moving." She ran her pretty brown hands through her locks again. "Hold on."

She peeked into the small cupboard that served as a closet for the patient's clothes. "His clothes are gone. Looks like this guy took a walk." She strode out of the cubicle. "I'll have to alert security just in case he's wandering around the premises, but it looks like he may have DAMA'd himself."

Shaking his big head, Dr. Peterson wrote Discharged Against Medical Advice on the top sheet of the medical chart in his hand. "Okay, I've got a GSW two rooms down. Now this one won't be getting up and walking away even if he wants to. The bullet crushed several vertebrae causing irreparable damage to the spinal column. This way, ladies and gents . . ."

5

"Man, this motherfucka done had us waiting all day! Fuck this bougie-ass nigga, SS."

Solemn Shawn leaned over to his longtime friend and second-in-command and spoke calmly. "Stay cool, bruh. It's just a stall tactic. These politician cats like to play this game. It makes them feel important."

Dante wouldn't allow himself to be pacified that easily. "SS, I don't dig this country-ass shit. Man, we put this motherfucka on. Mr. State Representative wouldn't be shit without us. I knew that we shouldn't'a fucked with this stud when he came crawling to us when he was an alderman. Now that he a big-time state rep, we got to sit out here and twiddle our fucking thumbs while we wait for him to get around to us. What kind of bullshit is this?"

Solemn Shawn removed his Cartier eyeglasses from his face and held them up to the light. From his back pocket he produced a silk kerchief and used it to wipe the lenses of his spectacles. Satisfied that they were free of dust particles and debris, he returned them to his face.

"Look, Tay, this can't be helped. I know that we are responsible for this cat being in office and he knows it too. That's not what's important. What is important is that he honors our friendship. See, when some people get placed in these positions of supposed importance, they develop a case of what I like to call convenient, selective amnesia. I've seen it many times before. They just need their memories jogged, you know?"

Grumpily Dante grumbled, "Yeah, whatever, Solitaire, I know the fuck that I'm tired of waiting for this nigga."

Solemn Shawn was in total agreement with that statement. He looked at the overflowing magazine rack in the corner of the room. He walked over to it and chose a *Time* magazine from between copies of *Sports Illustrated* and *People*. Sitting with his legs crossed, he thumbed through the issue while Dante chose to wait in silence and fume.

Another fifteen minutes passed.

Solemn Shawn closed the magazine and calmly got to his feet. He walked over to the receptionist's desk. Leaning over slightly, he spoke quietly to the young man fielding the office's incoming calls.

"Look, man, it's almost three thirty. I've been here since two forty-five for a three-o'clock meeting."

The man lisped, "I am so sorry for the inconvenience, sir, but you have to realize that State Representative Washington is an extremely busy man. He has been informed that you are waiting, but at this moment he's taking an extremely important conference call from the capital, sir."

Dante left his seat and joined Solemn Shawn at the receptionist's desk. He arrived just in time for some spittle from the young man's pronunciation of "sir" to land on the back of his hand. Disgustedly he wiped the back of his hand on his pants.

"Damn, man, we asked for the news, not the weather," Dante said.

Solemn Shawn continued, "Call Washington again and let him know that Mr. Terson and associate are here to see him. Let him know that we've been very patient so far, but our patience is wearing thin."

"You got that shit right," Dante added.

"As a matter of fact, I want you to take that headset off, get up, and go tell him."

The receptionist started to object, but he sensed that the calm man meant business. He deserted the receptionist's booth and quickly walked over to the state representative's office door. He knocked softly twice and entered the office, careful to close the door behind him.

State Representative Coleman Washington was sitting behind his massive oaken desk. His attention was divided between the telephone receiver glued to his ear and a small pile of cocaine on a black saucer, so he didn't notice his receptionist enter the office.

He continued his conversation on the telephone. " . . . look out for me. You know that money been slow. All of this government mole shit got everybody scared to offer or take." Sniff, sniff. "I know, I know. Yeah, that's what I was just thinking. We got to go back to block grant hustling, but it got to be some good shit." Sniff, sniff. "I got a few irons in the fire with a couple of shady preachers. Okay, I can do that, but I need you to get the ball rolling on that thing that we talked about." Sniff.

Washington looked up and noticed his receptionist. Sniff. He held the mouthpiece of the telephone to his striped dress shirt. "What the fuck do you want?" he whispered fiercely.

"Uh, sir, I, uh . . ."

"Spit it out, boy. This here is an important call."

"Well, sir, there are two men. Uh, a Mr. Terson and party, and they are demanding to see you this very moment. They say that they've waited long enough and that—"

"I don't care who the hell they are. You tell them I said—"

Suddenly the office door opened and Solemn Shawn casually strolled into the office followed by Dante.

"Tell them you said what?" the gang leader asked calmly.

Washington grabbed the saucer of cocaine and slid it into his desk drawer. He plastered a shit-eating grin on his face. He said, "SS, how have you been? Sorry about the wait. Just give me a moment to finish this call and I'll be right with you. . . . Uh, I'm sorry about that, Senator. Where were we? Oh yeah, I need . . ."

Dante walked over to the desk and removed the telephone receiver from Washington's hand. Without so much as a word, he returned the receiver to its cradle and took a seat on the corner of Washington's desk. The state rep was made noticeably uncomfortable by the Apostle's proximity.

"Hold Washington's calls," Solemn Shawn said to the receptionist.

The young man backed out of the room with his hand to his throat and returned to the receptionist's booth. He pulled an organizer out of his backpack and made a quick notation in it. "Pile of cocaine on desk, snorting it. Visited by two thugs." Satisfied, he closed the organizer and returned it to his bag.

"Job security," he clucked as he placed the telephone headset on his head.

In the state rep's office, Washington was trying to get Dante off of the corner of his desk. "Dante, wouldn't you like a seat?"

"I've got a seat, Coleman," Dante replied nastily.

Beads of sweat began to form on Washington's balding pate. Trying to appear at ease, he crossed and recrossed his legs, taking care not to wrinkle his tailored slacks. His shirt began to develop wet stains under the arms.

Washington said, "Sorry about the wait, SS. I had to take that call. I'm trying to line up all the people I can behind that project I talked to you about."

Solemn Shawn asked, "Why did you have me waiting out there in the reception area like I was here begging for your help or something?"

"It wasn't like that, SS. I'm telling you I had to take that call. These guys are pretty important and they can get me the kind of financial backing we'll need to get over the hump."

Solemn Shawn waved his hand. "Quit bullshitting me. Roll up your right sleeve."

"Come on, that isn't necessary."

"Would you stop talking and roll up your sleeve."

Washington held on to the cuff of his sleeve like it was going to fly away if he released it. "That isn't necessary; I understand."

Still Solemn Shawn persisted. "I want you to *over*stand. Roll up your sleeve."

This time Washington was silent; his pleading was more in his eyes, but Solemn Shawn didn't back down. Slowly he unbuttoned the cuff of his shirt and rolled up the sleeve. He had to push it to get past his elbow. On his biceps was a three-inch *A* with a halo—the Apostles' insignia.

Surprised, Dante laughed. "Well, I'll be a one-eyed motherfucka. I forgot you got that on yo arm back in the Charles."

Washington didn't say anything, he simply stared at the badge on his arm as if it were foreign to him. To him, that tattoo was a reminder of places where he didn't ever want to live again, things that he didn't ever want to be a part of again.

"I hate to say it but now you seem to have forgotten where you came from," Shawn reprimanded. "You wouldn't be here today if it wasn't for the Apostles. You've forgotten that those dudes back in Charles were taking your food every day and that they wanted to take your manhood. You seem to have forgotten all of the things we did on your behalf during your campaign."

Washington protested, "But I never asked you for help."

"You didn't have to, Coleman. You are our brother and regardless of what you may think, we wouldn't jeopardize that relationship. And you asked for my help on this one and I wouldn't refuse an Apostle any reasonable request."

Washington protested, "I'm the one taking all the risk by coming to you. You and I both know that over the years you've been involved with many illegal things. If who you are got out and that you were here now, the media would have a field day with this. They would crucify me. You know that they love to hang politicians out to dry. Especially Black ones."

Solemn Shawn didn't bite. "Really, you're insulting your own intelligence. You know as well as me that over the years as a politician you've done just as much dirt. Just of the legal kind. If you felt that meeting with me would jeopardize your career you wouldn't have me here now. You're not really an angel anyway. I'll be the first one to admit that if you stop looking for payoffs, and stop shoveling coke into your nose, you could truly be an asset to your people and community. All of that said, tell me what you're looking for from us to build this center."

Coleman Washington retreated into politician mode. "I'll tell you first that everything has got to be free to the people. It has to be a place where kids can go besides the streets. I want everything in this place. Swimming pool, full gym, state-of-the-art exercise equipment. Health and nutrition courses, accredited college courses, job program, trades. In short, everything we deem necessary to help heal our wounded community."

"I see," Solemn Shawn said, tenting his hands under his chin. "And just what stage are you at in the planning of this place?"

"First, I got my alderman cronies together to help us with the zoning and the building permits. Second, the place will cost about five million to build. I've got some people who will furnish the equipment. Hell, the Bears are donating a state-of-the-art fitness center in the place. The only problem we're experiencing is getting people to throw their hats in the ring initially. I mean . . . sure, people will donate after the fact, but we need cash to even fence off the land we're hoping that you're going to donate to this project."

Solemn Shawn began to speak, but Washington wasn't listening. He was too busy working the numbers in his head. He thought, *If I could get those dummies to give me at least $300,000, with the other people I have on the line I could come in with a few thousand more than $5 million. The contractors already told me they can do the job for $4.75 million. With the right amount of maneuvering I can keep the change. I'll call in Monty to crunch the numbers, then . . .*

Solemn Shawn's voice woke him from his thoughts. "Coleman, what's up, man? Give me a number."

"Well, you already know that we're going to need that lot of land," Coleman said, as he reached for his Rolodex. "That plus three hundred thousand dollars should get this thing off the ground."

"Done," Solemn Shawn said as he stood up. "We'll smooth out the details later. I'll be in touch."

Dante vacated his perch on the state rep's desk, walked over to the office door, and opened it for Shawn.

Coleman was already busy dialing a number on the telephone. He looked up at his retreating guests.

"SS, I'll make sure that I get you a copy of the plans as soon as possible."

"I'll be looking forward to going over them too. I'll make sure the deed to that land is dropped off here."

"Oh, and please don't leave it with the receptionist. Tell whoever is going to bring it to put it in my hands only."

"Will do, Mr. State Rep."

The two gang members exited the office and the building. Outside they climbed into Dante's new Maxima.

Dante spoke first. "It sounds like that joker is gone get right down to the fucking business, SS."

"I knew that he would," Shawn said.

"How?"

"Human nature."

"What?"

"Human nature, its tendencies and mercies. The man is a politician and a drug addict. That means he always needs publicity and money. He can use this project to easily win his reelection bid, and he's going to skim some money off the top. Personally I don't care. It's just that I really like the concept of the place he's trying to build."

For maybe the millionth time in his friendship with the quiet, well-spoken man beside him, Dante looked at him in awe. The man's mind and thought patterns never ceased to amaze him. Shaking his head, Dante put the key in the ignition and gave it a turn. Instantly it came to life. The mellow sounds of Main Ingredient filled the cabin as Dante pulled into traffic.

6

The boy bolted out of the doors of the Jewel's Food Store. He ran the four blocks to his home with his plastic Jewel's bag rippling in the wind behind him. The bag held a pound and a half of ground sirloin and a package of Twinkies to share with his younger twin sisters. The late-afternoon sun beamed onto the side of his caramel-colored face as he ran. His stride was easy and carefree.

At the age of fourteen the boy was of average size, but being a veteran of his stepfather's school of hard knocks, he was already tough as nails.

On the block of his home, the crowded two-bedroom apartment where he lived, the boy cut through the gangway and came out in the alley. He walked down the alley until he reached the garbage cans behind his building. From behind the foul-smelling cans he pulled his school books. After dusting off the knees of his pants, he easily vaulted over the four-foot chain-link fence surrounding the yard. The minute that the boy's feet touched the ground a blur of fur streaked out of the half-broken garage door. The blur streaked directly for him. Three feet from the boy the German shepherd stopped and bared its fangs. A menacing growl rose from its throat.

The boy stood face-to-face with the dog for a moment, then he whistled an intricate little melody. Instantly the dog's aggressiveness subsided. It bounded over to the boy and excitedly licked his hand. The dog literally danced in circles around the boy. A large smile, rather uncommon for the stoic youth, covered his face as he looked down at his dog. He hugged the wolf-looking canine and received a face full of wet dog kisses in return.

"Hey, girl," he whispered in the dog's large pointed ears, "did you miss me, girl? I know you ain't trying to act funny. Look what I got for you."

The boy held his grocery bag in front of the dog's moist, pointed snout. The dog sniffed the irresistible scent of the raw beef into her nostrils. Her already wagging tail sped up to near Mach speed. Her tongue lolled out of her mouth as she danced a jig in anticipation of her dinner.

There was a large stainless steel bowl by the wall of the garage. The boy walked over to it. He split the plastic wrapping on the meat package and dumped the contents into the bowl. The large dog almost knocked him over getting to the delicacy.

As she chomped, smacked, and licked her way through the meal, the boy stroked her coarse tan-and-gray fur. In a matter of seconds the entire meal was gone.

"You sure love that burger meat, huh, girl," the boy said as he scratched his friend's chest. "You ate it all. If I ate like that I would bust."

The dog cocked her head to the side and listened to her master. It was rare that the boy talked, so it always surprised the dog when he did.

Until dusk the boy remained in the backyard with his dog—petting her, training her, and playing with her. The boy knew from the disappearing sun that it was time to go inside. His good-byes to his friend were said more with his eyes than with words. The dog whimpered a bit as he began to retreat up the back porch stairs, then she turned and disappeared into the garage.

Inside the apartment the boy sat at the kitchen table and finished his homework. He helped his younger twin sisters with their assignments, then gave them their Twinkies. Dinner was quick, followed by television sitcoms until his mother declared that it was time to bathe and go to bed.

. . .

In the middle of night the boy awakened to the shouting of his mother and stepfather.

His stepfather shouted, "Let me the fuck go, Lillian! I don't give a fuck! I'm gone kill this motherfucker. This motherfucker done bit me!"

The boy heard his mother's high-pitched voice: "That dog didn't mean it, she was just protecting the house! Yo dumb ass came through the back way all drunk and shit. She thought yo ass was a goddamn burglar or something!"

"That motherfucking dog is stupid as fuck just like her dumb-ass master! That little quiet-ass nigga done taught that mutt to hate me! The dumb-ass mutt ain't even got no damn name! What kind of shit is that? That shiteater wanna bite me, huh? I got something for that ass!"

The boy sat up in his narrow bunk bed. The plain blue sheet slipped from his bare chest. He heard sounds of a struggle in the kitchen, followed by the crashing of what the boy knew had to be the porcelain cookie jar from the top of the refrigerator. He heard the screen door slam, then heavy steps on the creaky stairs of the back porch. Silence followed the footsteps. Then he heard his dog's throaty growl.

Five gunshots ripped through the night.

The heavy footsteps returned to the stairs. The screen door opened, then banged shut.

Again his mother's voice: "You didn't have to do that to that damn dog!"

"Shut the fuck up talking to me, Lillian! I done warned that boy that if that dog ever got out of pocket with me, I was gone kill it! It was a goddamn sooner anyway! The sooner off it got dead, the better off it is! I just put that motherfucker out of its misery!"

The boy's stepfather laughed at his own crude joke.

As his stepfather's laughter echoed ominously through his head, the boy slid out of bed. Careful not to wake his gently snoring baby sisters, he slipped into a T-shirt and pulled a pair of well-worn

Patrick Ewing sneakers onto his feet. His jogging pants made a slight rustle as he left the bedroom and headed for the kitchen. As he darkened the doorway of the kitchen his mother looked up at him. Across the table from her, his stepfather stared at him with a smug look on his face. His .38 revolver was on the kitchen counter.

"Go back to bed, Shawn," his mother said.

He ignored her as he pushed open the screen door and stepped onto the back porch. After his eyes adjusted to the darkness, he spotted the still form of his dog lying in the grass. He walked down the stairs and over to his furry friend. There were three immediately noticeable bullet wounds in his dog. Blood pumped furiously from the bullet holes. His friend was still breathing, shallow and labored, but breathing nonetheless. Tears began to crowd up in the boy's eyes. As he knelt on the grass, slick with his dog's blood, the floodgates to his soul opened up at seeing his friend in death's vestibule.

The dog recognized its master and began to whimper. The boy lifted the shepherd's head into his lap. Its pink tongue lapped desperately at the boy's face. A shudder passed through the dog's fur—it couldn't fend off the arctic temperature of death. The whimper subsided and her tongue ceased caressing the boy's face.

Using the back of his hand the boy wiped his face of the tears. By doing so he smeared the dog's blood onto his countenance. Gently he removed the dog's head from his lap. He climbed to his feet and walked into the garage. Amid brooms, rakes, and a snow shovel he found a large spade. In the middle of the yard the boy dug a grave. The tears streaming from his eyes turned the dirt and dog's blood on his face into a gruesome concoction.

Finally he was satisfied with the depth of the hole and climbed out of it. He knelt by his dog and scooped its limp body into his arms. The dog's head lolled to the side; the tongue escaped from between her frozen fangs. Gently he placed the dog in the grave. For a moment he stood on the lip of the open grave with his head bowed as he whispered a silent prayer for his friend. Unceremoniously he began to fill in the grave. When all of the displaced dirt covered his friend, he packed the dirt down with the back of the spade. Methodically he retraced his steps to the garage and returned the spade. He removed a tire iron from the hood of his stepfather's ruined hulk of an automobile. With meaningful strides he crossed the backyard and climbed the porch stairs. On the porch he paused and peeked through the screen door.

His stepfather was alone at the kitchen table. A dingy white T-shirt splattered with blood was crumpled on the linoleum floor. He was slumped down in the wooden chair, his chest and beer belly heaving as he snored.

The boy eased the screen door open, hoping that he wouldn't hear the telltale squeak of its old spring. Using his free hand he guided the screen door closed. Silently he stole across the floor and picked up his stepfather's pistol from the kitchen counter. Noiselessly he slid the pistol into his pocket. Spinning on his heels, the boy turned and walked until he was standing directly in front of his snoring stepfather.

"Wake up," the boy whispered harshly.

At the sound of the boy's voice, his stepfather awakened from his drunken slumber. He sat up straight in his chair trying to focus his sleep-logged red eyes. When the boy, covered in blood and dirt and clutching the tire iron, came into focus in front of him, his stepfather's eyes almost bugged out of his head. Terror shone in his eyes, through the inflammation lent by the alcohol. He looked at the boy's face and what he found there wasn't good. The boy's eyes were clear, but hard—no softness anywhere in them. Blood, dirt, and tears had transformed the boy's face into a primordial mask of some long-forgotten warrior tribe. Out of the corner of his eye he scanned the kitchen counter for his gun. It wasn't there.

He threatened, "Young nigga, you better get the fuck out from over me! Pussy-ass nigga, what the fuck you got that in yo hand for like you finta take care of some business! What the fuck, am I s'posed to be scared or something!"

The boy said, "You don't have to be."

"You bet to take yo punk ass to bed somewhere, before I stomp a mudknot out yo ass! Standing up here like you crazy or something. Nigga, you's a bitch just like yo bitch made-ass papa. I should take that tire iron from you and stick it up yo ass!"

He sat back and folded his arms across his bare chest, waiting to see if his bluff had worked—it hadn't. And he didn't have to wait long to find out just how much he grossly underestimated the boy's capabilities and his love for his dog.

Swinging the tire iron in a downward arc the boy crashed it into his stepfather's skull. Clunk. His stepfather spilled out of the chair onto the floor. The boy pounced on him; his stepfather screamed and tried to cover his head. In a blood frenzy the boy beat meaty patches out of his stepfather's head and flailing arms. Even when the man passed out the boy didn't stop whaling on him with the tire iron.

Somewhere in the fog of his bloodthirsty mind he could hear his mother's voice. "Hurry up! He's in the kitchen, he's killing my husband! Please, officers, stop him, he killing my husband."

7

BEZO STOOD BEHIND THE CANDY COUNTER. EXHAUSTED, HE mopped his forehead with the long sleeve of his shirt. He was the game room manager and today had been a long day, filled with noisy kids, loud rap music blaring from the CD jukebox, and petty arguments between the video game players. There was never any major commotion in here, maybe a few squabbles over who had the next game or quarters, but that was it. The neighborhood kids and the gangbangers alike knew this was his nephew Solemn Shawn's place and that any interruptions of business would be handled accordingly.

Affectionately known as "A-Land," the game room was a safe haven for the neighborhood kids; the Apostles treated the place like it was hallowed ground. No guns, drugs, or any contraband were allowed on the premises.

All day long Bezo doled out candy and potato chips, changed dollars into quarters, and kept the patrons from tearing up the games. His old buddy Jimmy Johnson kept the place clean. For a few bucks and a warm bed in the storeroom, the less than cordial rummy made sure that the arcade stayed spotless. The kids sure kept old Jimmy on his toes. They were always playing jokes on him. He claimed that he hated them all, but Bezo knew that Jimmy loved being there around all that young life. Plus the money he earned helped supplement his Social Security. It wasn't hard work, but at least he could be proud of the job that he was doing. His daily routine: sweep, complain, then take a sip from the eternal half-pint of Dimitri's gin in his back pocket.

Bezo looked at his old friend now, napping on two milk crates over by the pool tables. From beneath the candy counter, he pulled a bottle of cranberry juice. The red juice was spiked with Absolut vodka. He took a decent sip of the concoction and returned it to the bottom shelf—right next to the loaded Army Colt .45. It was an old pistol, but trustworthy. The belt of vodka warmed his stomach as it worked its magic. He shimmied a little to express the liquid enjoyment in his belly. As he was doing his little dance, the door of the game room was flung inward. Bezo raised his head to curse out the culprit who opened the door so roughly, but when he saw who it was, the expletives froze on his tongue.

Gang Crimes Detectives Bull and Grove stood framed in the doorway. Slowly they entered the room, making sure that everyone felt their presence. One young Apostle was so absorbed by the rap music blaring from the jukebox that he didn't notice the two detectives. His back was to them as he used the directional buttons on the jukebox to flip through the CD covers. An Oakland A's hat, the Apostles' trademark, sat on the boy's head at a rakish angle.

Grove walked up behind the youth and slapped his hat off of his head. Fired up, the youth wheeled, ready to attack, but when he saw the dangerous detective, the wind left his sails. Smoldering, he stared down at the toes of his Air Force Ones.

"Pick it up, Apostle, or should I say Asshole," Grove taunted the teenage thug.

The youth didn't move.

Grove took a step closer and placed his hand on the left side of the boy's chest. The teenager's heart was rioting in his rib cage.

Grove snarled, "You scared, huh? Yo tough ass is scared like a bitch. Tough-ass Apostle, pick up yo hat!"

"Nope," the youth mumbled.

Laughing, Grove turned to Bull. "This little fake thug must got some damn sense. He knew that I was gone kick him a new shit hole as soon as he tried to pick up that hat."

Bull was silent, his bored look plastered on his face.

Grove turned back to the kid. "Get lost, asshole!" he told him.

The youth sauntered out of the game room, leaving his baseball cap behind on the floor. Casually the duo made their way through the game room, similarly bothering the rest of the clientele. Bezo had to almost chomp down on his tongue not to say anything to the pair of men. He busied himself wiping the already spotless candy counter. Bull kicked the bottom crate from under Jimmy's sleeping form, causing the man to fall onto his behind.

Damn, I don't need this shit, Bezo thought. *Faggot-ass gang cops know that they can get on my fucking nerves with this bullshit.*

After harassing the entire cast of teenagers and young adults in the room the two men stood in front of the candy counter. Bull reached over and picked up a Twix candy bar. He opened the golden wrapper and broke one of the chocolate-covered cookie bars. He tossed it into his mouth. His partner walked over to the refrigerator behind the candy counter and opened it. He stood in the cool cavern for a moment before selecting an ice-cold plastic bottle of Code Red Mountain Dew.

Bezo waited with his arms folded.

Grove cracked open his soda pop and took a long swig.

Bezo waited—he knew it was coming.

"You really should try these new Dews, Bull. This shit is tight."

"Too much caffeine," Bull grunted.

"I don't give a fuck, I need some caffeine. What about you, Bezo, do you like these new Mountain Dews?"

Bezo said, "No, I don't, sir. I don't drink pop. It rots the teeth and kills the kidney."

Grove laughed. "You hear this nigga, Bull? I bet this nigga done drunk him a pint of vodka already today. And here he is talking about the dangers of drinking soda pop."

Bezo protested, "It ain't illegal."

"Bull, did anybody say anything about anything being illegal?" Still crunching his candy bar, Bull shook his head.

Grove belched. "Sounds like you guilty 'bout something. Whatever it is, we really don't have the time to beat a confession out of you. We just want you to pass on a message for us, Bernard. You tell Solemn Shawn that we want to talk to him."

"Hold on now," Bezo said. "I don't know where Shawn is or how to get him no message. So you really wasting yo time."

Grove snapped, "You little ex–dope fiend, ex-convict, drunk bitch! You better stop playing with us! We ain't got no time for yo bullshit! Nigga, you know how to get in touch with that mother-fucker! I bet if I put a pack on yo ass you would get in touch with him to bond yo funky ass out the county!" Grove pulled a business card from the inside pocket of his leather jacket. He tossed it on the countertop. "You get that card to him and tell him that I said he better get in touch with me. You motherfucka, I should..." He raised his hand as if to strike the shopkeeper.

Bezo didn't flinch. The cold, unyielding stare that he afforded Grove withered the detective's attempt to terrorize him.

The detective lowered his hand. "Motherfucka, I better hear from yo boss. Let's go, Bull."

Grove walked from behind the candy counter and headed for the door. Bull followed him, but not before grabbing another Twix.

If the two detectives had left the game room a few minutes earlier, they would've noticed the young Apostle they'd harassed leaning against their unmarked police unit. They also would have seen him open the gas tank door on the Crown Victoria's rear flank and unscrew the gas cap. From his pocket he produced two Snickers candy bars, which he stuffed through the little metal trapdoor in the gas tank neck. He screwed the gas cap back on and closed the gas tank door. With his hands in his pockets, the youth walked away humming the lyrics to 50 Cent's "Wanksta."

8

IT WAS SATURDAY NIGHT AND CHARLENE'S COOL CORNER WAS packed. Charlene's catered exclusively to the twenty-five-and-over crowd—no jeans, gym shoes, or baseball caps allowed. Bodies filled the dance floor and along the bar, and there was a line of people outside waiting to get in. The lights from the elaborate lighting system cut multicolored swatches through thick cigarette smoke. Scantily clad women braved the chill of the Chicago April night as they dashed from their cars in the parking lot to the lounge's entryway. In the DJ booth, a heavyset disc jockey with a mouth full of gold teeth made the crowd roar as he mixed cut after cut.

Tonight the VIP section was ruled by the Apostles. Solemn Shawn, Murderman, Big Ant, and a few other Apostles sat with a group of women enjoying themselves. Two almost impossibly huge bouncers warded off strays trying to join the VIP crowd. Without a nod from Shawn or one of the other heads it was impossible to enter this section of the lounge. Champagne and Rémy Martin cognac flowed like water as the revelers toasted the highlight of the weekend: Saturday night.

A young man walked through the crowd. The pair of dark glasses perched on his face did nothing to disguise his disfigured jaw. Courageously or foolishly he walked straight up to the bouncers guarding Solemn Shawn and his crowd and tried to push past them.

"Hold up, chief," the bouncer on the right said.

Wayne tried to ignore him.

The bouncer on the left put his large hand on Wayne's chest. "Nigga, I know the music ain't that loud! My partner told you to hold the fuck up!"

Impatiently, Wayne hissed through his teeth, "I need to talk to Solemn Shawn."

The two bouncers could barely understand him.

The bouncer on the right asked, "Man, what the fuck did you say?"

"I need to talk to Solemn Shawn," Wayne repeated.

"What's wrong with yo mouth, homie?" the bouncer on the left asked.

Unashamed, Wayne parted his lips to let the bouncers see the wires and rubber bands in his mouth holding his jaws together.

The bouncer on the right cracked, "Damn, mello, I don't know how you make it through no metal detector."

Wayne was not amused. "Nigga ain't shit funny," he hissed. With his Nike baseball glove–covered hands he lowered his sunglasses and let the bouncers get a glimpse of his eyes. A large blood clot circled his right pupil, giving him an evil look. "I'm trying to talk to the boss. I ain't got no time to be playing with the hired help, nigga. Now take me to him."

"All right, homie," the bouncer said, "get yo arms up." Thoroughly he searched Wayne's person. Satisfied that the man wasn't holding heat he told Wayne to follow him through the velvet rope. Ten feet from Shawn's table the bouncer stopped Wayne's progress. "Chill right here, homie. I'mma let the man know that you want to holler at him."

The bouncer mindlessly flexed his chest muscles in his tight, silver lamé shirt as he walked over to the gang leader's table.

"What's up, SS," he thundered as he reached over the table to shake Shawn's hand.

"How you feeling, Big Toby?" Shawn inquired.

"I'm cool, bro. Uh, this stud here want to have a sit-down with you."

"Is he on our team?"

"To tell you the truth, SS, I ain't never seen this stud before today. Somebody done gave this dude a punkinhead. His jaw broke up pretty bad."

Murderman leaned past the girl sitting between him and Shawn. "SS, that nigga is a Governor, one of them studs off of 71st Street. He fuck with Ditto's cousin, broad with a Indian name or something."

Solemn Shawn looked over at Wayne. "What this cat want with me?"

Murderman shrugged. "I don't know, but the Governors pushed on this nigga. They say that he a trick. They came through Ditto's cousin crib on some guerrilla shit and took all of this nigga shit. Disrespected her and shit."

Solemn Shawn looked at his old friend with admiration. Murderman's knowledge of underground events was unrivaled—he was like the CIA of street gangs.

"So how do you know all of that?" he asked.

"Ditto was telling me about the shit," Murderman answered with a smirk.

Solemn Shawn turned from his friend with a hint of a smile on his face. "I don't even want to know, Double M. Toby, tell the dude to come sit down and have a drink with us. It should be interesting to find out what my old friend Vee is up to."

Toby walked over to Wayne. He said a few words to him, then returned to his post. Wayne walked up to Solemn Shawn's table. Murderman stood up.

"Ladies, give us a minute," Shawn told the three women sitting at the table, who then excused themselves from the booth. "Have a seat, my man," Solemn Shawn told Wayne.

Wayne slid into the booth and Murderman sat on Wayne's right.

Solemn Shawn said, "You know who we are, but we don't know who you are."

"The name is Insane Wayne and I want some of y'all champagne." Without waiting for Shawn to reply, Wayne grabbed the ice-cold bottle of Moët from the ice bucket and poured himself a glass. To drink it, he had to hold his head back and pour the liquid through his wired teeth. A fourth of the glass wound up on the front of his shirt, but Wayne didn't seem to notice.

Solemn Shawn cut his eyes at Murderman; his friend returned his gaze.

Solemn Shawn asked, "Insane Wayne, huh? What is it that you want with me?"

Bluntly Wayne stated, "I want to be a Apostle."

"Why?" was the only thing Solemn Shawn could think to ask, still put off by Wayne's appearance.

"'Cause you niggas take care of y'all own. I don't see all that hating on each other shit going on between you studs."

A yell from the crowd made Solemn Shawn turn to the dance floor. At first he thought it was a fight or something, but then he saw a young lady getting especially loose on the dance floor. She had taken off her shirt and was going through a series of raunchy moves. He could tell by the glazed look in her eyes that alcohol or some other intoxicant had swept her up into the music thumping from the concert speakers at each end of the dance floor. A fellow who must have been her man or a friend stopped her before she could get her bra off. The irate man dragged her off the dance floor while the crowd groaned. He held up his middle finger as an answer to them.

Solemn Shawn turned back to Murderman and nodded his head.

Murderman snarled, "Nigga, what about the Governors?"

Wayne slammed his gloved hands down on the table, almost toppling the flickering candle in its middle. "Fuck the motherfuckin' Governors! Them niggas is the reason that my damn mouth is fucked up now! Fuck that bitch Vee!"

"Calm down," Solemn Shawn cautioned.

Murderman said menacingly, "Yeah, nigga, you better calm yo ass down!"

Sensing the malevolence in Murderman's voice, Solemn Shawn said, "Chill, Double M." To Wayne he said, "I take it that something transpired between you and the Governors."

Wayne answered evasively, "Just some bullshit." He reached for the champagne bottle again.

Murderman grabbed his hand and stopped Wayne from lifting the bottle. "Playboy, I ain't seent you drop no scratch while you trying to drink up all the champy."

From behind his shades Wayne stared at Murderman. He shrugged his hand free. Through his clenched teeth he said, "Dude, I came here to talk to Solemn Shawn. Now I don't know if you his bodyguard or his send-off man, but you need to keep your fucking hands off of me, pimp."

Murderman's face flushed. Before Shawn could stop him, his .44 Bulldog was under Wayne's chin. He snatched Wayne's glasses from his face. Angrily he spat, "Bitch-ass, trick-ass, dick-licking Governor! Nigga, I should make you lose yo memory right now! Who the fuck do you think you talking to? Pussy-ass nigga, you ain't gone never be no Apostle! We don't accept tricks or pancakes. And, nigga, you both! We know about you, bitch! You told on a nigga, now they done broke yo mouthpiece and you want to flip Apostle! Nigga, they should have cut yo fuckin' tongue out of yo mouth! Now if you don't get the fuck out of here, I'mma personally see to it that yo ass is in Gatlings by the morning!"

Wayne calmly asked, "So, Solemn Shawn, is that y'all final answer?"

"I would have to say that I echo his sentiments. I apologize, but we are not currently accepting any new members with questionable references. Murderman, chill with that heater."

Slowly Murderman lowered the pistol, but he didn't put it away. He stood up and allowed Wayne to slide out of the booth.

Wayne stood in front of the booth and stared at Shawn.

He said, "You motherfuckers is gone regret this shit. Bitch-ass Apostles!" Adding insult to injury, Wayne picked up the champagne bottle and walked away with it. With a sneer on his fractured mouth he walked out of the VIP section and out of the lounge. The bouncers started toward him, but Solemn Shawn waved them off.

In Insane Wayne's wake Murderman began to follow.

"Double M," Shawn called, "don't merc him. We don't need any more pressure than usual from the pigs."

Murderman smiled. "I ain't gone bite him, I'm just gone let my dog bark at him for all of that wolfin' he just did."

Halfway down the block from the lounge, Wayne was walking and sipping from the Moët bottle. He seemed to be holding a conversation with himself.

Suddenly the night exploded.

Blam, blam, blam, blam, blam, blam.

Like nothing had happened, Wayne kept on strolling, sipping champagne, and talking to himself.

Amazed, Murderman watched him walk to the corner, then turn and keep going. As he slipped his empty pistol into his pocket he thought, *Damn, that nigga really is insane.*

9

"STOP CALLING MY MOTHERFUCKIN' HOUSE!" SAKAWA SHOUTED into the telephone receiver, then slammed it into its cradle.

"Girl, who was that?" China Doll asked.

"Mind yo damn business, China Doll. And watch them damn blunt ashes on my couch, bitch!"

Nonchalantly, China brushed the blunt ashes onto the beige carpet. She said, "Bitch, ain't nobody finta burn yo little shit. And don't change the damn subject—who was that you just cussed out?" Holding the blunt in her ridiculously long, fake fingernails, China Doll took another hit of the weed. "This shit is some headache weed. Ain't been no good shit around here since Bing stopped working."

Sakawa was cross. "Bitch, I wish you would stop coming over here smoking that stanking shit in my damn house. I hate the smell of that shit. It be all in my clothes and hair."

"Saki, you is really bullshitting. When Wayne used to smoke all day in this motherfucker you didn't have shit to say."

"Wayne was my motherfuckin' man. You ain't my man, China."

A sly smile crossed China Doll's lips. She slit her almond-shaped eyes for a moment as she thought about the misfortune that had befallen the high-and-mighty Sakawa James. The Governors' robbing and damn near beating Wayne to death served her friend right. Shit, if Sakawa knew that Wayne used to give her money and try to fuck her on a regular basis she would flip. She decided to rub it in a little.

"You know what, Saki? I seen that nigga Wayne. Girl, he was talking to hisself with his mouth all wired up and shit. When I spoke to him I called him Wayne. He was like, 'Bitch, my name is Insane Wayne.' He scared the shit out of me. Them niggas must've fucked up some shit in his head when they beat him down. I hate the Governors."

Viciously, Sakawa retorted, "If you hate them so much, then why did you fuck so many of them?"

China tossed the blunt duck into the blown-glass ashtray on the coffee table. "I don't know what you talking about."

Sakawa laughed. "Bitch, stop lying. You know that they call you GP—Governor pussy."

China was unruffled as she flattened out her cherry-cola-dyed weave ponytail. She pulled off her camel leather, high-heeled boots and swung her legs over the arm of the sofa. Her Baby Phat pants fit like a second layer of skin. "I don't care. Motherfuckas can say what they want to say. They just be hating on a bad bitch like me. I bet can't none of the broke-ass niggas that be hustling packs say they hit this shit. As long as them niggas keeping paying for that new Altima parked downstairs, putting Prada on my feet, and putting Armani Exchange and Iceberg on my ass they can call me Governor pussy. All of us ain't as fortunate as you."

"What you mean by that shit?"

China rolled her eyes to the ceiling as she twirled a few pieces of weave around her finger. "Shit, we all ain't lucky enough to have a man like Wayne. That nigga gave you everything. He was a good man."

"China Doll, what you know about a good man? You give them some pussy so fast that you never find out if the nigga good or not."

"Whatever, bitch," China Doll said. She knew that she had struck pay dirt. Sakawa was pissed about her comments about

Wayne. She decided that it was time to change the subject before Sakawa made her leave. The weed she'd smoked had made her lazy and the couch was comfortable—she definitely didn't feel like going home. "How you been though, Saki? You know, since Wayne been gone."

For a short moment Sakawa's anger subsided. She sighed. "My fault for snapping you up like that, China Doll. It's just that since Wayne been gone that nigga Vee been trying to holla at me. He stop me on the street. He be calling all the damn time. Shit. That was him I just hung up on. I don't even know how that nigga got my number."

China knew—she had given him the telephone number for a hundred and fifty dollars. She tried to get him up to two hundred, but he wouldn't go for it.

Smoothing her shirt down, China said, "Girl, what's the problem? Shit, Wayne ain't got nothing. That nigga is fuckin' nuts. He ain't coming back, Saki. His ass gone be in Tinley Park, if anything, wearing one of those coats that make you hug yo'self. Is you trying to get that crazy nigga back?"

Disgusted, Sakawa replied, "Hell, nall, girl! I would love to spit in his fucking face. That nigga took my damn car and I ain't seen him since. That was about three weeks ago. I ain't tripping though—he bought it. I hope his ass die in a flaming car wreck!"

Both women laughed.

"What's wrong with Vee, girl? That nigga is the Head Governor. Shit, you was going with one of the soldiers. What is you thinking about?"

"Ain't nobody thinking about Vee. That nigga had his chance back a while ago, but he wanted to fuck with a hoodrat. I can't have that shit. At least if a nigga gone creep on his girl, he should get big—not little. I caught that nigga hugged up with some underage, baldhead, dirty little hood booger."

"Girl, if I had a man with as much paper as Vee, I wouldn't give a fuck what he did. Shit, I would help that nigga get some pussy, just keep my car note paid, and minutes on my cell phone. I would let that nigga . . ."

Sakawa drifted off into her own world, ignoring China. She thought, *Vee is the damn reason that my fucking man is out of his damn mind. Things used to be perfect with me and Wayne.* She thought of the engagement ring in her dresser drawer with the two-carat heart-shaped diamond. *We was gone get married and move to Atlanta and open up a business or two. Them niggas took the money we had saved up for our house. Wayne was ready to retire and have kids. Shit, I knew that everything was going too perfect. Now because of Vee I'm right back where I started—broke and looking for a way out of the damn ghetto. And this high-ass bitch sitting over here talking about I should holla at Vee. Shit, Vee already owe me. Wait a minute, that's right. That motherfucka do owe me. She said it, Wayne was just a soldier, Vee the damn general. I can take way more from that nigga than they took from Wayne. That nigga stupid too, plus he used to fuckin' wit these slum-ass bitches. I got some game for his ass. Yeah, I'mma take everything that nigga got. That should be payment enough for him fucking up my man and our future. I told Wayne stop fucking with them niggas, they petty. You can't get nowhere fuckin' with no loose-square buying-ass niggas. Shit . . .*

"Sakawa James!" China Doll shouted.

Sakawa looked over at China Doll. "Girl, why is you hollering in my damn house like you crazy?"

"Bitch, you musta caught a contact high or something. I was sitting here talking to you and yo ass drifted off into space. I was telling you that you betta holla at that nigga Vee. Shit, that nigga got that new Lexus, the 430, I think. And got a Excursion with all them TVs, DVD players, video games—all that shit. That nigga got some paper. You better get that money, girl."

Slyly Sakawa said, "I just might listen to what the nigga got to say next time he try to holla."

"You better, bitch, because it's all about the paper in the new millennium. Shit, I tell 'em, spend a gee on me, you can pee on me. I needs my paper. Shit, if he got the scratch, we can have a wrestling match. A bitch like me is high maintenance. I need to—"

"Girl, shut yo ass up and go in the bathroom and get that air freshener from under the sink. You got my whole damn house smelling like weed."

Juvenile criminal court Judge Geneva Sehorn looked down from the imposing bench at the boy. He looked like every other Black man-child that was dragged in front of her—poor and lost. As a Black woman she supposed that she should have felt some iota of mothering instinct for these ghetto spawn, but she didn't. In them she always saw the faces of the two boys, high off of happy sticks, who had broken into her parents' home, killed her father, and then taken turns raping her and her mother.

"Your Honor," the juvenile court state's attorney said, "this young man is a serious threat to society. The charges that he is facing are of an extremely grave nature. The unlawful possession and concealment of a firearm by a minor. Also we have upgraded the previous charge of assault with a deadly weapon to attempted murder. Your Honor, though the defendant cannot be charged as an adult, the state would like to pursue the maximum penalty for these charges."

Judge Sehorn pointed her gavel at the public defender and the boy. "How does the defendant plead to these charges?"

The boy's public defender thumbed through her yellow legal pad, then stood. Ms. Tiena Hernandez was a pretty, petite Latin American woman with shoulder-length reddish-brown hair. She was also in need of a vacation. Before she opened her mouth she knew that her case was lost. Sehorn had that look on her face that she had come to recognize. That look that said that no matter what Tiena said, the judge had already made up her mind, and that it wasn't going to go well for her client. Judge Sehorn was hiding something serious in her past—something that made her hate young Black boys. Tiena was determined to find out what it was so that justice could be served.

"Your Honor, I am not truly prepared for this case. I have had little or no cooperation from the defendant in this matter. It is obvious that he has behavioral and psychological deficiencies. At the time of his arrest, the defendant was covered in so much blood that the police sought medical attention for him along with the victim. The defendant wasn't injured at that time, but the medical personnel who examined him found evidence of long-term physical abuse. He obviously suffered this abuse at the hands of the victim, his stepfather. Your Honor, before you, you will find a notarized affidavit that attests to this."

Judge Sehorn took a cursory glance at the affidavit, then tossed it to the side. "Ms. Hernandez, we are not here for that. We're here today about the charges on this docket."

Tiena protested, "But, Your Honor, that is a vital part of my defense. I'm trying to establish to the bench that my client was severely beaten over a long period of time. I need that document entered into evidence, Your Honor. Furthermore—"

"I know what you're trying to do, Ms. Hernandez. You're trying to garner sympathy from the bench for the defendant, but I won't allow it. Do you have any real evidence to help these proceedings?"

Tiena was noticeably flustered. She reached into her briefcase and pulled out a sheet of paper with the clerk's seal on it.

"Your Honor, I have a motion to lessen the charge of attempted murder to assault with a deadly weapon."

Sehorn banged her gavel. "Granted."

"Also, Your Honor, I have a motion to suppress the firearm as evidence against the defendant. His stepfather's fingerprints were on the trigger and the spent shell casings in the revolver."

Sehorn banged her gavel. "Denied."

"But, Your Honor . . . ," Tiena tried to argue.

"Ms. Hernandez, if you don't have any real, presentable evidence, may we proceed?"

Stumped, Tiena closed the case file on the table in front of her and looked over at the boy. As usual he seemed to be totally oblivious of his plight, showing no emotion. She leaned over and whispered in his ear.

"There's nothing I can do, Shawn."

The boy's lips parted in a slight smile as he looked up at her. He motioned for her to bend her ear.

He whispered in return, "I know. Thank you for your compelling, but ineffectual argument on my behalf."

Tiena straightened up and looked at the boy for a moment. With a sad smile in her eyes she turned back to the judge.

"Your Honor, the defense rests with hope for leniency due to the defendant's tender age and lack of criminal history."

"I'll take that into account," Judge Sehorn said dryly. "I find the defendant guilty of assault with a deadly weapon and unlawful possession of a firearm. Does the state have anything else to present before sentencing?"

The state's attorney stood. He buttoned his suit jacket, then riffled through his case file until he found a handwritten note. Clearing his throat, he motioned to the bailiff. "Your Honor, the bailiff is handing you a letter from the defendant's mother. His mother states that the defendant no longer has a place in her household. Essentially she has washed her hands of the defendant because of his actions. Also, Your Honor—"

"All right, Mr. Davidson, I get the gist of the letter. Mr. Terson, obviously you are a threat to society, sir. The danger that you represent is leagues beyond your fourteen years on this planet. I wish the law books would allow me to charge you as an adult. Were that possible, I assure you that any one of my colleagues that you stood in front of would give you a fitting sentence. However, since that is not possible, I will impose the maximum sentence for a juvenile offender. You are to be remanded to the St. Charles Boys Reformatory until the age of eighteen. Mr. Terson, do you have anything to say?"

The boy shook his head.

11

FROM HIS GIRLFRIEND'S APARTMENT WINDOW BING USED the remote start on the automobile alarm keypad to fire the ignition of Wayne's Buick Regal. Though it really wasn't a huge car, it was comfortable as long as he slid the leather power seat all the way back and tilted it. Every time that he looked at it, he knew that Wayne had to miss this car. It was painted a sparkling black cherry and sat on nineteen-inch fans. The interior was soft black leather with a dashboard television and two more televisions in the headrests for the rear passengers. Four ten-inch subwoofers in the trunk in a custom bass box made the sound massive.

Bing held the blinds open for a moment longer than necessary, staring at the Regal. The night they had robbed and beaten Wayne had proved quite fruitful. They seized thirty-one thousand in cash, a quarter key of coke, and the title and keys to his Regal. Bing gave Toobie and Tonto nine ounces of cocaine and two thousand dollars as a thank-you. After bailing his woman out of the County, he still had about twenty thousand in change—enough to buy a lot of weed. The only problem was his connect was still dry. He told him to hold out though—it would be all good soon.

The night was warm, with a soft breeze. He reached for his leather peacoat in the closet, but decided against wearing it. He could hear his woman in the kitchen gossiping while she braided the hair of the fat girl from the apartment below. He hollered, "Baby, I'm gone. I'll be back in a couple of hours!"

"All right, Bing! When you come in make sure you bring me some Pralines 'n' Cream ice cream from up there at Dunkin' Donuts!"

He yelled in return, "Girl, all yo pregnant ass think about is that damn ice cream! It might be late when I come in!"

"I don't care! Just bring my ice cream, I'll wake up!"

Bing laughed as he left the apartment. As he walked out of the building's entrance he could hear the quiet humming of his Regal's engine. He crossed the street and popped the door lock with the remote. Inside the car's cabin, the stereo remote was clipped to the sun visor. Bing pulled it down and used it to turn on the stereo. The sounds of DMX came thumping from the trunk. Checking his rearview mirror, he got ready to pull out of the parking space. Ahead of him a pair of headlights halted his progress. The car was slowly driving down the narrow street—in the wrong direction.

Must be some dumb-ass clucker looking for some shit, he thought.

With his hand on the steering wheel, Bing waited for the car to pass. As the silver Honda Accord got closer it slowed down, then stopped.

Bing tried to make out the driver. Whoever it was had a fisherman-style hat pulled down low on his head, successfully concealing most of his facial features.

The driver of the Accord rolled down his window and motioned for Bing to do the same. Bing thumbed the pause button on the stereo remote, then used the power switch to slide the glass out of the way.

Bing asked, "What's up, homie, you lost or something?"

Through his teeth the driver of the Honda replied, "Nall, homie, you just lost."

Bing said, "What the fuck did you say?"

Then he recognized the wires and rubber bands in the mouth of the man driving the Honda.

Insane Wayne hefted a chrome .357 onto the Honda's door to steady the heavy pistol. Grinning, he said, "You just lost your life."

"Damn!" Bing exclaimed as he closed his eyes and braced himself for the shots. A few seconds passed. He peeped out of his scrunched eyelids. Then they came—fast, loud; then hard and painful; then nothing. Bing couldn't tell how many of the slugs from Wayne's gun hit him—the first one removed the part of the brain that used to help him count. His fingers flexed for the last time, pushing the pause button on the stereo remote in his hand. Music escaped from the speakers again as Bing fell over across the seat rest. The Regal lurched forward as his quickly stiffening foot slipped off the brake, causing the Regal to crash into the rear of a U-Haul truck ten feet away.

Wayne tossed a green baseball cap with a gold embroidered *A* on the pavement near the rear wheel of the Regal. Making sure that it didn't shatter, he flung a Moët champagne bottle in the weeds by the car. Mimicking DMX, Wayne put the Honda in reverse and backed down the street.

12

"SOMEBODY GET THE DOOR!" SAMANTHA YELLED FROM THE kitchen. With one hand she swept her microbraids from her face as she pulled hot dogs from a large pot on the electric range. A few seconds later the doorbell rang again, startling her. She dropped the tongs into the boiling water and a little of it splashed on her hand.

"Fuck!" she shouted. Her hand came to her mouth. "Oh, I'm sorry, Mama," she said as she remembered her mother was sitting at the kitchen island, smoking a cigarette and drinking gin.

"Don't mind me, Sam," her mother said. "Shit, you already acting like I ain't even here. You might as well keep on cussing with that foul-ass mouth. Don't you or your twin pay me the least bit of attention. Y'all been acting like I'm in the way or something since I got here. Tabitha ain't said shit to me and here you is cussing, like you ain't got no damn home training, right in front of yo mother."

Samantha walked over to the stainless steel sink and rinsed her burned hand under the cold water. While her back was turned to her mother, she rolled her eyes to the ceiling and whispered, "Help me, somebody." She patted her hands dry with a towel and turned back to her mother.

"Mama, please don't start. Not today. This is your grandson's birthday party. Tabitha is out there in the yard trying to keep all of those kids entertained. You came in here to help out, I thought."

Lillian Terson-Liston dismissed her daughter with a wave of the hand. "Sam, you can gone 'head along with that bullshit. I came over here to get drunk and spend some time with my grandson."

"Well, why don't you go out in the back with Tabby and the kids then?" Samantha headed back to the stove and used a large fork to remove the tongs from the pot. When the tongs cooled off she began removing the remainder of the hot dogs from the pot.

Lillian said, "Girl, you got to be crazy. The two things in this world that I'm scared of is clowns and animals. As long as them damn ponies and them fucking clowns is out there, I'll be my high-yellow ass right in here. You know that I don't fuck with clowns and animals so you have hired them motherfuckers on purpose, trying to keep me away from my grandson."

Samantha was busy stuffing hot dogs into the buns and lining them up in a foil pan. "Mama, sometimes you say some stuff that I can't even believe you would say. These ponies and clowns are for my son and his friends, not to scare you. I didn't even order them. His uncle paid for them. The jumping jack, the ponies, and the clowns."

"Humph," Lillian said and took a sip of gin. "I wonder who that motherfucker killt to get the money for that shit."

"I didn't kill anyone, Mother dear," Solemn Shawn said from the doorway of the kitchen.

A look of fear shadowed Lillian's face. Quickly she took a gulp of gin to steel her nerves before turning to confront her eldest child. "You still sneaking up on people, huh? I guess that's what you gangsters do. Sneak up on people to steal their shit and take their lives. Once a sneak, always a damn sneak."

"I don't know how I was sneaking and I was dragging this," Solemn Shawn said, pointing to an engine-powered go-cart by the kitchen entrance. The go-cart was bright orange with racing-stripe stickers and fat, knobby tires. A colossal blue gift bow was mounted on the steering wheel.

"Ooh, Shawn," Samantha bubbled. She rushed over to hug Shawn and give him a kiss on his clean-shaven cheek. She hit him on the chest. "Boy, you gone spoil my doggone son. He already be walking around here smelling his own butt, talking 'bout what his uncle gone buy him."

Solemn Shawn let his eyes smile as his sister bent down to get a better look at the go-cart. When she stood, he pulled an orange crash helmet from behind his back.

Samantha hugged him. "Boy, you know me. I was just about to ask you where was his helmet."

"Well, ain't that sweet," their mother said sardonically. She left her seat and brushed past Shawn and Samantha on her way to the bar in the living room to refill her glass with gin.

"Forget her," Sam whispered.

Solemn Shawn looked glum. Samantha slid her arms around his waist as if to hug him. Instead she tickled him. He smiled and gave her a gentle stiff-arm.

"Girl, don't be tickling me."

"Yeah, don't tickle him," their mother said as she reentered the kitchen. "God forbid that you make Mr. Gangbanger laugh. Shit, then he might have to have you killed. Or he gone have a couple hundred of his thugs beat the hell out of you." Lillian walked back to the stool by the island and perched on it. With her elbows on the marble top she took a sip of her drink.

Just then Tabitha, Samantha's twin, burst through the patio doors. Except for a few pounds around the hip and bust area that Samantha gained and never lost during her pregnancy, Tabitha was her carbon copy.

"Sam, you better get those hot dogs out here. These damn kids is hungry. I saw the little fat girl from down the street looking at that cute gray pony like a steak. In a minute she gone have that little horse on the barbecue grill. Shawn!" she screeched as she noticed her brother. Tabitha ran and jumped into Shawn's arms, kissing him all over the face.

"C'mon, Tabby," he said bashfully. "You gone knock me over. And you getting slob all over my glasses."

"This is so touching," their mother said. "It makes me want to throw up, but I don't want to waste perfectly good alcohol. I'd rather go outside with them nasty-ass donkeys than stay in here and witness this bullshit. Y'all up in here acting like this murdering motherfucker is the damn pope or something."

"That's what you need to do, Mama," Tabitha said. "You need to go outside instead of sitting in here drinking up all the gin you can get your hands on and talking crazy. But knowing you, if you went out there you would have the clown crying. I can see him now, his face paint running." Tabitha turned to her twin. "I was coming to tell you that the ponies is about to leave. The guy said that everything was cool and that him and his people would clean up any hay or boo-boo before they leave the premises. The photographer got some nice shots of the kids on the ponies and he's going to shoot a couple more rolls of film when the clowns start the magic show. The clowns are ready to start but the kids are squawking for hot dogs."

Samantha covered the hot dog tray with Saran Wrap. "Let me run these out there," she said. She dipped through the patio doors.

In the kitchen they could hear the children chanting for the hot dogs.

Tabitha laughed. "I told her they was hungry. It sounds like they about to kill her out there. So what's up, big brother? I ain't gone even ask you about this go-cart. I just know you be getting the bomb gifts. What you been up to?"

Before Solemn Shawn could answer, their mother said, "What you think Mr. Big-time Gangster been up to? Stealing, killing, and drug dealing. And not always in that order. Motherfucker don't know how to do shit else. Always trying to act like he so calm and shit, with his violent ass. I'm ashamed to know that you came out of me. You the reason why I drink. I be trying to forget that my only son is a murdering-ass thug."

"C'mon, Shawn," Tabitha said as she grabbed his arm and pulled him through the patio doors. "You know how Mama is when she get drunk. She always looking for a scapegoat. That's why I had to move out."

The huge backyard was colorfully festooned. Multicolored streamers hung from the trees and bordered the fence. Several clowns congregated in a small tent preparing for their magic show. Children milled around the picnic table covered with the birthday party spread. An elaborately decorated chocolate sheet cake was the centerpiece of the table. Samantha, assisted by a couple of the children's mothers, was trying to make sure that all of the kids got a hot dog. The children were pushing, shoving, and yelling. Amid all of the confusion, Little Shawn, the birthday boy, saw his uncle Shawn and raced to him. He dove into Solemn Shawn's arms.

"Uncle Shawn, Uncle Shawn!" he spouted. "We been riding ponies and I got clowns. The clowns are about to do some magic tricks, but all these dumb kids is hungry. Uncle Shawn . . . and I got a jumping bag. We been bouncing around."

"Boy, slow down," Solemn Shawn said. "Tell me, how old are you today?"

"I just made eight today, Uncle Shawn," Little Shawn responded proudly. "Grandma said that you weren't going to make it. She said that you were too busy doing stuff, but I knew you were coming. I know that you got me the ponies and clowns and stuff, Uncle Shawn."

"How do you know that?"

"Because I know that my mom, Aunt Tabby, or Grandma won't go anywhere near any kind of animal."

Solemn Shawn and Tabitha laughed.

Little Shawn grabbed his uncle's hand. "Are you going to stay for the magic show, Uncle Shawn?"

"I'll have to see about that. Where's your father?"

"Mom said that he was flying in tonight. He was finishing up some architect stuff on a building in Denver. I talked to him today though. His son—I mean my brother is here too. But forget about that, Uncle Shawn. What's up with my present you said you were going to get me?"

Solemn Shawn covered his mouth with his hand. "Oops, I must have forgotten it."

Little Shawn punched his uncle in the stomach lightly. "C'mon, Uncle Shawn, stop kidding."

"All right, all right. Go look in the house and tell me what you think."

Little Shawn let go of his uncle's hand and dashed for the patio doors. Bright-eyed, Solemn Shawn waited with Tabitha for Little Shawn to return. They were distracted by Samantha at the food table.

"Y'all better get over here and help me serve these kids!" Samantha yelled.

They smiled as they walked over to the food table. Solemn Shawn was handing a juice box to a little girl with missing front teeth and a million colorful barrettes in her hair when Little Shawn came hurtling out of the house. He jumped into his uncle's arms, almost bowling him over for the second time that afternoon. As his nephew hugged his waist, Solemn Shawn looked over his head and directly into his mother's eyes. She was standing in the patio doorway with her drink in her hand. She spit into the flower bed beside the doorway, then retreated inside.

Little Shawn broke loose from his uncle and bolted for his mother. "Mom, Uncle Shawn bought me a go-cart. Can I ride it, please? Please?"

"You see what you done started, Uncle Shawn?" Samantha said. "Now I'll never hear the end of this until he gets a ride."

Solemn Shawn winked at his sister. "I'm way ahead of you, sis. I only put enough gas in that thing so that he could get a few rides. By the time the kids finish eating he'll be through. Plus you won't have to worry about all of the kids wanting a ride. A couple of rides up and down the alley and it'll be kaput. And of course he'll have on his helmet."

With pleading eyes, Little Shawn looked up at his mother. "C'mon, Mom. You heard him. A couple of rides and I'll be back in time for the magic show. These ole hungry kids won't even miss me."

"Okay, okay. You already know that I can't resist when you and your uncle gang up on me. Just make sure that you take it easy and wear that doggone helmet."

In the kitchen, Solemn Shawn's mother was still rooted to her stool. As her son and grandson walked past, she asked, "What you gone teach him to do, drive-bys on that thing? Can't never teach them too early, you know."

Solemn Shawn ignored her and the questioning look on his nephew's face. He led his nephew over to the go-cart. "Little Shawn, you need to pay attention so I can show you how this thing works. It looks like a toy but you can really get hurt on this thing if you don't know what you're doing. You see this switch here. This is the cutoff switch. You just flip it to 'on,' next . . ."

Lillian poured herself another glass of gin from the bottle she had transplanted from the bar to the living room. She set the bottle down on the island top with a loud thunk. She sneered, "Gangbanging-ass murderer up in here trying to act like you worried about my grandson's safety. You would probably kill him for a couple of dollars."

Solemn Shawn again chose to ignore his mother's drunken ravings.

"Bitch!" she screeched. "I'm sick of you ignoring me! I'm your gotdamned mother!"

"You don't act like a mother," Solemn Shawn countered.

"Fuck you!" Lillian screamed. She threw the gin bottle at Solemn Shawn.

Solemn Shawn straightened in time to avoid being hit with the bottle. It shattered on the wall behind him, showering him and his nephew with gin and glass. Little Shawn howled as gin splashed into his wide-open eyes. Samantha and Tabitha ran into the kitchen, followed by several of the children's mothers.

Furious and wet, Solemn Shawn took a step toward his mother.

"What happened?" Samantha asked frantically.

Lillian ran behind her twin daughters. "That drug-dealing bastard threatened me in front of my grandson. He called me a bitch and said he would slap me in the mouth."

Solemn Shawn was astonished. "Woman, what's wrong with you? I haven't said anything to you."

Little Shawn ran over to Samantha. He was crying and rubbing his eyes. "Mom, my eyes are burning," he wailed.

Samantha led her son over to the sink and rinsed his eyes with cold water.

With a piteous look on her face, Lillian beseeched, "Sammy, you believe me, don't you? You know how violent your brother can be. He's just trying to mess up my only grandson's birthday party. He's crazy. He was muttering under his breath about how much he hated me. Talking about shooting me if I wasn't his mother. I bet you he has a gun with him now."

Samantha was patting Little Shawn's face dry with a towel, but her ears perked up at the mention of the word "gun." "Shawn, do you have a gun on you?" she asked her brother.

Solemn Shawn looked into her eyes for a moment, then averted his gaze. He looked at Tabitha and at his drunken dramaqueen mother. He looked back at Samantha. For a microsecond his anger threatened to boil over, but he managed to keep it in check.

Calmly, Solemn Shawn said, "I think it's time for me to leave, Sam. Happy birthday, Little Shawn. Tell your dad I said what's up." He turned and walked to the front door. He made it out of the house and was almost to his pickup truck when Tabitha came running out of the house.

"Shawn, slow down, big brother!"

He turned with a slight smile. "What's up, Tabby?"

"We know Mama be tripping with her drunk ass. I know you ain't said nothing to her. She just be needing the attention, you know. That stanking-ass husband of hers don't be paying her no attention."

Solemn Shawn unlocked the doors of his F-150 Harley-Davidson pickup truck. He already knew that Tabitha wanted something, but he didn't mind. She would always beat around the bush whenever she needed him. He didn't know why though, because he never refused her a thing.

"What you need, Tabby Cat?" he asked as he climbed into the leather interior of the pickup truck.

Tabitha sighed. "Boy, you know me. I could use a couple of bucks for clothes and shit. I'm 'bout to do the summer semester thing so I can get out in January. Then I'll have my master's degree. Then I can start earning the big bucks and repay you some of the money I owe you. A sister want to be looking good for the summer though. I might catch me a husband or something."

"Girl, can't no man put up with your crazy butt. Just call me in the morning. Sometime this week we'll grab some breakfast, then I'll take you shopping and put a few bucks in your pocket. Is that cool?"

"Hell yeah, big brother. I'll call you in the morning."

"Now get back in there and help out Sammy."

Tabitha leaned in the truck and gave Shawn a kiss on his jaw. "Small things ain't nothing to a giant, big brother," she said. She watched as he backed the truck out of the driveway and made a left at the stop sign. Already she could hear her mother inside whining to Samantha as she stepped back up on the porch.

"Lord, give me the strength," Tabitha said as she entered the house.

13

BULL AND GROVE PULLED UP IN THEIR GRAY CROWN VICTORIA. Grove parked alongside the portable Chicago Police forensics lab. The GCU detectives left their vehicle and ducked under the yellow crimescene tape. They continued past a throng of police officers to a ring of suit-and-tie-wearing detectives. They were forming a wall around the open door of a late-model Buick Regal, where a police photographer was snapping pictures like crazy. Before Grove could get close to the car, a beefy homicide detective put his hand on Grove's chest.

His face was beet red even in the dim streetlight and his necktie disappeared into his jowls. It looked like it was cutting off the circulation of blood to his face. "Whoa there, Detective," the homicide detective said. "No sightseeing. This is a homicide investigation."

Grove looked at the hand on his bulletproof vest—covered chest. Grove looked at Bull. "Why do we have to go through this shit with every new guy that makes the homicide squad? These O'Briens drive me crazy. You would think they would tell these new cats that everybody that drops in occupied territory the GCU get a gander at."

The overweight homicide detective's red face turned a deeper scarlet. "Hold on there, slick. My name isn't O'Brien, it's Lonihan. I've heard about you GCU guys. More like criminals with badges."

"Fuck you very much," Grove said with a smile. "You just jeal-

ous 'cause the only little Black boys you get to feel on are already dead, homo-cide dick."

"You son of a bitch!" Lonihan choked out. He looked like he was ready to charge at Grove.

"What the hell is going on, Lonihan?" an authoritative voice barked.

Lonihan turned to see Homicide Captain Matthew Hartibrig taking in the scene. As usual the captain was attired in an expensive suit. His handcrafted leather shoes reflected the streetlights like mirrors. His hair was a dirty blond with just a hint of gray at the temples.

Lonihan complained, "Cap, these GCU guys came stampeding up in here. I told them this was a homicide investigation. And that they need to get the hell out of here."

Hartibrig straightened the knot in his tie, which was already perfect. "Lonihan, is this your crime scene?"

Lonihan hung his head. "No, sir."

"That's right. This isn't your crime scene. In homicide we do not go out of our way to alienate other department units. We are all on the same team. The GCU is one of the most cooperative and lucrative units in the department when it comes down to homicides of this nature. Are you out here on these streets every day, Lonihan?"

"No, sir," Lonihan mumbled.

"Well, they are. They know these guys, so when something like this happens they often can give us behind-the-scenes details that shine some light on such matters. Is that understood, Lonihan?"

"Yes, sir."

"Good, Lonihan. Now why don't you see if you can scare up any eyewitnesses. It's unlikely, but you never know. Grab a couple of the guys and start canvassing the crowd and the block. And try to be polite."

Lonihan started to protest about being assigned such a menial detail, but Captain Hartibrig was already ushering Grove and Bull closer to the Buick Regal. Grove turned to Lonihan and smoothed

down his eyebrows with his middle fingers. If the captain noticed he didn't say anything about it.

As they neared the car containing Bing's lanky body sprawled across the front seat, Grove asked, "Captain, what are you doing out here on a local body?"

Hartibrig wiped his forehead with a pearly white handkerchief, then returned it to his trouser pocket. "The body happens to be the son of an aide to our illustrious mayor. When the mayor gets woke up, he wakes up everyone down the line. I think he has a hard-on for the kid's mother. I was on my way home from a late dinner when I got the call."

Bull inquired, "So, I guess they want you to head this thing up, Captain?"

"Unfortunately I'm the point on this one. It's been a while since I've been out here in the trenches so I'll appreciate any input the GCU can give us. Make way, fellas."

A herd of homicide detectives parted to let Captain Hartibrig and the two GCU dicks near the car. On the ground next to the open door of the Regal was an Oakland A's hat.

Grove looked at his partner and muttered, "Apostles."

"What was that, Hargrove?" Hartibrig asked.

"I said Apostles. Solemn Shawn's crew. Pretty big and well organized. A lot of them wear these baseball caps. Mostly the Oakland A's or Angels, any fitted cap with an *A* on it. The shooter must have dropped it."

Bull walked past them and looked in the car. He leaned in close to the stiff figure. "Grove, check it out."

"What is it, Bull?"

"Looks like Governor Bing. I'm guessing because this kid's face is so fucked up. But this guy is tall like him. He used to stand out like a sore thumb when he was hanging on the block because he was so damn tall."

Hartibrig consulted his notebook. "Driver's license says James Bingham. The pregnant girl over there in the ambulance is his girlfriend. She kept calling him Bing. What do you guys know about him?"

Grove scratched his head. "Seemed like a halfway decent kid. He used to sling a little weed. He wasn't even on our radar until one of his boys gave us his scent. We hit his crib and found a few pounds of weed. Nice haul. He jumped out the window on us and we gave his girl the case. He ran with the Governors. A lightweight crew. Not many members, but pretty vicious."

Hartibrig was making notes. "You don't think this could be retal for the stuff you guys busted? Like maybe he was working for the Apostles?"

Bull asserted, "No way, Cap. Governors and Apostles don't mix. This looks like it may be the end of something or just the beginning."

"Why do you say that?" Hartibrig asked.

Grove fielded the question. "Well, it's been kinda quiet on the streets lately. We got the feeling that something big is in the works. We don't have anything concrete, but there's something going on. I mean these dudes are carrying on business as usual, but there's something in the water. The Apostles especially haven't been making any noise. They're playing their cards real close to the chest. That's why if this was an Apostle and Governor thing as the hat indicates, then it doesn't make sense. What you say, Bull?" Bull simply shrugged.

One of the homicide detectives walked up to them. "Captain Hartibrig, we've got a champagne bottle in the weeds by the car. We've got prints on it, too. It's bagged and tagged, sir."

"Thanks," Hartibrig said to the detective, then turned to the GCU cops. "I sure could use any help you guys could give me on this body. I know you don't take orders from me, but I would consider it a real personal favor if you guys would keep your ears to the ground for me. Okay?"

Ever ready to have someone prestigious owe him a favor, Grove willingly agreed. You never knew when your fat would be in the fire, especially when you worked the Gang Crimes Unit. It would be a definite plus to have a homicide captain ready to go to bat for him if things ever went bad.

"We'll do what we can, sir," Grove responded.

The two GCU cops shook hands with Captain Hartibrig and headed for their car. They ducked under the yellow tape again. Grove detoured to the open doors of the ambulance. Bing's girlfriend was sitting on the gurney receiving oxygen from one of the EMTs. As the GCU detective neared her, she looked up and recognized him through her tears.

Grove took off his hat and said, "Sorry about your boyfriend. I'm glad that you got out the County before you had that baby. We'll see you in court, sweetie."

"Fuck you!" she screamed. "Fuck you, motherfucker!"

Grove replaced his hat and rejoined his partner. Bing's girlfriend continued to scream, cry, and curse in the back of the ambulance.

14

"Aw, c'mon, Hardy," Big Ant Hamilton said to a tall, dark-skinned corrections officer. "Man, I'm finta go home in a few months and you giving me a cellie. A young dude at that."

Department of Corrections Officer Hardy looked at Big Ant with a smirk. He liked the husky youth. There had been days when Big Ant had his sides aching with laughter from his jokes; plus he seemed to have his head screwed on straight. That was why Hardy decided to let Shawn Terson bunk with him. The quiet, slim youth with the schoolboy looks was going to have enough problems on his hands already, without being unable to sleep comfortably at night for fear of booty-hole bandits.

"Sorry 'bout this, Big Ant," Officer Hardy said, "but you know that shit is going to get crowded as hell around here. We're almost at capacity now and summer is just starting."

Big Ant agreed, "I know, I know." He got up from the steel desk and began removing his personal items from the top bunk. He looked at Shawn. To him the boy looked rail thin with big, serious eyes. He stood quietly holding his toiletries.

"All right, Terson, step on in," Hardy commanded. He really didn't know what to make of Shawn. The boy was silent, but he didn't seem to be afraid; more like he was anticipating and adjusting to his situation. Hardy knew that he would have to keep his eyes on the quiet boy, if for nothing else but to try to keep the dogs off him.

After Shawn stepped into the small cell, Officer Hardy clanged the heavy steel door shut. Whistling, he retreated to his station and his freshly confiscated issue of Black Tail. Shawn stood facing Big Ant in the small cell.

"What's your name, my man?" Big Ant asked as he took his seat at the desk again.

"Shawn."

"Well, they call me Big Ant, little fella. I ain't gone act like I'm happy to have no roommate and shit. The last silly little stud I had for a cellie kept getting us set up for shakedowns with all the bullshit he was on. I told that little nigga to get hisself sent to another house or I was gone mop his ass. I can't be letting no dumb-ass stud jag off the little time I got left on my fuckin' bit, you dig. The last stud that was up in here before that didn't believe in taking no showers. You believe in taking showers, don't you?"

"Yeah," Shawn said.

"Well, we off to a good start then, cat daddy. You ain't got to stand there holding yo shit. The top bunk is yours, take a load off. The top shelf is yours, too."

Shawn walked over to the bunk and deposited his bedroll there. He placed his few toilet articles on the shelf and walked back over to the bunk and began making the bed. When he was through he turned to Big Ant.

"Any other rules?" Shawn asked.

Big Ant looked at him quizzically.

"I mean are there any other stipulations that I need to be aware of so that I can at least make our time together cordial?"

Big Ant laughed. "Nigga, yo little ass sound like you done swallowed a dictionary. That was a real mouthful. Nall, there ain't shit else, but if something come up then I'll let you know, you dig."

Shawn turned and prepared to jump up on his bunk.

Big Ant said, "Oh, there is one more thing."

Expectantly, Shawn turned. Big Ant jumped up from the desk and came toward him. The older boy faked like he was going to steal on Shawn, but the younger boy didn't flinch. Big Ant backed off, laughing. He sat down at the desk again. Shawn did not appear amused.

"What was that supposed to be?" Shawn asked stone-faced.

"Just checking yo nuts, little partner. No harm, no foul. You gone get tested in here. That's how this shit go. Shit, I remember when I was on the new. Cats be trying to take yo food, yo asshole, anything they feel they can take and get away with. How did you know that I wasn't going to hit you?"

Shawn turned back to the bed and jumped up on his bunk. "Ant, do you mind if I borrow one of your books?"

Big Ant chose Donald Goines's White Man's Justice, Black Man's Grief and tossed it up to Shawn. "That's a good book there, kid. All right, now tell me. How did you know I wasn't gone jaw you?"

Shawn caught the dog-eared novel and propped himself up on his pillow. He opened the novel. "It's simple really. You don't strike me as being a stupid dude."

Shawn's answer ruffled Big Ant's feathers. "What the fuck you mean by that?"

"Calm down," Shawn said in his usual dry monotone. He never took his eyes off the first page of the novel. "I meant that only an idiot would go out of his way to provoke his cellmate."

Big Ant couldn't see the boy's face but he was already beginning to like his character. He felt it was his duty to hip the naive youngster to the ways of jail. "Well, I'm sorry to bust yo bubble, but this place is full of idiots. But you don't have to worry about that shit in this cell. Like I said, I'm out of here in a few months. I got a crazy weed connect from my Mexican buddy that was up in here wit me for two years. When I get out of here, I'm get rich wit the prices this stud done told me he'd give me the shit for."

Shawn sat up on his bunk. He looked at Big Ant earnestly. "Mind if I ask you a question?"

The look on Shawn's face made Big Ant laugh. "Man, you's a

solemn little cat. That's what I'm gone call you—Solemn Shawn. Yeah, go ahead, Solemn Shawn, ask me anything you want."

"How do you survive in this place?"

Tilting his head, Big Ant gave the question some serious thought. Finally he said, "Most dudes would never ask a question like that. That's why so many of them come in here and jag they bits off. I would have to say there's a number of ways. You got to learn to go with the flow mostly. Like you gots to be hard but not too hard. You gots to be cool but not too cool. Just like everything else I learned about in life. If you don't take yo time then you gone be giving up time.

"Also you got to learn to mind yo own business. That don't seem like it'll be a problem for you. You got to learn to read situations and adapt to the shit that's going on around you, you dig. But even after that, I ain't gone lie to you, Solemn Shawn. Motherfuckas is still gone try you up in here. A lot these cats be selling wolf tickets though. Punks be having a little crowd around and try to get tough with you.

"Man, if that shit happen you better blast one of these studs out the water, you dig. If you don't they gone think you a poot-butt. I know you heard that shit they say about one chance to make a first impression."

Solemn Shawn looked at Big Ant earnestly, as if he were committing his every word to memory. "Is there anybody in particular that I need to be on the lookout for?" he asked stoically.

This little motherfucker ain't no joke. I got to sneak into the files and see what he in for, Big Ant thought.

"Nall, ain't nobody in particular. You got to watch out for all these studs. Don't trust nobody. I don't know how much time you got and I ain't ask, but my advice is not to even worry about returning to the world. You'll get there when you get there. It's natural to get homesick, but you can't let that shit fuck yo head up. You got to be watching yo ass twenty-four/sev, you dig?"

"I will," Solemn Shawn replied as he reclined again and resumed reading.

15

"Hello," Vee said into his cell phone as he exited the Dan Ryan Expressway on 95th Street. He headed westbound on the large thoroughfare.

"Uh, hello," a female voice said. "May I speak to Vee?"

"This is him. Who is this?"

The voice purred, "Oh, you don't remember a sister, huh? You always said that you would never forget me."

Pulling the phone from his ear, Vee looked at the caller ID, but it read "No ID." He put it back to his ear. "Shorty, I don't know who you is, but you sound sexy than a motherfucka. What's the deal, is you gone tell me yo name?"

"Damn, player. You got that many women that you don't know a sister's name. You kinda making me jealous. This is Sakawa."

Vee almost dropped his cell phone. "Who did you say?"

A seductive sound that would have to be called a laugh escaped from Sakawa. "I said this is Sakawa James."

"What you want?" Vee asked, his voice dripping with suspicion.

"Damn, Vee. Why you say it like that?"

"'Cause the last time I called you, you japped out on me and shit. Told me not to ever call yo fuckin' house again."

Sakawa apologized. "I'm sorry 'bout that. It's just that I had a lot of shit on my mind at the time, you know. But if I'm bothering you..." Her words trailed off.

"Nall, it's cool," Vee said hurriedly, afraid that she might hang up. He heard only silence on the other end, so he said, "Sakawa?"

"Yeah, I'm still here."

"I thought you hung up on a nigga again, shorty. What you up to?"

Sakawa sighed. "Nothing heavy. Really, I was just laying back at the crib all by myself and I got to thinking about the old times we had."

Vee wasn't lured in so easily. "What old times, girl? You stopped fuckin' wit yo boy over some bullshit. You ain't even give a nigga a chance to get back, you know what I'm sayin'."

"Vee, you need to stop bullshitting yo'self. 'Cause you shole ain't bullshitting me. I caught you up in the party with a nasty, bald-headed, ran-over-shoe-wearing hood booger. What was I s'posed to do. I couldn't have my man going out like that. How do you think that make me look?"

Vee conceded. "Yeah, you is right, shorty. I was trying to hit, shorty. It was only 'cause you wadn't gone give me none."

"How did you know what I was gone do? I was gone give you some that night. I was gone let you take my virginity, but you fucked that up. I come up in the party and you hugged all up with a hoodie-hood."

"You was a virgin?" Vee asked incredulously. "Stop playing."

"I was," Sakawa assured him.

Vee banged the steering wheel with the palm of his driving hand. He took the cell phone's mouthpiece away from his lips and mouthed the word "fuck." He decided to test the waters with Sakawa. "So what's up now, shorty?"

Sakawa wouldn't bite. "What you mean by that?"

"Are you still fuckin' wit that nigga Wayne?" Vee asked as he steeled himself for a sharp-tongued reply.

It never came.

Sakawa said, "I don't fuck with Wayne no mo'. That nigga ain't gangster enough for a bitch like me."

Vee had to chuckle to himself at her answer. He said, "I always did wonder what you saw in that soft-ass nigga. But anyway, like I said, what is you doing right now?"

"Like I said. Nothing. Just laying back at the crib and I got to feeling like I wanted to holla at somebody, you know."

Vee licked his lips. His voice lowered an octave. "What you got on?"

"You get straight down to it?" Sakawa asked seductively. "Well, I wasn't on nothing, so I really ain't got on nothing."

"What you mean by 'ain't got on nothing'?"

"I mean a baby T and some thongs. Nothing exotic like thigh-high stockings and high heels, though I do have some of them."

"Um-um," Vee muttered.

"What you mean by 'um-um'?" Sakawa asked coyly.

"Nothing. It's cool. When can I see you in them thongs, shorty?"

"One day. If you act right," she said.

"What you mean if I act right?"

"I mean if, and only if, I decide to give you another chance. To get another chance I need to know that you gone act right, Vee."

The call waiting signal on Vee's celly clicked in his ear. "Sakawa, give me a second to clear this other line." He clicked over to his other line. "What's up?"

"Vee, this is O."

"What's the deal, O?"

"Bing got killt last night, family."

Vee snapped, "What the fuck you mean last night and I'm just hearing about it!"

"My fault, family. I tried hitting yo horn last night but yo shit kept going straight to voice mail, fam."

"Nigga, hold on a minute." Vee clicked back over to Sakawa. "Shorty, I got to call you back. Some business just came up," he told her.

"All right, hit me later," she said.

He clicked back over to O. "What the fuck happened?"

"We don't know."

Vee's face screwed up in thought for a moment. "Get the State Department together. We gone meet at the garage. I'll be there in fifteen minutes. Let them niggas know they better be there or every one of them is gone be wearing Governor glasses!"

Vee slammed his cell phone shut and tossed it on the passenger seat. "Fuck!" he shouted. He had been on his way to the Evergreen Plaza and Breyer's for a quick shopping spree, but it would have to wait. Hanging halfway out of the Excursion's window he busted a tire-screeching U-turn. Several drivers honked their horns furiously at him. He barreled down 95th to the expressway. He was at the garage in a little over twenty minutes. He parked his large SUV alongside a brown Chevy sitting on twenty-inch Daytons. He grabbed his celly off the seat and slammed the door.

In the garage the Governors' State Department lounged on old car seats, overturned buckets, and milk crates. Cigarette and blunt smoke thickened the air in the already musty garage. Vee eased through the door and took the seat reserved for him, an old leather lounger. Mentally he took attendance; everyone was present. Idle conversations stopped as the State Department looked to their leader. One of the blunts being passed ended up in Vee's clutches.

"So what the fuck happened?" Vee asked as he filled his lungs with smoke from the sticky green.

Governor Ornell "O" Jones blew Black & Mild smoke toward the center of the room. He said, "Last night I was bending a couple of corners in my whip, when I drove down upon a gang of pigs and shit on Bing's block. First I was gone keep on sliding, but when I weeped the yellow tape and shit and saw a crowd, I decided to check the shit out.

"I parked my whip and walked over to the crowd. As I got closer I could see that the yellow tape was around the whip that Bing took from Wayne's pussy ass. I could see Bing slumped on the steering wheel and they wadn't trying to get him no help, so I knew that somebody had rolled his carpet back. The pigs kept pointing at something on the ground and when they moved I could see that it was a A's fitted hat."

Vee jumped to his feet. He moved so fast that he startled the Governor sitting next to him, causing him to topple off the bucket he had been using for a seat.

"Bitch motherfuckin' Apostles!" Vee bellowed. "I know them ho-ass niggas ain't kill no Governor. I'mma off one of those bitches!"

Teddy, one of Vee's staunchest followers, sat watching the proceedings. He was a smart man and partly responsible for the Governors' survival. It could be said that he was the mastermind behind Vee, but the Head Governor would never admit it. Teddy resembled Snoop Dogg with the exception of his brown teeth and the razor bumps covering his chin and neck. That he was particularly vicious was a quality that slid him through the ranks of the Governors. His long hair was pulled back into a ponytail covered by an Akademics cap. "So what's up with these niggas, Vee?" he asked.

"Fuck you mean?" Vee snapped.

"Do we get to merc a few of these assholes or what?"

Vee retook his seat. He tugged weed smoke into his lungs. A smile crossed his lips as he kicked back in the recliner and exhaled. The State Department sat quietly and waited for him to speak. He sat up suddenly and tossed the lit blunt to Teddy, who fielded it easily and righted the blunt before it could burn his palm.

"One of ours, two of theirs," Vee said evenly as he looked into Teddy's eyes.

16

VANESSA HENRY ROLLED OVER ONTO HER STOMACH. THE olive green jersey sheet poofed around her for a moment, then settled down, framing her curves. A slight snore escaped from between her pouting lips. Her micromini braids were pinned under a silken scarf wrapped securely around her head; only the mahogany tips peeked from under the scarf. The sheet toppled from her shoulders, baring her arms. Her caramel-colored skin looked soft to the touch where her camisole failed to cover her.

Solemn Shawn stood in the shadows and watched her sleep. He had done so on many occasions, but it never failed to amaze him just how angelic she appeared when she slept. He loved to watch her sleep. To him she seemed like she left this physical plane and returned to Heaven.

A smile invaded his heart and forced itself upon his lips. Outside of his sisters, his nephew, and his reading, Nessa was one of the few pleasures he allowed himself. The woman was pure energy and bustle, but she also knew how to chill and relax. Really she was his exact opposite and it showed. Where he was quiet and brooding, she was talkative and outgoing. He could keep a secret to himself, but Vanessa couldn't wait to shatter her friends' confidences by regaling him with tales of who was cheating on whom.

Noiselessly Shawn slipped out of his pants and shirt and placed them carefully on the leather settee in the corner of the bedroom. Wearing his multicolored boxer shorts he approached the gigantic platform bed. He placed his eyeglasses on the ebony nightstand, then he slid under the jersey sheets. Vanessa stirred.

"Shawn?" she said, reaching back and touching his arm.

"Yeah, baby," he answered.

"Come closer," Vanessa demanded playfully. "You act like you scared."

Solemn Shawn rolled over onto his side and propped his leg across the backs of her thighs. "Thought you was sleep, Nessa."

"You know I wake up when you get in the bed."

"I be trying not to wake you. I know you got to get up for work in the morning."

"I'm the boss," Vanessa said. "If I'm a little late what are they gone do to me?"

Shawn had to agree with her, but he said, "Just like a Black person, you give them a little power, then you can't tell them shit. Don't be around here getting big headed just 'cause you run the joint."

Vanessa snuggled back against Shawn. For the first time he realized that she wasn't wearing any panties under her short nightie. His manhood stirred as he rubbed her naked thighs and round, smooth buttocks.

"Girl, why you ain't got no draws on?"

"I was expecting company," Vanessa teased.

"Yeah, who?"

"You don't know him," she answered slyly.

In a mock-angry voice, Shawn said, "You better stop playing with me, woman."

Without warning Vanessa sprang from under Shawn's leg and rolled on top of him in one quick movement. In a husky voice she challenged, "What you gone do if I don't stop playing with you?"

Shawn threatened, "You better quit playing with me, woman, before I do something to you."

"Oh yeah?"

"Yeah."

She leaned forward and kissed Solemn Shawn on his neck. She

nuzzled his ear, then licked behind it. With a gentle breath she blew on the wet path she kissed down to his throat and chest. Entirely at her mercy, Shawn shuddered. As Vanessa licked a path from one of his nipples to the other, his manhood threatened to rip his boxer shorts off.

"Damn, Nessa. What you trying to do?"

She didn't answer. Instead she balanced herself on one knee and reached behind her to free Shawn from the confines of his boxer shorts. She swung her leg back over him as he reached for her satin-covered breasts. He gently squeezed and massaged her breasts until the hardened nipples raised the fabric from her chest. Vanessa moaned as she kissed her way back up to his throat. She locked her soft lips on his and slid her tongue into his mouth. While she kissed him, she reached behind herself and grasped his joint with her fingertips. Using her French-manicured hand she inserted him into her moist slit.

In unison they groaned.

"Damn, baby, you wet," Shawn muttered, as he moved his hands from her breasts to her hips to guide her up and down.

Vanessa rotated her hips. "You know you make me wet, daddy."

She pushed herself up into sitting position using Shawn's abs. She stripped her camisole off and flung it across the room. She leaned back down and teasingly dangled her nipples inches from Shawn's face. He grabbed her ass tighter and craned his neck to capture the tip of her luscious fruit in his mouth. He bit, licked, and sucked the taut skin of her nipples until she had to bite back a scream.

"Just like that," Vanessa groaned as she rolled her hips from side to side. "That's my spot, daddy. Uhhh, that's my spot. Right there, daddy."

As Shawn plunged upward into his woman, simultaneously he licked and blew on her nipples. She sat upright and ground her hips down against his pelvis with an intimate urgency. Her hands came up to knead and massage her own breasts. Half-closed, her eyes fluttered. A low, guttural moan escaped her—it came more from her throat than her mouth.

"Daddy, grab my ass, I'm coming!" Vanessa announced.

Shawn complied by palming the smooth, firm cheeks of her behind.

"That's it, daddy!" Vanessa moaned. "I'm coming. Uhhh, I'm coming! Do you feel my juice, daddy?"

Vanessa's erotic movements and animal-like grunts and groans inspired Solemn Shawn. He held her ass tighter as he pumped furiously, lifting up off the bed. Sensing that her man was about to come, Vanessa egged him on. "C'mon, daddy! Nut in this pussy! This is yo pussy! Empty yo nuts in this hairy pussy, daddy!" She rolled her hips clockwise then counterclockwise and pinched Shawn's nipples.

"Damn, Nessa," Shawn grunted. "I'm coming, baby!" He pumped even faster as semen shot upward into her womb. She responded by grinding even harder on him.

Vanessa's voice fell to a whisper as she said, "That's it, daddy. Get it all out. Put it all in me, daddy."

As Shawn spent himself, he stopped moving and fell silent. Vanessa collapsed on his sweaty chest and began gently kissing his neck. After a few moments she rolled off him. Without saying a word, Shawn got up and went to the bathroom. He turned the hot water on and stepped into the shower. With a hand towel he lathered himself. Seconds later the glass shower door opened and Vanessa stepped in behind him. She ducked past Shawn into the fine spray of the warm, reviving water.

"I said I better get up and get in there before you use up all the hot water," Vanessa said.

Shawn chuckled. "I was finta call you to wash my back anyway."

Vanessa pursed her lips, but took the soapy cloth from Shawn and washed his back. She handed him back his cloth and began to soap her own body. She moved to the rear of the shower so Shawn could rinse himself. As he was letting the water run down on his body, Shawn looked Vanessa in the eyes.

"Nessa," he said.

She continued to soap herself. "What, baby?"

"I got some stuff I'm working on. When I'm through, I'm out the streets. When I'm done I want you to be my wife. You want to get married?"

Vanessa's mouth fell open. "What did you ask me, Shawn?"

"I know I ain't get you no ring yet. I just wanted to know if you would before I went and got one. I didn't want you to take it and throw it back in my face. I just want to know, will you marry me?"

Vanessa rushed forward and hugged Shawn so suddenly that he had to put a hand on the wall behind him to prevent himself from falling. "Damn, girl. You 'bout to knock me over."

"Yes, baby," Vanessa cooed. "I'll marry you, daddy."

Shawn hit her on the behind lightly. "Well, shut up and kiss me then."

With a mischievous twinkle in her eye, Vanessa detached herself from Solemn Shawn. "I'll do more than kiss you," she said as she squatted down in front of him.

"You gone get yo braids wet," Shawn cautioned.

"I got a blow-dryer," she countered as she took him in her wet, pouting lips.

"Oh shit," Solemn Shawn muttered as he leaned back against the shower wall.

"Baby," Vanessa whispered in Shawn's ear. She was dressed in a navy blue pinstripe suit. Her braids were pulled back in a Chinese comb. On her shoulder was slung her attaché case. In her hand she clutched the keys to her Lexus IS 300.

"Shawn, I have to go. I'm already running late. Before you leave, pull some lamb chops out the freezer so they'll thaw in time."

Shawn's voice was full of sleep as he said, "All right, Nessa."

She leaned over and kissed him on his forehead, nose, and lips. "I'll call you, daddy."

As his wife-to-be departed, Shawn maneuvered the pillows around and reached for the television remote. It was a habit of his to listen to the news in the morning when his woman left for the office as he got back to sleep. Ten minutes into the CLTV broadcast he was snoring again. His cell phone began humming on the nightstand. After a few seconds it began to ring. It rang for a few seconds, then stopped. Solemn Shawn stirred and reached for it. As he detached it from the charger, it vibrated again in his hand. He opened it and put it to his ear.

"Hello," Solemn Shawn rasped.

"SS, this is C-Dub."

Solemn Shawn pulled a pillow over his head with his free hand. "Yeah, what is it?"

"Meet and potatoes."

"Watch?" Solemn Shawn asked.

"Half-and-half."

"Loc?"

"S and I."

"Cool," Solemn Shawn said. He hung up the telephone and swung his legs out of the bed. Thirty-five minutes later, he pulled into the underground parking garage at the Museum of Science and Industry. State Representative Coleman Washington winked the headlights of his car as Solemn Shawn passed him in his truck. Solemn Shawn caught the signal and parked a few spaces away. A moment after the pickup was in its parking space, Coleman hopped in.

"SS, how you been?"

"Can't complain," Solemn Shawn said. "What you got for me?"

Coleman looked around the parking lot before he spoke. He rubbed his hands together like he was trying to warm them up.

Solemn Shawn looked over at him. "Spit it out, man."

"All right. It's like this. I got the ball rolling. I've been down to Springfield and got this thing out of the shed."

"What does that mean, C-Dub?"

Coleman pulled a cigarette from his blazer pocket and was about to light it until he saw the look on Solemn Shawn's face. He returned the Kool to his pocket. "What I'm saying is that we've got an agreement for the funding as long as we come up with the facility. I've got a few irons in the fire with the city council, so zoning shouldn't be a problem."

Solemn Shawn raised his hand. "What do you mean, 'shouldn't be a problem'?"

Coleman replied, "I don't know if you know how these things are done in the political arena, but you've got to spread the love around. Especially when you're trying to do something of this magnitude."

Solemn Shawn had to chuckle at Coleman's words. "Spread the love, huh. I've never had it put to me quite like that, but I expected as much. Now I need for you to tell me just how much this 'love' is gonna cost."

"Well, SS. Truthfully. I can pull us through the aldermen for about forty or fifty stacks." *Really, it's more like twenty or twenty-five,* Coleman thought.

The gang leader surprised Coleman by saying, "Okay, what else?"

Coleman jumped out there. "Well, I had to figure out some way to handle the cash. I've got a friend that runs a casino over in Indiana. Any cash I bring she'll turn over for 5 percent off the top. It'll come back in certified cashier's checks. That way we won't have a problem. It can be traced but it'll look like a donation. If there are any inquiries they'll have to come through her, so she can say what we program her to say."

Having spun his web, Coleman sat back to see if Solemn Shawn would fly into it. Really the friend that he spoke of was his girlfriend. Two years ago she wouldn't have dreamed of doing something as underhanded as laundering money. But a person could embrace her dark side when she had the proper motivation—cocaine was the motivating factor for her. She was only charging two cents on the dollar, but Coleman planned to line his pockets with the gapper. His arrangement with his old gang was looking like it could turn out to be extremely lucrative.

Solemn Shawn broke through Coleman's greedy musing. "C-Dub, how does this thing really look to you?"

He caught Coleman completely off guard with the sincerity in his voice. Coleman looked at Solemn Shawn and said, "What you mean, SS?"

"I'm saying, I'm not really second-guessing myself but this thing can be really big. Bigger than I imagined. The money isn't really the issue. This is really a grand idea. To have a place like this that's totally free would be like an oasis in the desert, you know. I'm wondering will it really make a difference in some kid's life. I mean, will it really be an alternative to the streets."

Coleman thought about Solemn Shawn's query for a moment. "I can't really say, SS. Maybe it'll save some lives, you know. I hate to say it but a lot of kids these days are too far gone. The streets are eating them alive. They playing for high stakes and they ass-betting. I don't know how much of an effect this place will have."

Solemn Shawn was quiet for a moment. He looked away from Coleman. "So are you saying that you don't want to do this?" he asked.

Coleman felt his ship sinking. He had spoken too frankly at first, but there was no way that he was letting Solemn Shawn off the line. He had to coax him back on the hook.

"No, no, SS. I ain't saying that. God forbid. This is exactly the type of place we need to save the few who want to be saved. We can't worry about the knuckleheads. Hell, jail, or a bullet will straighten them out. This place will be an oasis. An oasis for the few who want to get out of the desert.

"We really don't have to concern ourselves with saving the masses. The masses don't want to be saved. We need to concern ourselves with that one boy or girl who wants to use this place to their advantage. We need this place for that one boy or girl who wants to get out of this cesspool. That's who this place would be for."

Solemn Shawn smiled a little. "Spoken like a true politician," he said. "Okay, I just needed a little reassurance."

Mentally, Coleman wiped the sweat from his forehead. Just to make sure, he asked, "So I can still count on you for the whole three fifty?"

"Yeah, C-Dub. Full speed ahead. I'll start getting that cash to you to get it washed. I'm trusting you to make sure everything goes smooth."

"As silk," Coleman added. He hopped out of the pickup truck and headed for his CTS. Solemn Shawn bumped the horn lightly as he drove past the state representative.

17

REGINALD "REG" PARKER PUT HIS HAND TO THE SIDE OF HIS mouth and yelled, "Yo, Ghost! Ghost, come to the window, A!" he hollered up to the third-floor windows of the apartment building on the corner of 67th Street.

There was movement at the windows. The miniblinds rose and a light-skinned youth stuck his head out the window. Canton "Ghost" Tyson said, "Reg, what's the deal, A? What you on?"

"I just came through to kick it with you, A."

"I got Moo-Moo," Ghost said. "She just went to sleep and shit. Sherry had to go to a job interview downtown and shit. You can come up though. Let me whup on that ass in some NBA Street."

"Get the fuck outta here, A," Reg replied. "I'm the one that be whupping yo ass in Street. Last time we played I beat yo ass about ten times straight." With that Reg bounced up the three steps to enter the building's hallway. He scampered up the three flights of stairs to Ghost's apartment. At the apartment door he used the brass-plated knocker to tap lightly on the door. "Open up, A. I'm finta spank those cheeks," he said.

"You betta quit all that woofin', A," Ghost said with a gap-toothed smile as he opened the door. A small gold cross dangled on a thin gold chain on his bare chest. His only apparel was a pair of And 1 basketball shorts and some white socks.

Reg brushed past him and headed for the bedroom that Ghost shared with his little brother. In the small bedroom, Reg was about to take a seat on the bottom bunk when Ghost rushed into the room.

"Hold up, A," Ghost cautioned. "Watch Moo-Moo."

Reg looked behind him and saw Ghost's daughter on the bed. She was sleeping peacefully, sucking on a pink pacifier. He apologized, "Oh shit, A. My fault, fam. I didn't even see her. You know I ain't finta to sit on my goddaughter."

"It's cool, A," Ghost said as he gently rolled his daughter closer to the wall. "Shid, Moo-Moo would have still been sleep even if you would have sat on her. This girl could sleep through a Jigga concert."

While Ghost straightened out the covers around Moo-Moo, Reg busied himself with turning on the PlayStation 2 console. Moments later the two friends were competing fiercely with each other. Several games later, Reg dipped into his sock and pulled out a long, thin blunt. He brandished it. "Let's hit the back porch and blow this, A."

Ghost grabbed an Ecko sweatshirt off the top bunk and led the way to the back door. He picked up the cordless telephone off the kitchen table along the way. On the back porch, they both took a seat. Reg lit the blunt; he puffed and passed.

When Reg exhaled the marijuana smoke with tears in his eyes, he said, "You better be careful with that, A. That's some 'dro right there. That Governor that got killt, dude Bing, used to have tight 'dro like that. That was a cool stud to be a Governor. He wadn't set-tripping. He was 'bout selling that green to get some green, A." Reg had to laugh at his own little play on words.

In between puffs of weed, Ghost commented, "The nigga should have been an Apostle, A."

Reg leaned back against the cool bricks. "Man, this shit is crazy. I be wondering is we gone make it out this shit alive, A. I mean, my grandmother get to preaching at me and shit about the streets and I be wanting to tell her, damn, I know that shit. I can't even front, A. She be telling the truth."

"When I talk to my pops he be on the same shit," Ghost said. "But that nigga in the joint for the rest of his days, A. I be wondering how that shit must feel. I ain't trying to fly like that, A. I'm 'bout to graduate from high school this year and I been talking to my guidance counselor about going into the service or something."

Reg's cheeks were puffed up like Louis Armstrong with weed smoke. When he exhaled, he said, "Fuck that, A. I ain't joining no army-type shit. I would be done wiled out on one of those redneck-ass drill sergeants. Them motherfuckas be all up in yo face talking shit. Shid, the way this motherfucka Bush be picking fights with motherfuckas ain't no telling where a nigga would end up. A, we living in a war zone now. I ain't finta fly no zillion miles to be fighting some no-English-talking, towel-head, camel-riding motherfuckas over some gotdamn oil that don't none of us own."

Ghost almost fell off his crate laughing. When he sobered up, he said, "I ain't trying to fight no war, A. But I just made seventeen and I already got a kid. I got to do something, A. I wish I could just go to school, but my grades ain't shit and I don't play no sports or shit. Unless they come up with a scholarship for motherfuckas like me, then I'm dead in the water, A.

"The way I see it is, if I go to the service, when my time is up them motherfuckas will at least pay for my schooling. Plus after I been there awhile, they give you a tip on the base and shit. That way Sherry and Moo-Moo can come stay with a nigga, A."

Reg interjected, "That's if you ain't overseas with some chemical warfare shit in yo ass, A. Some of that shit that have you pissing on yo'self and shaking."

"Fuck you, A," Ghost said with a smile. "Shid, if I was in one of those motherfuckin' countries, all you got to do is give me a gas mask, a heater, and a bag of bullets and I guarantee you I'm gone make it back alive."

"How you gone do that, Ghost?"

"I'm gone clap the shit out of anything that don't speak American. Women, kids, camels, whatever, A."

Reg laughed again. "You a fool, A. They gone bring yo trigger-happy ass up on war crimes like one of them Nazi punks."

"Well, at least I'll be alive to stand trial, A."

"True dat," Reg agreed.

The two friends finished smoking Reg's blunt and decided to go inside and continue playing the video game. The weed had definitely affected their demeanor if not their motor skills. Now they spent more time concentrating on playing offense and defense on the street basketball game than talking smack to each other.

A half hour into their second gaming session, Reg said, "Damn, A. I'm hungrier than a hostage. I'm 'bout to bounce to the sub joint and grab me that two–pizza–puff special, A. Want me to bring you something back?"

Ghost stood up and stretched. He grabbed a pair of pants off the top bunk and began pulling them on. "I'mma walk wit you, A," he said.

Reg looked back at Ghost's daughter. "What about Moo-Moo?"

Ghost grabbed his pair of blue leather six-inch Timberland boots and tugged them on his feet. "She ain't finta wake up, A. She just went to sleep right before you came through. Plus her mother-fucking teeth is bothering her. She cutting like four teeth at once. That shit be having her acting her fool. I just gave her some medicine for her fever so she gone be knocked out for like three or four hours. By the time I grab me a gyro cheeseburger and make it back here she still ain't be awake, A."

Reg stood up and yawned. He asked, "You sure, A?"

Ghost grabbed a fitted Angels cap and put it over his do-rag. "I'm the daddy, A. I know what I'm doing. Now come on 'fore you wake her up with all that whining, A."

They left the apartment and headed for the submarine shop on the corner. In the small restaurant Reg ordered two pizza puffs. Ghost stepped up to the bulletproof window after him.

"Habib, listen up, motherfucker!" Ghost snarled through the hole in the glass. "Motherfucker, I want a gyro cheeseburger. I don't want nothing on that shit but cheese, gyro sauce, and onions. Last time yo stanking ass put ketchup and mustard on my shit. I started to come back up here and smear that shit on yo fucking windshield!"

The Arab sandwich shop owner smiled. "Fuck you, Meester Ghost. Motherfuck your ass. I'm an Apostle, I'll have you fucked up, beetch!"

Ghost and Reg nearly split their sides laughing at the Arab's mispronunciations. Ghost turned back to the window and he said, "You know what, Habib? You all right, A." Ghost pulled his slim bankroll from his pocket and peeled off four singles. "That's three-fifty right, for the burger, right? And give me one of those loose squares, A."

With the Newport 100 in his mouth, Ghost walked outside the restaurant—Reg followed. They stood in front of the sandwich shop making small talk while they waited for their orders.

Neither of them noticed the rusty white Chevy Celebrity as it putt-putted past them. But the driver of the Celebrity noticed the two Apostles standing in front of the sandwich shop. Behind the steering wheel of the Celebrity, Teddy watched the two young men without staring at them. He looked over at the young Governor Cave and said, "Don't look but there go two Assholes in front of that sandwich spot. It's perfect too. They ain't even watching they ass. We can bend this block and come up in the alley. You gone get out and walk back around this bitch. When you walk up to them, just be like, 'What's up, A?' Then as soon as they hit you up back, let they ass have it. You got me, Cave?"

Cave's lint-ridden cornrows bobbed up and down as he nodded.

Teddy pulled a 9mm from under the seat and handed it to Cave. "Give them studs the whole clip, shorty. You got that?"

Again Cave nodded his head to answer. His mouth was too dry to speak. Teddy nosed the Celebrity around the corner and into the alley. He crept to the edge of the alley and stopped. He looked over at Cave. "Take care of that state business, Governor."

Cave pulled on his hood and opened the car door. Rubber-legged he walked to the mouth of the alley. The weight of the pistol in the front pocket of his hooded sweatshirt seemed to give him courage, and by the time he gained the lip of the alley, he was walking with confidence. He stepped out of the alley. The mouth of the alley was right next to the sandwich shop entrance. He saw the two Apostles.

Reg was saying, "Then shorty told me she was going to the bathroom, but she never came back. I was so high sitting on the couch zoning that I didn't even notice. She had been gone about fifteen minutes before I realized this bitch done gave me move, A."

When Cave materialized out of the alley, Reg's back was to him, but he noticed the look on Ghost's face and turned around. He saw the young boy standing there with his hood on his head.

Cave greeted them. "What's up, A?"

Ghost looked Cave up and down, then he looked over at Reg to see if he recognized the hooded boy.

If Reg sensed something was amiss, he didn't give away his intuitions when he responded amicably, "Just chilling, A. What you on?"

Cave looked around before answering.

That made Ghost even more suspicious. Reg seemed to have read his mind as he asked with a little more caution in his voice, "Where you from, A? I ain't never seen you before."

Momentarily Cave almost panicked and ran, but the thought of Cold War brought him back to the task at hand. "I know you ain't trying to talk shit, A," Cave spurted.

Reg looked at Ghost with a stupefied look on his face. He turned back to Cave. "Nigga, what the fuck is you talking 'bout?"

Cave's face turned into an ugly mask. "Asshole, who the fuck you think you talking to!" His hand started to clear his pocket with the gun.

Reg turned, put his hand behind his head, and bolted.

Ghost stood transfixed with a look of fear plastered on his face.

His mouth framed the word "shit" but it couldn't be heard over the barking of the pistol in the hooded youth's hand. The sound of the slugs being launched from the semiauto gave Reg wings on his feet. He was halfway down the block when he felt something blur past him. Then he sensed more than felt a bullet disintegrate the tip of his middle finger and graze his ear. The cool wind felt good on his burning finger and ear as he raced across the street and cut through a vacant lot. Ghost finally willed his feet to move and he ran into the sandwich shop.

"Habib, Habib!" Ghost screamed as he beat on the gate that led to the kitchen of the sandwich shop. "Let me in, Habib!"

The Arab sandwich maker was nowhere to be seen. Cave stuck his hand in the door of the restaurant and fired several shots at Ghost. Two of the bullets struck the bulletproof glass, but the third slammed into his back. Ghost pitched forward into the counter, then fell backward onto the floor. Cave walked over to him and stood over him. With his eyes partially closed, Cave made the pistol bark and jerk until it was empty.

When the pistol in Cave's hand fell silent, Cave opened his eyes and peered at the dying youth at his feet. He felt faint, but the thought of being captured made him resolve to carry himself out the door of the sandwich shop into the waiting safety of the Chevy Celebrity. Two blocks from the shooting, Cave threw up all over the dashboard of the Celebrity. He was assured by Teddy that if he didn't pay to have the car cleaned he would be wearing Governor glasses for a month.

In the sandwich shop, on the floor, Ghost was turning into his nickname. He trembled as he watched the credits on the short film of his life roll in front of his eyes as he bled out on the floor among the cigarette butts, blunt guts, and old french fries. *I hope Sherry get that job,* he thought as he went to sleep.

Underneath the porch where Reg was hiding, his heart was colliding against his rib cage. The burn of his dinged ear was nothing in comparison to the throbbing pain accompanied by the pouring blood of his fingertip. As scared as he was, his thoughts were of his friend and fellow Apostle, Ghost. He knew that his friend was dead; he didn't move fast enough. Reg sat there under the porch with the spiders until he heard police sirens in the distance. His mind drifted as his adrenaline began to subside. The sirens reminded him of something. They almost sounded like a baby crying in the stillness after the shooting. "Moo-Moo!" he said as he scrambled from under the porch and began to run again.

A LIGHT, STEADY RAIN FELL ONTO THE BLUE-AND-WHITE Chicago police cars that blocked off both ends of the avenue. Bull and Grove pulled up to the police cruiser on the north end of the street. The officer in the blue-and-white wasn't paying attention, so Bull tapped the siren lightly. The dreadlocked policewoman behind the wheel looked up and saw the two GCU dicks. She dropped her vehicle into reverse and noiselessly glided out of their path. Once their car went past, she guided her vehicle back into position.

In the middle of the block in front of the sandwich shop, an area of twenty feet in either direction had been cordoned off with yellow tape. On the sidewalk beyond the yellow tape barrier a crowd of about fifty people stood, ignoring the slight rain in their curiosity. There were numerous police vehicles parked in the middle of the street, including a paddy wagon. Bull and Grove knew the large police truck was there to transport a dead body.

Bull glided the Crown Vic over to the gaggle of department vehicles and cut the engine. Dressed smartly, Grove wore a navy blue tailored suit complete with a Dobbs hat, and Bull was in an expensive sweater with nice slacks and size-fourteen alligator shoes. The two gang detectives exited the vehicle and made their way under the yellow tape. They received nods and even some cat-calls from some of the officers and detectives, which they returned. Inside the sandwich shop several homicide detectives stood to the side smoking cigarettes, while a fourth instructed the crime scene photographer. Two uniformed officers with white surgical gloves on their hands were positioning Ghost's body in a black body bag.

Homicide Detective Lonihan was behind the bulletproof glass in the kitchen area of the restaurant finishing up a field interview with Habib. The frightened Arab was babbling in a strange mixture of Arabic, English, and street slang. Shock was still etched across his bearded face. Lonihan turned to his partner, Clara Casey, a fiery redheaded woman with a stern schoolmarm face, and said, "I can't understand a thing this guy is saying. Put him in a unit and have them take him to the station. Maybe if we can get him to calm down a bit we can begin to decipher this shit."

Detective Casey nodded. She helped Habib up off the case of vegetable shortening he had been sitting on and escorted him out of the kitchen. Lonihan walked over to one of the deep fryers and lifted a wire basket containing two charred pizza puffs from the smoking grease. He wiped his hand on a towel and exited the kitchen to the lobby of the sandwich shop. There he saw Bull and Grove. Lonihan started to walk past them, but the captain's last stinging reprimand rang in his head. The Irish detective swallowed and walked over to them.

"How's it going, Detectives?" Lonihan asked evenly.

"Well if it ain't our old buddy O'Connor," Grove said jovially.

Detective Casey walked back into the lobby.

"That's Lonihan. And this is my partner, Detective Casey. Casey, this is Detectives Thensen and Hargrove."

Casey offered her freckled hand to the two GCU detectives. "Nice to meet you, Detectives Thensen and Hargrove," she said politely.

"Bull and Grove, ma'am, GCU at your service," Grove said as he touched the brim of his hat.

"You guys seem a tad overdressed for GCU," Casey commented.

"On our way to get a commendation," Bull grunted.

Grove smirked. "Another commendation."

"Congratulations," Casey said as she reeled her hand back in. She blushed a bit when she realized these two detectives were the ones her partner had ranted on and on about. Grove noticed her slight reddening and the self-conscious look on her face.

He laughed it off. "Ah, don't believe anything O'Brien says about us. He's just mad 'cause he can't be Black and pretty like us."

This time it was Lonihan's turn to blush. Vowing to not let Grove get under his skin, he turned and walked over to the bagged corpse. "If you guys will take a look at this, I'll give you what we got so far." He whipped out his small notebook. "Teenage, Black, male. No ID. The owner of this fine establishment called him 'Ghost.' Habib Salaam, that's the owner, said he was an Apostle. We already figured that because of the locale and the stiff's headgear." Lonihan pointed a fat pink finger at an evidence bag on the counter. In it was a bloody fitted hat with an *A* on it. "Do you guys know this kid?" Lonihan asked as the two GCU detectives joined him over the unzipped body bag.

Bull and Grove both stared at the body for a few moments before answering.

"I've never seen this kid before. What about you, Bull?"

The large gang crimes dick shook his massive head.

Grove looked up at Lonihan. "He was probably some foot soldier. He wasn't big or anything or he would have been on our radar. Might have been one of their shorties hustling on the block or something. Did it look like a robbery?"

Casey fielded the question. "Near as we could tell, no. His jewelry is still on his neck and he had a couple of bucks in his pocket. Now I was thinking this may have been—"

Lonihan cut her off. "We're on our way to interview Habib at the station. Maybe he can shine some light on this thing. I think he knows more than he was saying."

Grove wasn't so easily put off. "Casey, what were you saying?"

Slightly startled that Grove asked her opinion, Casey looked at Lonihan. She was unable to read his beefy face so she went ahead.

"I was thinking this may have been retaliation for the Bingham murder. I was on vacation when it happened, but my partner gave me the details. I know that someone wanted us to think that it was an Apostles hit for sure, but I couldn't really swallow that. It just seems too neat. Then this kid here, 'Ghost,' gets it. Seems to me that this is too much of a co-inky-dink."

Lonihan didn't want to seem stubborn, so he offered, "We got the prints back on the champagne bottle we found at the Bingham scene. Partials from Shawn Terson aka Solemn Shawn and Michael Moore aka Murderman. We're going to pull them in for questioning."

Grove looked at Bull. To the homicide detectives, he said, "If we bump into them, then we'll bring them in. I think the captain would appreciate that. What you think, O'Brien?"

Lonihan swallowed again. "I'm quite sure that he would appreciate that," he said dryly. "Come on, Casey."

Bull and Grove watched them leave. They took one last look at Ghost before the officer zipped up the body bag, then they left too.

19

"WHAT YOU WANT, TABBY?" SOLEMN SHAWN ASKED HIS SISTER as they stood in line at the Cajun Kitchen in the food court of the Orland Square Mall. He shifted the numerous shopping bags he was carrying as he turned to her.

"I want some bourbon chicken, rice, and vegetables, with lemonade."

"Sounds good. I think I'll have the same," Solemn Shawn said as he stepped up to the cashier. "I'd like two number twos with lemonade."

When their food was ready, they made their way to one of the iron table sets in the seating area.

In between forkfuls of bourbon chicken, Solemn Shawn commented, "I don't know if all this shopping done made me hungry, but this chicken is tight. I must be starving too 'cause even the vegetables is nice."

"Yeah and you getting old, so you need all the veggies you can get."

Solemn Shawn pointed his fork at her. "You better watch your mouth, young lady. Especially while I still have all the receipts to all your stuff."

"Just kidding, big bro. You as young as one of R. Kelly's girlfriends."

At her comment Solemn Shawn almost spit out the lemonade he was sipping. "Get your ass out of here. I ain't in preschool."

They both cracked up and continued to eat.

"Seriously though, big bro, I got to thank you for all the new hotness you copped me."

"Can't have my little sister at school looking like somebody's bum. I told you when you first went away to school that as long as I was around and you were in school that you wouldn't have to worry about a thing."

"You ain't never lied," Tabitha agreed after slurping some lemonade. "I haven't wanted for a thing since I started school. Then you copped me a truck for graduating. That was love right there."

"You sure you aren't burning yourself out by going straight through the summer? Usually it's good to take the summer off to get some rest."

"Hecky nall, big bro. I'm straight. I'm trying to get up out of there and get back to the real world. The only reason I'm going is because you've got to have at least a master's to be talking about any kind of money in corporate America. Even then you got to hustle and be willing to cut a nukka's throat to make it."

"You know, Tabby Cat," Solemn Shawn began softly, "I've always been proud of you. Your willingness to learn and take control of your own destiny. We're alike in many ways. I really am proud of you. I love you."

Tabitha blushed. "Dag, big bro. It sound like you catchin' feelings and shit. I know you're proud of me and that helps me a lot. It's not always about money either. A lot of times when I call I just want to hear your voice. That and a few bucks. No, seriously, it's just that you've been like a father to me. Somehow I know that you will always make everything all right when I call you.

"I don't even get that from Sam and she's my twin. Sometimes you make me think about what our father would have been like if he woulda made it, you know. I know you're proud of me. You should have seen how you were looking at my college graduation. You were looking like you were about to burst at the seams from happiness."

"Get outta here, Tabby Cat. Really, I was happy 'cause I thought yo butt was gone get out of school and get a damn job. Then you turn around and go to grad school on me. If I paid taxes, I could file you as a dependent."

Tabitha rolled her eyes and pursed her lips. "Yeah right. I never seen you that happy in my doggone life. That's what had me crying—the look of joy on my brother's face that I'd never seen before. That and my truck."

Remembering that day, Solemn Shawn responded sourly, "Then your crazy mama had to go and start talking greasy. Auditorium full of people gathered together on what's supposed to be a joyous occasion and somehow she finds a way to be fucking with me."

The pain in her brother's eyes at the mention of their mother was so strong, Tabitha had to look away.

"Big bro, you got to stop letting Ma rain on your parade," she stated comfortingly.

"Tabby, that lady finds some way to embarrass me anytime I'm around her. I used to think as the years went by she would let the past go, but she hasn't. You don't know what it feels like to have your mother hate you. Like the shit she pulled at Lil Shawn's party. That was sick."

"Awww, man. Don't nobody pay no attention to her. Sam knows that you ain't going to do anything to hurt your nephew. She was just worried about you having a gun in her house. You know she's straitlaced. Me though—I want you to protect yo neck. Do what you gotta do. You told me that shit a long time ago when I snuck and accepted a collect call from you when you was locked up. Man, Ma saw the charge for that call on the telephone bill and she beat the shit outta me."

"Sorry 'bout that, Tabby Cat. That must have been one of the few times that I got homesick while I was in there."

"It wasn't your fault. I knew what I was doing. I just wanted to talk to my big bro. I hated it when you got locked up. Didn't have nobody to do my homework for me no more."

"Get outta here. I know you thought you was slick by trying to get me to do your homework. I knew what you was on."

Tabitha laughed and blew bubbles in her lemonade with the plastic drinking straw. "But it was fun trying to get you to do it. Plus it was faster. I used to be trying to get to that damn TV. You ain't know it but Woody Woodpecker was my boyfriend."

Both of them laughed. When the laughter diminished, Solemn Shawn dug into his rice and asked, "You think you got enough clothes?"

Tabitha looked at all the bags from different stores. "Yeah, this stuff should hold me."

"You sure? 'Cause you hardly put a dent in me. You barely made it to a stack and I'd planned on at least spending two thousand on you. Then I was gone drop a stack in your pocket so you won't have to be out there eating Oodles of Noodles."

Tabitha paused with a piece of chicken halfway to her lips. "Are you trying to tell me that I got a thousand more to spend?"

"Something like that. But first you got to take care of some business for me. I have to warn you that it's real serious. You might not be able to handle it."

"What, big bro?" Tabitha asked eagerly.

Solemn Shawn leaned forward over his food tray and motioned for her to do the same. In a stage whisper, he said, "I need you to go over there to that McDonald's and get me a caramel sundae with nuts."

"Boy, you stupid," Tabitha said as she got out of her seat and headed over to the Mickey D's.

"Mission accomplished," she announced when she came back and set the sundae on the table.

Solemn Shawn picked up the sundae and snapped his fingers. "My fault, Tabby. You took off so fast that I forgot to tell you that I wanted an apple pie."

Again Tabitha jumped to her feet to make the short trip.

Laughing, Solemn Shawn said, "I was just joking, Tabby Cat. Sit down, girl."

Tabitha sat down. "Shid, I woulda baked you a pie if you wanted me to."

"Girl, you crazy."

"You think I'm playing, try me," Tabitha assured, as she polished off her last few bites of chicken. She picked up a napkin on her tray to wipe her mouth; underneath the napkin was a small jewelry box. Her eyes bucked as she looked up at her brother; he was playing innocent, eating his sundae and avoiding her eyes.

Picking up the box, Tabitha asked, "What's this, big bro?"

"I never seen that before. Why don't you open it and take a look."

As she removed the small lid from the box, the sparkle of diamonds hit her eye. The precious stones were mounted on a small golden cross. An elaborately linked but thin gold chain completed the necklace. Tabitha's hand flew to her mouth.

"Good lord, Shawn!" she exclaimed. "This is so nice, big bro!"

Shoppers at the nearby tables gazed curiously at them. Some of them instantly decided that it wasn't a lovers' quarrel or a marriage proposal so they quickly became disinterested.

Happy at his sister's reaction, Solemn Shawn polished off the rest of his sundae. "Put it on, Tabby Cat."

Tabitha was so giddy at her gift, she couldn't open the small, delicate clasp. Solemn Shawn wiped his hands on a napkin.

"Give it here before you break it." He stood up and walked behind her chair to place the necklace on her neck.

Her hand went to the cross. "Thanks, big bro," Tabitha bubbled. "I'm loving this. This boy is so phat. I'mma have motherfuckers jelly when I get to school."

"Okay, that's enough, Tabby. Now let's go finish spending my money."

Happy as a pardoned death row inmate, Tabitha hugged her brother. She was all smiles as she helped him collect her shopping bags.

20

Officer Hardy looked up from the sports section of his newspaper and scowled. He was sitting at the security post in the main cafeteria of the juvenile prison. Today the boys were making an excessive amount of noise.

"Smallwood, sit you ass down and cut that shit out!" Hardy shouted to a tall light-skinned boy who was juggling several oranges.

Startled, Smallwood dropped one of the oranges and grinned sheepishly. "My fault, Hardy." The boy took his seat after retrieving the fruit.

"Yo fault, yo mistake," Hardy said. "I can tell you motherfuckers is frantic to be eating lunch out them damn cells again. That lockdown be having y'all asses going crazy."

"You ain't lying, Hardy," Dante commented as he walked by with his plastic food tray in his hand. "A week on lockdown feel like a damn month or something. It's bad enough being locked up, but being locked down is a bitch. Good thing that me and my cellie is cool or I'da done been snapped, crackled, and popped."

Officer Hardy laughed. "Keep it moving, Dante."

Dante smiled as he headed for his customary table. It was a long one, seating about twenty inmates on the long benches that were attached to the table. Chairs were considered weapons and had been removed from the cafeteria years before.

"Solemn Shawn, what's happening, bro?" Dante said cheerfully as he took a seat across from the stone-faced youth.

"Nothing to it, but to do it, Dante," Solemn Shawn answered.

"I heard that," Dante said as he handed his small carton of chocolate milk to Murderman.

Grinning with his mouth full of food, Murderman said, "You always give me yo chocolate milk. What you got against brown milk, Dante?"

"Nothing. I just like things to be the way they should be. Milk is supposed to be white and motherfuckers be trying to change it and shit. Putting that nasty-ass Ovaltine shit in it. I know it's s'posed to be white, so that's the only way I'm gone drink it."

Mimicking Malcolm X, Solemn Shawn ranted, "See, brother. That's what the white man wants us to think—that milk shouldn't be brown, chocolaty, and good, brother. The cow that gives the white milk is celebrated. He's invited to breakfast with Captain Crunch. But the brother cows—the soulful cows—the ones with the Afros, they are shunned by their cow brethren."

The boys broke up in laughter—partly because it was funny, partly because Solemn Shawn was telling a joke.

"What the fuck is so funny?" a small skinny-faced boy named Weezie asked as he squeezed onto the bench next to Dante.

Putting his mirth aside, Dante became all business. "I hope you got our scratch for them three joints we gave yo ass on credit," he growled at Weezie. "Yo lying ass. I really didn't think about it when you said it was yo birthday. Later on I realized that this was about yo third birthday this year, motherfucker. I should kick yo butt just on GP, nigga."

"Dante, my man. You ain't even gotta act like that. I got something that's worth more than a few funky greenbacks."

"Nigga, you fulla shit," Murderman said. "I don't know of nothing that's worth more than dough, nigga. You must be losing yo damn mind. You tell me what's worth more than scratch."

"Information," Weezie stated smugly as he reached for Murderman's extra chocolate milk.

Murderman smacked his hand. "Don't make me beat you up,

Weezie. What type of info you got that's worth more than the money you owe us, nigga?"

Solemn Shawn appeared nonchalant, but he was more than interested in what Weezie had under his cap.

Weezie tried to keep his hole card hidden. "I wanna know what my information is worth to you cats. Since all of y'all work for Big Ant my information is valuable to all y'all, but mainly Solemn Shawn in particular."

"Nigga, you can't even spell 'particular,' " Murderman said. "And if yo info is good, then it's worth us not kicking yo damn head in."

Solemn Shawn zoomed in on Weezie. "Cut the theatrics and lay the shit out. If it's good then you can forget about your debt."

Weezie instinctively knew that Solemn Shawn wasn't the one for his bullshitting. "When I was in the gym under the bleachers—don't ask me what I was doing there—I overheard some cats talking shit. Cats was talking 'bout since Big Ant was gone how sweet this shit was gone be. Cats was talking about robbing you and fucking you up bad. One of them said they was gone get the quiet punk.

"First I thought it was just some motherfuckers bellyaching 'cause they ain't got cop money, but these studs been around the building trying to get their hand on shanks and shit."

Solemn Shawn held his hand up to halt Weezie. "How many of them is it?"

"Four."

"Did they say when and where?"

Weezie reached for Murderman's chocolate milk again, but a glance from the youth with the high-top fade stopped him. "In the rec room on Thursday. Two of them plan to start a fight outside of the rec room to keep the guard distracted while the others take you offa here. They know they ain't no way for Dante or Murderman to get rec room privileges on Thursday 'cause they got different house numbers. Plus, they know that you be holding heavy on rec room day."

Toying with his orange, Solemn Shawn asked, "Who are these cats?"

"Ben, you know Bad Breath Ben, Frito, and I don't know the other two cats by name. One of them I think is called Freddy. They stay on some bullshit though. Stealing out of niggas' cells and shit. Them niggas think they hard too."

Solemn Shawn looked around. He noticed four of the kids sitting at the table had got in the wind at the mention of Ben and Frito. Several more looked ready to bolt, and the last four looked ready to spread news of his cowardice, if he showed any. He could even see that Murderman and Dante were trying to play it off, but they were looking at him expectantly—looking at him to make a decision, to be a leader.

Big Ant had groomed him for this day. He had told him over and over again this day was coming, especially once he'd left for the world. This was a direct challenge to his existence, and if he didn't meet it head-on, Solemn Shawn knew he was through gambling. He thought about the few months of training in the art of prison warfare that Big Ant had bestowed upon him. It was time to put some of the cruel, brutal methods into action. He hated being picked as the weak one out of the crowd, but he would definitely show Ben and his buddies they had seriously underestimated him.

"Weezie," Solemn Shawn said, "I thank you for sharing this information with us. Your slate is wiped clean. Next time you lie to get some weed from us, we gone stomp yo ass. Now excuse yourself."

This is a cold-blooded motherfucker, Weezie thought. He dismissing me like I'm a damn peasant or something. Well, that's cool, I don't owe these motherfuckers no more. This nigga acting all arrogant and shit. I hope he don't write no check that his ass can't cash.

Weezie stood up. "I'm glad that I could be of service to y'all. You know I always liked you cats. Watch y'all back."

Dante spoke first. "We can't be up in that rec room wit you, so what you gone do? The niggas in yo house ain't gone help you. You need to chill until we can bust them niggas' heads together. Or we can get on the phone and rap with Big Ant and maybe he can point us in the right direction."

Solemn Shawn began to peel his orange. "Can't do that, Dante. We got to stand on our own two feet. Inside here and outside, weakness is a sin. I must stress that I have to deal with this head-on. Like Chaplain Brown says, if our cause be divine, everything'll be fine."

"Later for that preacher-man shit," Murderman snapped. "Sounds like you starting to believe all that 'meek shall inherit the earth' shit. It's gone be two niggas in that room with shanks, and Chaplain Brown and his God ain't gone be nowhere around, you dig."

"What would you propose I do," Solemn Shawn asked. "Run from these dudes? Look around you, my man. There isn't anywhere to run. Should I call Big Ant sniveling like a coward and try to get him to pull a few strings? If I did then he would think we couldn't take care of our own problems in here. I know that if I don't handle these punks, then we might as well give our weed away, because ain't nobody gonna wanna cop from a punk-ass dopeman. The shanks they're going to have only pose a minor threat because they're walking into a room full of pool sticks. I can already tell these dudes aren't too bright—greedy but stupid."

Frustrated, Murderman asked, "Dante, you heard this nigga?"

"Yeah, Shawn, you is starting to sound like you off you damn rocker."

"Trust me," Solemn Shawn said as he ate his orange. He collected his food tray and walked away without looking back.

"That nigga is losing his damn marbles," Murderman said. "Going up against two niggas with shanks just for the hell of it. That nigga so smart, he stupid."

Pensively, Dante said, "That's just him. Ain't no kind of way he gone let that shit ride. As long as I known him, he ain't never fucked with nobody, but he ain't never allowed no motherfucker to fuck with him. Stop worrying about that nigga. He'll come to his senses. Now bring yo ass on, I'm ready to work out. You gone hit the weights wit me?"

"Hell nall. You know I don't lift no fucking weights. The only iron I lift is the kind that go bang and that's what got me in here in the first place. You gone on ahead, I got to go check on something."

Outside the recreation room, Solemn Shawn whispered a silent prayer under his breath before he pushed open the door and entered the room.

"Good," he said to himself. He had made it here before his antagonists.

Quietly he began making his rounds and peddling his joints of the best green stuff this kiddie pen had seen in a long time. Several boys by the Ping-Pong table signaled to him to get his attention. Warily he walked over to them, his eyes scanning the room. He noticed one youth over by the Foosball table leaning on a mop in a bucket, staring at him. The boy had a menacing scowl on his face. Solemn Shawn made a note to keep his eyes on that kid.

He stepped to the kids playing Ping-Pong. "What's up, y'all?"

"Got some reefer?" Billy, the taller of the Ping-Pong players, asked.

"Yeah, man," Solemn Shawn answered in clipped tones.

"The same good shit like last time?" the other player asked. "I mean is it that fire bo that make yo hair grow?"

"Money-back guarantee," Solemn Shawn stated impatiently. They knew he had the good stuff. He had known it would be risky pretending to carry on business as usual, but the way these dudes were questioning the obvious was ridiculous. "So what's up? Y'all copping or window-shopping, baby?"

"Yeah, give us four of 'em. Tone, pay the man," Billy directed. Tone looked like he wanted to protest, but Billy gave him a look. "Nigga, I know you ain't trying to renege on our bet. You lost four times—that's four joints. Now pay the man."

Reluctantly Tone coughed up the money, including a dollar's worth of change that Solemn Shawn didn't want to take, but hey, money was money. Once the transaction was made, Solemn Shawn headed over to the pool table area. There were three pool tables and all of them were occupied. He picked his marks and slid up to them.

"A Johnny and Bread," he said to the two pool-playing boys. "Let me put a bug in y'all ear."

Bread stopped aiming at the seven ball and looked up. "Solemn Shawn, what's up, baby?"

"I need this table here and I'm willing to pay you cats two dollars and two joints for it."

"'Nuff said," Bread replied. He and Johnny laid their pool cues on the table, accepted the payoff, and made for the game closet to get high.

After making sure the guard wasn't watching him, Solemn Shawn broke one of the pool cues across his knee as quietly as possible. He attracted only minor attention from the other inmates. The skinny end of the pool cue he tossed in the garbage can; the heavy weighted end he placed on the side of the pool table in the space where the unracked balls were stored. As he prepared himself for battle, Solemn Shawn kept an eye on the door and the boy who was leaning on the mop. The boy hadn't moved from his initial spot. From his pocket Solemn Shawn pulled a double tube sock. Palming two balls from the table, he dropped them in the sock and tied a knot right over them. He stashed the pool ball sock with the broken pool cue. When he looked up, the kid by the mop was still watching him.

Still keeping his eye on the door, Solemn Shawn walked back over to the Ping-Pong table. "Billy, dig it. Let me ask you something, man."

Without putting down his Ping-Pong paddle, Billy stepped a little ways away from the Ping-Pong table. "Yeah, man. What's popping?"

"Billy, who is this chump that's leaning on that mop over there?" Solemn Shawn asked. "That stud keep pinning me while I'm trying to take care of my business like he a junior narc or something."

"Dude name is Vee. Shorty been here for a minute. You probably ain't never seen him 'cause he spend so much time in the hole for doing bullshit."

"Yeah. What's the 411 on him though?"

"Shorty be trying to make a name for hisself. Starting fights and shit. He ain't shit."

"Thanks, Billy," Solemn Shawn said. He slapped Billy five before making his way back to the pool table loaded with his mini-arsenal.

At the pool table, Solemn Shawn racked the balls, and through his nervous anticipation he managed to make a few shots. He was trying to sink a two-cushion shot when he heard a commotion outside the rec room.

This is it, he thought, as he moved around the table to the side where his weapons were stored.

Sure enough, Ben and Frito burst into the rec room. Ben shouted, "Them niggas is out there boxing! Dre is mopping Tyrone! Check it out, y'all!"

All of the inmates and the rec room guard bolted for the door to see the brawl. Solemn Shawn stood his ground.

The empty room gave notice to Ben that the first stage of his plan was successful. He started toward the seemingly uninterested Solemn Shawn. Behind Ben, Frito closed the door, pulled the guard's chair over and secured it under the doorknob.

"Quiet-ass nigga, drop that stick!" Ben ordered as he pulled a six-inch shank from his waistband.

Solemn Shawn dropped the pool cue and stood up. "What's happening, man? What, you niggas want to buy some weed?"

"Frito, you hear this nigga talking about do we want to buy some weed?"

Frito snickered. "Nigga must be stupid, Ben, or he losing his got-damn mind."

"Yeah, something like that," Ben agreed. "Let me make it where he can understand this shit. Nigga, this is a stickup, don't make it an ambulance pickup."

The boys were only a few feet from Solemn Shawn, coming at him from both ends of the pool table with their knives out in front of them.

In a blur, Solemn Shawn filled his hands with the pool ball sock and broken pool cue. Looks of amazement leaped to his attackers' faces as they saw their mark was prepared for them. Across the room, Vee stepped from behind one of the room's columns holding the metal mop bucket filled with hot water.

"Ahhhh!" he yelled as he charged across the room.

Vee's yell caught everyone off guard. As Ben and Frito turned to see who the hell was yelling like a fool, Solemn Shawn sprang forward and tried to cave the back of Ben's head in with the pool ball sock. There was a dull thunk as Ben grabbed his head. He dropped his knife and melted to his knees. The boy with the bucket was almost upon him so Solemn Shawn had to disregard Frito momentarily so he could defend himself against Vee.

But instead of heading toward Solemn Shawn, Vee heaved the bucket of water on Frito. Drenched in the hot water, Frito began to dance around, all the while bellowing in pain. Vee hopped toward him and slapped him alongside his head with the metal bucket. As Frito fell, Vee pounced on him and began beating him with the bucket.

Amazed, but relieved, Solemn Shawn went to work on Ben with the pool cue. With the heavy end, he mechanically beat Ben. The would-be robber writhed on the floor in pain as he tried to cover his face and head with his arms and hands. With surgical precision, Solemn Shawn brought the pool cue down on his wrists, arms, and hands over and over again. The smacks of the wood were punctuated by the sound of fracturing bones. One of the bones in Ben's left wrist began peeking through the flesh. Solemn Shawn aimed the stick at Ben's right shoulder and swung hard. There was an awesome crack as the pool cue and Ben's collarbone met. Satisfied with his handiwork, he backed off. Solemn Shawn looked over at Vee, who was taking his time kicking Frito's unconscious face to pieces.

The soggy, bloody boy looked to be disfigured, but Vee wasn't through. Vee spotted Solemn Shawn's discarded pool ball sock and scooped it up. With it, he began aiming blow after blow at Frito's ankles and knees.

Solemn Shawn knew from the awful sound of the pool balls striking Frito's kneecaps that the boy wouldn't be walking normally any-time soon—if ever again.

Worried that they would be missed, Solemn Shawn called out to Vee, "A, man, that's enough. We need to get out of here before every-body come back."

Vee ignored him and kept whacking Frito with the sock.

Solemn Shawn walked over and grabbed his flailing arm. "Man, I said that's about enough," he said forcefully.

There was a slight glaze in Vee's eyes as he looked up at Solemn Shawn. It seemed to take him a second or two to fight down the blood-lust. Solemn Shawn released his arm and started for the door. Vee looked over at Ben, unconscious of pain. Almost as an afterthought he swatted Ben a few times in the head and groin area with the pool ball sock.

"I said that's enough, man!" Solemn Shawn spit through his teeth. "We need to book before we both be in the hole or get our privileges took for the rest of our sentences. Now come on."

Vee gave Ben one more hit, and then after kicking him in the ribs, he dropped the sock and joined Solemn Shawn by the door.

"One thing, man. Why did you help me?"

Breathing heavily, Vee said, "Murderman sent me. I owed him a favor, plus he paid me a couple of joints to give you a hand in here. I hate that punk Frito anyway, so really it was a pleasure. Murderman said not to hip you that I was s'posed to help you out. That's why I hid behind the wall when everybody ran out in the hallway."

Note to self, Solemn Shawn thought, I got to thank Murder for sending such a wildcat.

"All right, Vee, now we got to get out of here. We gone mingle in the crowd around the fight, then when ain't nobody looking we gone scram. Got it?"

"Uh-huh," Vee said.

After peeking through the glass, Solemn Shawn pulled the chair from under the doorknob. He examined Vee's clothes and his own. Both of them had blood on their clothing, but it couldn't be helped.

Outside the door the rec room guard was having the damnedest time trying to break up the staged fight between Ben's lackeys. The hallway contained more inmates than were originally in the rec room. Most of them had wandered on the scene, hoping for a chance to see some bloodletting.

Using the melee for cover, Vee and Solemn Shawn slipped into the hallway unnoticed. For a hot second they pretended to watch the fight.

"It was a business doing pleasure with you," Vee said, before walking away.

Solemn Shawn watched him for a moment, then began heading for his own cell to clean up and change clothes.

21

"Sorry I'm late, A," Solemn Shawn announced as he dropped his bowling bag and looked around.

The huge bowling alley was full of families, bowling teams, and spectators. Children ran to the video games, quarters clutched tightly in their small fingers. Teenagers lounged at the snack shop. At the bar, women drank, smoked cigarettes, and cursed while their husbands, boyfriends, and future bedroom conquests battled one another on the smooth lanes. Sprinkled in the crowd were three young men. Instead of bowling equipment in their bags, they carried MP5s with fifty-shot clips. They were the security team for the Head Apostles.

"You ain't miss shit, A," Big Ant said, as he took another swallow of his beer.

Dante spoke up. "The office is ready for us. I'll have Nick send back some pizzas and a couple of longnecks."

As the others headed for the management office, Dante went toward the bar. He ignored the hungry glances of women as he had a few words with his brother, Nick, behind the bar. In the office, Murderman and Mumps sat on a futon, while Big Ant and Solemn Shawn chose two reclining chairs. When Dante entered the office he took a seat behind the glass desk. Few people outside of the five men in the room knew that the bowling alley was really owned by them. If the church leagues, police officers, and fine upstanding members of the community knew that their chief recreation center was owned by Chicago's most notorious gang, they would be more than a little angry.

There was a tap at the door, then Nick entered the office carrying two boxed pizzas and a twelve-pack of beer. "Pies and suds," he said cheerfully as he set the food and beer on the table in front of the sofa. "There's paper plates and napkins in the cabinet behind the desk," he said before turning to leave.

"Any problems, Nick?" Dante asked his brother before he could get to the door.

Nick stopped and wiped his hands on the apron tied around his waist. His face twisted up in thought before he answered. "Nothing major but this cat that used to work here. I had to fire the dude for stealing. Dude was stealing liquor and shit so I got rid of his ass. Little motherfucker got to talking crazy and shit. Said he was gone burn the place down."

Murderman's voice was a cold wind. "What's his name?"

"Little short dude named Troy. I'll give you his address and shit before you leave."

"As soon as you do, it's taken care of, A," Murderman assured Nick.

"All right, I'll get that to you, M1. If you guys need anything else just ring the bar," Nick said as he left the office.

The five Head Apostles joked around as they helped themselves to pizza and beer, but the moment they were seated again it became all business.

Solemn Shawn asked, "Tay, how is the paper looking for the community center, A?"

Dante wiped his mouth and answered, "We already got a hundred in cashier's checks. We got about one sixty to one seventy stacks on the streets, and Benito from the Westside is bringing me another hundred, A.

"The yay is doing all right, so is the diesel, but the thing that's really bringing in the dough is that hydro shit, A. That fucking weed shit sell like heroin used to sell back in the days."

Big Ant toned in, "But it be hard to find somewhere to store all that shit. Shit, my motherfucking junkyard was full of that shit. The fumes from that shit be a bitch, A. My goddamn dogs was walking around high as hell off that shit, eating up big bags of Eukanuba in one day."

Everybody laughed.

Big Ant continued, "With the money Dante gave me to cop wit I almost scared my connect. They wasn't used to me grabbing fifty pounds, but because I been fucking with them so long they went on and did it. The turnover is crazy. We might be making between three and half, four stacks off of every pillow. That way we paying everybody that getting rid of it for us real lovely. We only paying four thousand for a pillow, while anybody else, even if they could get it, would be paying about anywhere between five thousand to fifty-five hundred for a pound."

Mumps asked, "Is the shit gone dry up on us, A?"

Big Ant said, "Not no time soon. My guy will let me know if it's gonna go bad and let me buy everything he's got until he gets some more shit in. Plus when I told him what we were trying to do he said that he would let a lot of his cats dry up while we made this move. That's guaranteeing that we got this shit on lock. I suggest when this shit is over we keep on getting it like this, A."

Solemn Shawn wiped his mouth and hands with a napkin, then balled it up and shot it at the garbage can halfway across the room and missed. As he left his seat and picked the napkin up off the floor, without looking at Murderman, he asked, "Double M, why you got rocks in yo jaws, A?"

Murderman's voice kept its cold edge as he answered, "One of the young cats got merced, A. He was up at that gyro spot on Sixty-seventh. Him and another Apostle. The other cat got clipped on his finger and his ear."

Solemn Shawn took his seat and zeroed in on Murderman. "Why am I just hearing about this?"

Murderman was a bit uneasy under Solemn Shawn's intense

glare. "This just happened the other day, SS, and I been trying to find out where this shit came from, A. Me and Yo-Yo, the Under Apostle for that section, been checking this out. The young cat's name was Ghost and the cat that was with him is name Reg. Me and Yo-Yo hollered at Reg, A. Reg said that the stud that rolled Ghost's carpet back approached them like he was family. Said he didn't really get a good look at the dude but that he knew something wasn't right. Reg said this kid just upped his heater and started letting loose for no reason."

Big Ant asked, "You sure them shorties wadn't trying to wile out or something on dude and he got the best of them, A?"

Dante answered for Murderman. "Don't make no difference if they was in the wrong. The stud that killed our little brother is dead wrong, A. Ain't no cat s'posed to be on no Apostle set offing one of ours."

"You right, A," Big Ant agreed. "Why I'm saying that is maybe if we knew what provoked this shit, then maybe, just maybe, we would know who this stud is that cooked our little brother."

Mumps drawled, "We ain't even got to discuss this shit, A. When an Apostle goes to Heaven, somebody else goes to hell. M1, all you got to do is use some of those CIA-type informants you got to find out who did this shit, A."

Nodding, Murderman said, "I already got my feelers out there now. Does the Council of Head Apostles agree that when I find this dude and whatever crew he from I can push some buttons?"

Everyone cast their eyes downward, a prearranged signal that meant death.

22

"I'm downstairs," Vee said into his cell phone.

"Here I come," Sakawa said into her telephone. She hung up the cordless telephone and tossed it on the bed. She walked to the mirror on her closet door and took a look at herself. On her last trip to the beauty shop, Mrs. Dunn's Get It Dunn, she had her stylist clip her long hair to a short, wavy bob that accentuated her beautiful face. Her Native American ancestry was easily recognizable in the reddish hue of her skin and her high cheekbones.

Sakawa was wearing a maroon, short-sleeved tight sweater that hugged her chest. Underneath her sweater the bra from Victoria's Secret was doing its thing. Her skirt was a long smoke gray, made from an almost sheer material that hung down to her ankles. On the right side of the skirt, a long split displayed her shapely thighs, thin ankles, and smooth skin. A pair of maroon Donna Karan sandals were tied up her well-muscled calves.

Satisfied with her reflection, Sakawa grabbed a pair of oversize Donna Karan sunglasses and her Donna Karan purse. She checked her purse to make sure she had her cock-blocking kit—tampons and Midol.

Slyly, she chuckled. *If this nigga think he getting some pussy, he got another think coming,* she thought. The telephone jangled, breaking her train of thought. Without picking up the telephone she looked at the caller ID—it was Vee.

"I'm gone have to train this nigga," she said to herself as she picked up the telephone.

"I'm coming, baby," Sakawa said sweetly.

"That's what I want to hear you say," Vee said lecherously.

Nigga, you wish, she thought. But she said, "Stop playing, boy. I'm on my way down. I had to make sure that I was looking good for you, baby." Sakawa pushed the End button on the telephone and threw it back on her bed.

At the curb in front of her building, Vee was sitting behind the wheel of his Excursion. He had Musiq Soulchild's first CD playing softly on the sound system. He knew that he was looking good in a white-and-orange-trimmed Akademiks jogging suit with a pair of white-and-orange-trimmed Air Force Ones. Though he was looking fly he wasn't ready for just how lovely Sakawa looked with her new hairdo.

"Gotdamn, girl," Vee commented as she climbed into the SUV. "You look good than a motherfucka with no hair. Like Halle Berry or Toni Braxton or something. Shid, I should skip dinner and go straight to the telly."

"Stop playing with me, Vee," Sakawa said with a seductive flash of her white teeth. "The only way you got me out the house after a long day of work is because you said we was going out to eat. Hungry as I am, you better take me straight to the restaurant."

Sakawa's refusal of his proposition to go to a motel didn't make Vee angry. He had hoped she would say yes, but deep down he knew she wouldn't, well, not before dinner anyway. They had been out on about six dates so far and she never seemed like she was on the verge of pulling down her panties. Around the fourth date she had offered him a polite peck on the cheek, but not much more. One night he had gotten up his courage to palm her butt and she hit the ceiling. She had actually cursed him out and made him drop her off at home. For a few days Vee said fuck her, but soon he found himself sending her flowers and candy. After that date Vee knew to keep his hands to himself.

My day will come though, Vee thought. *And when it do, I'mma take me some ginseng and tear that pussy up.* Smiling, Vee turned the music up until the bass resonated through the truck, and he headed for Lakeshore Drive.

The day was pleasant with a mild breeze blowing off Lake Michigan.

Sakawa signaled for Vee to turn the music down. "Where are we eating?" Sakawa inquired.

"This little spot called Ron of Japan," Vee answered. "It's a fancy-schmancy Japanese restaurant. People be making a big deal out of it, but I only like this batter type of shit they put on the shrimp and lobster. Why you looking like that? Like you think all niggas know is J&J Fish, McDonald's, and on special occasions Red Lobster."

Laughing, Sakawa said, "That's all you niggas know. Y'all be all up in Red Lobster trying to get the all-you-can-eat shrimp and trying to act like you balling." She imitated a man's voice, "You know what I mean, I want a gang of them skrimps and bring some more of them biscuits, yo."

They both laughed.

"Girl, you crazy than a motherfucka," Vee said.

It took them fifteen minutes to reach the Japanese eatery in downtown Chicago. A red-jacketed valet drove the Excursion away as Vee held the restaurant door open for Sakawa. They were a few minutes early for their reservation so they sat at the bar. Vee ordered Super Mai Tais for them both. Over the bar, the television was on the Sports History Channel showing an old basketball game. It was the Detroit Pistons from the Bad Boy era beating up on the pre-championship Chicago Bulls.

As the barkeeper set their drinks in front of them, Vee commented, "Damn, look at those little-ass shorts Isiah and them got on. Them motherfuckas look like they got on biking shorts or something."

Sakawa removed her sunglasses. "Shit, if Zeke try to do a crossover his nuts gone pop up out them little-ass shorts."

Vee roared with laughter. He cracked, "Look at Rodman, that motherfucka looked fruity even back then. I bet Laimbeer and them used to let his ass shower first."

Sakawa joked, "I know the Microwave used to be like, 'Nall, Dennis, you gone head, family. I'll wait.' "

It was Vee's turn to be surprised. "The Microwave? Girl, what you know about basketball?"

"Shit, I love me some ball. I played for my high school. Power forward. I was all-city, too. Tore up my ACL. No college wants a wounded duck. Dropped out of high school and hit the streets. After that I got locked up. Now I'm trying to get myself together and get in the league. You know the drill."

Vee looked at her. "You was locked up?"

"Nall, man. I was just bullshitting. You know that's what all the athletes be saying on them SportsCenter whatever-happened-to-what's-his-name specials. I did play for my school though and tore up my knee. Finished school though. You ever play basketball?"

Vee took a sip of his Mai Tai. "Girl, you stupid. I was 'bout to say. Nall, I can't really play. I love to watch though. Shit, one of my shorties, this nigga named Bing, could fly. He used to be up in the gym dunking on any motherfucka that got in his way. Shit, I done won stacks betting on that nigga. And the stud had a pure jump shot. Every time he touched the ball it was like he was a sniper or something. He coulda made it to the NBA or something. Motherfucka killt him not too long ago." He fell silent.

For the next few minutes they watched the game quietly, content to sip their drinks. The hostess walked over and announced that their table was ready. Throwing a ten-dollar tip on the bar, Vee grabbed their drinks and they followed the hostess to their table. The table was a semicircular booth that housed a fully functioning grill. Each booth could seat eight people comfortably. Part of the ambience of Ron of Japan was that you would usually end up sharing dinner and sometimes politely strained conversation with complete and total strangers. It was the early supper hour and patronage was light, so Vee had managed to secure a private booth for them by tipping the hostess two extra C-notes.

At their private booth, Vee and Sakawa chatted while they watched the Japanese chef work his magic with the grill, cutlery, vegetables, rice, and seafood.

"Girl, I hope you as tight in the kitchen as this dude," Vee said.

"That's all you men want. Y'all can't wait to get a sister in the kitchen and have her fucking up her hair, slaving over a hot stove for y'all asses."

"You damn right, Sakawa. My mama and all my aunties can get in that kitchen and burn some shit. And any woman that gone be my girl or wife got to be able to cook, too."

Sakawa rolled her eyes and killed her Super Mai Tai. "Your wife? Now I know that player, gangster-ass Vee ain't talking 'bout getting married."

"Yeah, I'm gone get married one day. My mama and daddy still married. Both of my grandparents is still married. My big brother and little sister is married. My uncles and aunts is married. Shit, marriage run in my family."

"So why you ain't married yet, Vee? You 'bout thirty, thirty-one. What you waiting on?"

Vee looked around the restaurant like maybe the answer was written on the wall somewhere. After a gulp of his Mai Tai, he said, "Really, it ain't me. I just ain't found the type of woman that I could marry and be happy with for life."

Running her finger around the rim of her empty glass, Sakawa asked, "And what is the type of woman that you would marry?"

Before he answered, Vee ordered them another round of Super Mai Tais. He looked Sakawa straight in the eyes and said, "You."

His answer caused her to choke on her drink. After slapping her lightly on the back, Vee waited for her to get her bearings before asking, "Damn, would it be that bad marrying me? Just the thought got you choking up in this piece."

Sakawa wiped her mouth with her linen napkin and answered in a somewhat raspy voice, "It ain't like that, Vee. You just threw me off with your answer. Made my drink go down the wrong pipe, shid."

Still offended, Vee cracked, "It ain't like I was proposing or nothing. I was just saying that you the kind of girl that a nigga should marry. Not none of these rats that be out here trying to hit a nigga up for some cheese."

Sakawa sensed that she needed to smooth down Vee's ruffled feathers. She put her hand on his arm and said, "I didn't think that you were proposing. Actually I'm quite flattered that you could consider me marriage material. You just caught me by surprise with your answer, that's all. I wasn't trying to make fun or belittle you. You want me to keep it real with you, Vaton?"

"I always want you to keep it real with me."

"Vee, for you to have someone like me for a wife, you'd have to change certain things about the way you're living."

Vee pulled his arm away from her hand and picked up his drink. "Just like a woman. They ass always want you change. A nigga ain't never good enough for y'all. You always got to try and make a motherfucka be the way that you want him."

His remark lit a fire under Sakawa. She said, "Just like a nigga—afraid to change. Nigga, you a gangbanger. Only one of them rats that you claim you don't like would have a gangbanger for a husband. One of these dumb-ass rats wouldn't mind having to bury yo ass or come visit you in the joint 'cause you done got caught up. A real woman doesn't want to see her husband go through some shit like that. A woman like me don't want no husband that's out there in them streets every day and night.

"So when I say you need to change, I ain't talking about changing into some square-ass chump. I don't like soft men. You just got to learn how to gangbang on a different level. Gangbang in some-body's boardroom 'cause that street shit ain't gone last forever. You got to take that shit to the next level."

Silence reigned as Vee soaked up what Sakawa had to say. As they sat and watched the chef, Sakawa's cell phone vibrated in her purse. She didn't want to seem rude by answering her phone in front of Vee so she excused herself to go to the restroom.

In the bathroom she called back the missed number. "What's up, China Doll?"

China Doll was her usual loud self. "Bitch, where you at?"

"I'm out."

"Out where, bitch?"

"Bitch, you ain't my mama. I said that I'm out. I'm at a restau-rant having a nice dinner, bitch."

China Doll couldn't resist. "With who, Saki?"

"Bitch, you nosy. I'm with none-ya."

China Doll was lost. "With who?"

"None-ya business, bitch," Sakawa cracked.

China Doll was hardly taken aback. "Oh it's like that. You a sneaky bitch, Saki. Don't think I don't know you. You think you slick, bitch."

Sakawa feigned innocence. "I don't know what you talking 'bout, China Doll. I'm just out having a little dinner with a friend."

"Whatever you say, Saki. Do yo thing, bitch. Make sure you know this: Don't let that nigga see the trim if his pockets is slim."

"China, bitch, you know a nigga can't see this cat if his pockets ain't fat. Now, girl, I gotta go. I'll call you when I get in. Meow."

"Meow, bitch," China Doll said.

Sakawa dumped her cell phone back into her purse and checked her reflection in the restroom mirror. She smoothed down her arched eyebrows. To her reflection, she said, "Girl, remember don't be catching feelings. This man is a pigeon. He is responsible for taking away yo future. You ain't playing deuces wild at granny's house, this is high-stakes poker in Vegas, bitch. Now get this nigga open like butt cheeks. Meow."

Back at the table she slid into the booth. She moved real close to Vee and squeezed his thigh. "Sorry I took so long. You know the ladies' room be packed."

"It's cool, ma. Dude just finished with the appetizers and shit. The shrimp be good as hell with this batter on them. Taste them."

Hungrily, Sakawa dug into her appetizers. They joked and laughed as the different courses of the meal were prepared and placed in front of them. It had grown dark outside by the time dessert, gigantic chunks of fresh pineapple, was served. They had occupied the booth for quite a while and the hostess was pacing back and forth shooting Vee little looks that he completely ignored. After Sakawa finished her third Super Mai Tai, Vee finally decided it was time to leave. He paid the bill and left the chef a sizable tip.

Outside the restaurant, Vee put his arm around Sakawa's shoulders as they waited for the valet to bring his Excursion. After tipping the valet with a sawbuck, Vee held the truck door open for Sakawa. He caught a glimpse of her bronze legs when the split in her skirt opened as she climbed in the truck. Instinct made him reach out and rub her smooth thigh. She didn't smack his hand away, but she did ease it off her thigh, then she readjusted her skirt.

The feel of her leg was enough to give Vee a wood. After he closed her door, he walked behind the truck and adjusted the erection in his jogging pants.

On the way to Sakawa's house, Vee was all smiles as he anticipated bedding her down for the first time. He knew that she had to be drunk after three Super Mai Tais. He flipped through the CD changer until he hit a Slow Grooves disc and turned it up.

Sakawa reached over and tapped Vee. She signaled for him to turn the music down and asked, "So would you change?"

Vee was caught off guard by her question and answered without thinking. "Hell nall. I'm already married to the streets. I ain't gone never change. I love this street shit. You said you don't want no soft-ass nigga, right? Well, I shole ain't soft. You like you a thug nigga, don't you?"

Wrong answer, Sakawa thought, but she said rather dryly, "Yeah, I like a thug nigga. Don't ever change."

Misreading her sarcasm, Vee smiled, thinking she had bought his thug bravado. To celebrate he hit the remote to change to a selection from Trick Daddy. "Baby I'm a Thug" blasted from the woofers.

When he pulled over in front of Sakawa's apartment building, Vee asked, "So what's the deal, shorty? Can I come up to the crib?"

"For what?" Sakawa asked a little more coldly than she planned. As she opened the truck to get out, she saw the dejected look on Vee's face and realized that she was blowing it. Drunkenly, she stumbled a little as she walked around the truck to the driver's side. She leaned into the open window and said, "I'm sorry if I'm mood swinging. Aunt Flo is visiting."

Vee apologized, "My fault, shorty. I didn't know that you had company at yo house."

"Nall, man. Not my auntie. Aunt Flo—the red curse. My period, boy."

"Ohhh," Vee said bashfully. "I get it. It's cool." Mentally he was already digging through his cell directory for a chicken to spend the night with.

Sakawa climbed up on the truck's running board and gave Vee a kiss on the jaw. "Thanks for the dinner and conversation, player. I really enjoyed myself. But now I got to go change my pad before it overflows."

She jumped down and walked to the steps of her apartment building. As she was pulling her keys out of her purse, Vee called her name. She turned and waited.

"Shorty, if yo aunt wasn't visiting would I have been able to come up and spend the night with you?"

Hell nall, popped into her head, but she held her tongue. Instead she said, "Maybe."

That was good enough for Vee. He pulled off with a smile on his face.

Sakawa turned back to the building's door and keyed the lock and went inside. Watching them, Insane Wayne sat on the roof of the industrial garage across the street.

Sakawa dreamed that Wayne was home—home and in bed with her. His strong hands lifted her T-shirt up, actually it was one of his shirts, and looked down at the imprint the lips of her womanhood made in her cotton briefs. He lifted the T-shirt even higher and stared at her well-endowed chest. Like a starving wolf he covered her breasts in saliva as he licked and sucked them.

In her sleep Sakawa moaned. She knew that it had to be the three gigantic Super Mai Tais she'd drunk that had her hallucinating that her man was making love to her, but she didn't care.

The dream was perfect. Her nipples stretched and pointed toward the ceiling under his oral caresses. From her breasts, he kissed and licked his way down to her firm thighs. Gently, Wayne pulled her panties down and spread her thighs and she didn't resist. Just like old times, he gave her a few introductory kisses on the lips down there, then dove in. Up and down, around and around he swirled his tongue on her clitoris until she was squirming and pushing his head down.

I'm having the most delicious dream, Sakawa told herself. *My man is here and he's eating my kitty just like I like it.*

Faster and faster Wayne flicked his tongue around her clit while playing with her taut nipples. After what seemed like an erotic eternity of his tongue calisthenics, Sakawa grunted as she began to orgasm.

"Keep licking my kitty, daddy! I'm coming!" she squealed in her sleep.

In response to her cries, Sakawa could almost feel Wayne stick his tongue into her pussy and lap deeply to make her orgasm even harder. He kept lapping until her last vibration stopped.

"Daddy, you know that mommy loves yo tongue in her kitty," Sakawa murmured dreamily.

Without answering, Wayne flipped her gently on her belly and pulled her T-shirt over her head. He began to rub her back and shoulders to release any tension in them. As Sakawa lay on her stomach with her love juices dripping from the pouting lips of her womb, she felt the imaginary hands stop their gentle caresses and she had to remind herself that it was only a dream. A few feet from her head she thought she heard a ripping sound. Then she felt the hands again. Firmly but gently the hands bound her wrists and ankles separately to each bedpost until she was secured spread-eagled on her stomach.

Still asleep, she asked in a childlike voice, "Why you tying me up, daddy? Did yo baby do something wrong?"

There was no answer. Of course there wasn't an answer—this was a dream.

She felt something warm and oily dribble down onto her lower back and buttocks. The smell she recognized as baby oil and it felt wonderful as her dream lover massaged it into her lower extremities. Then she felt the hands grasping her butt cheeks and spreading them. Next she felt what had to be the head of her lover's organ press against the tight, round circle of her anus.

Sleepily, she warned, "Daddy, you know I don't like it when you try to get in my ass."

"Shut up, bitch!" Insane Wayne hissed as he forced his dick into her asshole.

"Ahhhh!" Sakawa screamed as she jolted awake. With a scream she tried to buck Wayne off of her but her range of movement was restricted by her bonds.

Ignoring her cries of pain, Insane Wayne pumped in and out of her butt. Through the broken wires and rubber bands in his mouth he hissed in delirium.

"Ahhh, please stop!" Sakawa begged as she felt the tissue in her rectum tearing. "Please, baby, don't do me like this!"

Her pleas for mercy turned Insane Wayne on even more. He hissed, "Bitch, you wasn't telling me to stop when I was eating yo pussy!"

"Wayne, I love you. Why is you doing this to me?" Sakawa sobbed.

He didn't answer as he concentrated on getting his nut off. Harder and harder he slammed into her ass until he felt the sensation begin to gather at the base of his testicles.

"Oh yeah, bitch!" Insane Wayne croaked as he began to ejaculate. "That's it, bitch. Do you feel me coming in yo ass?" Finally he stopped pumping and lay there on top of her for a moment.

"Get the fuck off of me!" Sakawa screamed. "You didn't even have to do me like that! You is crazy! You sick motherfucka!"

Insane Wayne laughed as he climbed off of her. "That's right, bitch. I am crazy and you need to remember that," he said as he wiped his dick on a teddy bear he had given her for Valentine's Day one year.

"Untie me, you motherfucka!" Sakawa yelled. "Crazy motherfucka let me out of this shit right now!"

"Tell Vee to let you loose, ho," Insane Wayne said as he began to pull his pants back on. "Matter of fact, you make sure that you tell him that he may get the pussy, but I'mma get the ass whenever I want it, bitch."

He sat on the bed beside Sakawa and began to put his boots on. She stared at him with an intense hate-filled glare, and he simply smiled at her. He stood up and rubbed her short hairdo. "I been meaning to tell you that I don't like yo new haircut, bitch."

"Fuck you, nigga!" Sakawa shouted as she struggled against her restraints. "I hate yo nasty, freakish ass!"

"But I like yo ass," Insane Wayne retorted and patted her on her ass cheeks. "Thanks for letting me get shit on my dick, Saki. I love you, baby."

Against her will, she winced in pain.

When her eyes were closed, Insane Wayne leaned over and licked her forehead. "I'll be seeing you, boo," he said before he stood up. As he headed for the bedroom door, he stopped and blew her a kiss. "Tell Vee that I left the back door open for him," he teased as he left.

Sakawa could hear him laughing at his sick joke as he left the apartment. She turned her head and sobbed into the jersey sheet until she fell asleep. Later, in the fog in her head, she heard someone calling her name. Thinking it was Wayne returning, she threatened, "Motherfucker, you bet' not touch me again or I'm gone call the police!"

"Saki, it's me, girl," China Doll said from the bedroom doorway.

Sakawa couldn't remember a time she'd been happier to see her friend.

"Saki, is you all right?" China Doll asked dubiously.

"Just get me aloose," Sakawa wailed.

As China Doll came closer she could see the blood and dried semen on Sakawa's behind. Gingerly she began to untie her friend. "Girl, what happened? Did Vee do this?"

"It was Wayne," Sakawa sobbed. "I was drunk and I woke up and he had me tied up. Then he gone rape me and leave me tied up."

When China Doll finally set her free, Sakawa hugged her friend and began to cry hysterically on her shoulder. China Doll didn't know what to do aside from pulling the sheets around her naked friend.

"Man, fuck this nigga!" Dante whispered harshly.

Solemn Shawn gave him a reproachful look. "Watch yo mouth, Tay. This is a church."

"My fault," Dante apologized, "but what I'm saying is this nigga is getting on my last damn nerve. Ever since this big punk came through the door he been acting like he crucial or something. Ain't that right, Murderman?"

Murderman turned his youthful face to his friends. "Tay is right, Shawn. This dude got an attitude problem. He be trying to bully everybody. I had to stay in the bathroom with that kid Coleman 'cause he was about to try and rape him. Then this dude got in my face at lunch. I was about to jaw him. I ain't finta be playing wit no punk. Then this dude was all in the gym talking that yin yang and saying what he was gone do to anybody that don't like it."

Solemn Shawn thought about it for a minute. "We got to be cool until we can get this stud and get away with it. Everything in its proper time."

Just then the chapel door opened. A husky, brown-skinned teenager walked in, followed by a few of his nondescript lackeys. He sat down in the pew across the aisle from Solemn Shawn and his boys. The three friends remained silent. Tension filled the small chapel. Corey, the aforementioned bully, peeked across the aisle at the three boys.

To his cronies, Corey stage-whispered, "Look at these faggot-ass niggas. I always heard my granny say if you scared then you need to go church, but this is ridiculous."

Corey's followers laughed like they were listening to Eddie Murphy do a stand-up routine. Chaplain Brown woke up from his nap and looked up from the Bible on his lap. He gave the boys a reproachful look. Instantly they quieted down. Solemn Shawn could feel Murderman seething in anger beside him. The two crews sat eye-balling one another while they waited for the chaplain to drift off to sleep again.

When he heard the chaplain snoring softly, Corey sneered, "Punk-ass marks sitting up in here like some bitch-ass Apostles praying for Jesus to save them. That's what I'm gone call these church boys, the Apostles."

Again Corey's group laughed their heads off at his remarks. Murderman had to be physically restrained by Solemn Shawn and Dante.

"This ain't the time, Murder!" Solemn Shawn whispered forcibly. "You ain't gone do nothing but get all our privileges took."

"F-F-Fuck this nigga!" Murderman sputtered. "I'll fuck this stud up!"

Corey and his followers laughed at Murderman's anger. Corey whispered, "You punk-ass Apostles better keep burying y'all nappy heads in them Bibles. This camp is mine from here on out. Next time one of you ho-ass Apostles stick y'all nose in my personal business, I'm gone stick my dick in one of y'all. If I hear so much as a peep out of one y'all I'm gone get in that ass." To his crew, Corey said, "C'mon, y'all. Fuck these Apostles."

Corey and his crew exited the chapel, leaving behind an angry threesome in their wake. Murderman was so angry that tears began to roll down his boyish cheeks.

"Why you let him talk that shit like that?" Murderman sobbed to Solemn Shawn. "I don't care if you don't do nothing, I'm gone kill his bitch ass. He ain't finta keep talking that smack to me."

Solemn Shawn was almost moved to tears himself by the passion in his friend's voice, but he knew it was best to keep a level head. "Look, Murder, we gone get that dude, but we need to hold up. You still ain't healed all the way from the knife you took in the back for me. Plus we ain't trying to push no moves until we finish getting rid of all that reefer Big Ant sent us. We can't stand for no searches until we finish this package."

Dante added, "Listen to Shawn, man. You know the drill. We can't get busted for fighting or we gone get confined. If we in trouble we ain't making no money. With a pipeline like Big Ant we can be living right when we get out this kiddie camp. I ain't finta blow all this scratch over some poot-butt. I ain't saying that we gone let this shit slide, I'm just saying we got to play our cards right. Shawn, you keep yo nose buried in that Art of War book, what you got to say about this dude?"

Solemn Shawn sat back and his trademark stoic smile danced at the corners of his mouth. "I ain't mad at Corey. Really, I need to thank his punk ass."

Murderman stopped wiping his tears and looked at his friend like he had lost his mind.

Rather coldly, Solemn Shawn said, "Yeah, we all need to thank him. I knew that we was gone need a name for us, and that big goofy just gave us one. Albeit he might have thought the shit was a joke, but we gone show him and anybody else that get in our way that the Apostles is gone have to be respected. Loved by none, respected by all."

"That's cool, now that you mention it," Dante commented. "I like that—Apostles. What you say, Murderman?"

"I dig that."

"Tay, how much time you think you gone need to finish up this last load of cess?" Solemn Shawn asked.

Swiftly Dante calculated the task in his head. "Give me 'bout a week to ten days at the most. I got about two hundred five-dollar joints and about seven hundred dollar joints left. What you got in mind, Shawn?"

"Well, I'm gone tell Big Ant to hold off for a few days when we get through with this shit. So he won't trip, I'm gone let him know that we plan to double our order on the next go-round. You make sure you get your brother to get them money orders for our cash."

Dante looked dubious. "That's a lot of reefer, baby. We can barely handle all that we getting now."

"You worry too much, Tay," Solemn Shawn assured him. "As long as the guards keep letting us bring it in, ain't no problem. Our stash spot in the mop closet wall is safe. Plus, after we take care of this stud Corey, dudes is gone be waiting in line to get down with the Apostles. And we gone put they butts to work. Dante, from this day forth, you the Apostle of Finance. Murderman, from this day forth, you the Apostle of War."

"And what is you?" Dante asked.

"I'm the Head Apostle. Any objections?"

Dante and Murderman didn't protest.

Solemn Shawn continued, "Good then. As soon as we done with this reefer we gone take care of Mr. Funnyman, Corey. In the next two weeks I need y'all to get hold of a few items. We gone need some fresh candy bars, a blindfold, a plastic bag, some shit turds, some vise grips, some lye drain cleaner, and a piece of pipe."

"What the hell you up to, man?" Murderman asked. "What we gone do wit all that stuff?"

Solemn Shawn looked up at Chaplain Brown. The priest was still dozing with his large Bible on his lap. "All right, check this out."

Murderman and Dante moved closer. As Solemn Shawn began explaining, Murderman's face lit up with glee. Dante, on the other hand, looked like he was about to throw up.

Captain James T. Bellows looked at his lunch bag and sighed. The delicious cold roast beef with American and provolone cheese, thinly sliced, ripe, juicy tomatoes, lettuce, and mayo would have to wait a few more minutes. Bellows hit the intercom button on his telephone and barked, "Send Shawn Terson in here."

Solemn Shawn unceremoniously waltzed into the captain's office.

Every time Captain Bellows saw him, he had to admit to himself that the kid definitely had charisma. Then again most killers, con men, and gangsters did.

"Take a seat, Terson," Bellows commanded.

Solemn Shawn sat in the hardback chair directly facing the captain of correctional officers.

Longingly, Bellows fingered the paper bag containing his sandwich. "Mr. Terson, or should I call you Solemn Shawn?"

"My name is Shawn Terson, sir. And what's this about, sir?"

"You think you're pretty smart, don't you, Terson. I just wanted to see you so you could look at a few pictures with me. You don't mind, do you?"

Solemn Shawn hunched his shoulders. "I don't mind, sir."

Bellows opened the file folder on his desk to reveal a set of eight-by-ten color photographs and a typewritten report. He picked up the pictures. "I must admit, Terson. This is a piece of work. Actually it's the best I've seen, and I've been doing this for about seventeen years. The culprits even had the knowledge to do this on my day off. Know anything about this, Terson?"

Solemn Shawn never missed a beat. "Know anything about what, sir?"

Bellows tossed the pictures on the desk in front of Solemn Shawn and picked up the report. "Go ahead and take a look at your handiwork, kid. I've got to tell you. You guys are good. Corey never saw a thing."

Solemn Shawn picked up the pictures and began to look at them one by one.

Bellows watched the boy's seemingly unconcerned face over the report in his hand. "Report says that they found traces of feces in his mouth, nose, and ears. He had chemical burns on his genitalia and a steel pipe was lodged in his rectum, which required surgical removal and thirty-four stitches. He also suffered a dislocated jaw, a skull fracture, and the letter A was carved into his forehead and chest. Still don't know anything about this, Terson?"

Never looking up from the pictures, Solemn Shawn said, "No, sir, Captain, sir. I still don't know anything about this."

Not expecting the crafty teenager in front of him to admit to the beating, humiliation, and degradation of another inmate, Bellows said, "I didn't think you did. I can't prove it, but somehow I know that this is your doing. If you didn't participate, you had it done."

Feigning a wounded look, Solemn Shawn tossed the pictures back onto the captain's desk. "Captain Bellows, I don't know what you're talking about."

"Cut the Oscar-winning performance, Terson. I watch your crew. I've read up on you, too. I know full well what you're capable of doing to someone. I also know that this kid has been talking shit to everybody since he got here. Also, Corey has raped or attempted to rape at least three other inmates. So I'm not saying that he was an angel. I know that because of the behavior he exhibited he had to incur some enemies. I also know that he threatened at least one of your little gang. I know that you hoodlum motherfuckers did this to this fuck. Come clean now, give up your homeboys and I can assure you that I'll be lenient with you."

Solemn Shawn sat forward in his chair, a steel glint in his eyes. "Captain, are you charging me with something?"

Bellows bellowed, "You know you little motherfuckers didn't leave any evidence for me to charge you with anything!"

Solemn Shawn sat back in the chair again. "Well, sir, if you're not charging me with anything then I don't see the point of this meeting."

Captain Bellows was taken aback. This kid had the poise of a mob hit man and he was only seventeen years old. He felt a prickle of fear at the fact that soon this little monster would be released back into society. "You think you so gotdamn smart, don't you, Terson. Well, you're on my radar now, you little fuck. If you step out of line once, I'll be there to run you through the fucking wringer. Now get the fuck out of my eyesight before I decide to suspend your privileges on GP. On your way out send Michael Moore in."

Solemn Shawn opened the office door and stepped out. He nodded his head at Murderman, indicating for him to go into Captain Bellows's office. Dante was there too, waiting to see the captain. As Murderman stood and headed for the office, he mouthed the word "Apostles."

24

THE ENTIRE STREET WAS QUIET. SO QUIET YOU COULD ALMOST hear the electricity powering the streetlights. The sun was just beginning to turn the sky purplish orange as it pushed night's blanket off the bed. Jermaine "Maine-Maine" Hayes looked at his watch as he walked to the stoop of an abandoned building in the middle of the block. Maine-Maine quickly skipped up the steps of the building and ducked into the dark maw of the hallway. With care he removed his pistol from under his Denver Nuggets jersey and tucked it in the mailbox in the hallway. Stepping back onto the porch, Maine-Maine looked up and down the block, then at his watch. Six a.m. on the dot.

With his fingers in his mouth, Maine-Maine whistled twice. The loud, shrill sound echoed up and down the dark street. In response to the whistle the light popped on in the second-floor hallway of the building across the street from him. From the hallway window a whistle sounded. Maine-Maine looked at the cars lining the curbs on both sides of the street. Again he put his fingers in his mouth and whistled two times—the all-clear signal. Maine-Maine climbed to the concrete porch shoulder and shouted, "Shop's open! Nod Squad got a bomb!"

The street came alive as the sun began to tiptoe across the eastern sky. Car doors began opening, ejecting heroin addicts onto the pavement. Early morning sounds of birds and distant traffic could no longer be heard as the small stampede of dope fiends headed for the hallway with the light on the second floor.

One teenage drug dealer stepped out of the hallway. His job was to keep order, though the look of his baby face would have made that seem like an impossible task. In his hands the young Apostle carried a small black White Sox bat from a Comiskey Park giveaway. His black Angels hat sat on his head with a rakish tilt. His big brown eyes weren't soft and the ragged, sparse growth of a beard was just beginning to show underneath his chin. While the youth outside the hallway kept the fiends in line, another youth right inside the hallway collected the money. Once the money was given over, a third boy, the pitcher, would give the customer the appropriate number of bags and the consumer would exit the building. No muss, no fuss—keep it moving was the order of the dope line.

"Get the fuck in a straight motherfuckin' line!" the youth outside shouted. "You ain't got to push, it's enough for all you motherfuckas! If y'all get to acting rowdy ain't gone be no wake-ups in this bitch! White boy in that little-ass shirt! Take yo raggedy ass and that nasty bitch of yours and get to the back of the fuckin' line."

The Caucasian youth the drug dealer was addressing looked around. The young white dope fiend whined, "Hey, bro, I ain't done nothing. I was right here."

With a grimace on his face that would have made Tupac proud, the young Apostle said, "Bitch-ass honky! I'll bust yo motherfuckin' head if you don't get yo ass to the end of the line! You know what— fuck that! If you don't get yo ass to end of the line ain't no blows being sold, funky-ass cracker!"

The other addicts in the line began to turn and glare at the white youth. They would be damned if he would prevent them from getting their sick off. A lot of them were functioning addicts and had to be at work in a while; it would fuck up their schedules to have to try to go somewhere else to cop, especially while the

Nod Squad had some of the best dope in Chi-town. No, that definitely wouldn't do.

A tall dope fiend ten places in line behind the white boy assured him, "If they shut down 'cause of you, we gone whup the shit out you out here."

That was enough for the offender. He told his girl, "C'mon, Peggy." Her dirty sundress swished as she followed her boyfriend to the end of the line.

Feeling like he had struck a small blow for Black people everywhere, the young drug dealer shouted, "Now you motherfuckas better get this damn line straight before I bust somebody head!"

Magically the dope line became straight as an arrow. It wasn't the threat of physical violence that scared most of them, it was the thought of not being able to purchase one of those good early morning blows. The cruel little bastard with the bat could have told them to take off their clothes; 98 percent of them would have done it—anything for a good-ass bag of diesel.

Maine-Maine was still across the street on the stoop. He removed a Black & Mild cigar hanging from the NBA headband on his head. He peeled the wrapper off the cheap cigar and rolled it between his fingers to remove some of the tobacco to make it smoke more easily. Proudly, he looked at the dope line of fifty plus and smiled as he lit his cigar. He had reason to be proud; Nod Squad was his operation. After he paid the crew and broke the Apostles off their 10 percent every week, the rest was all his. Right now he was making close to ten thousand a day. He was definitely getting his weight up.

He didn't even have to get up and come out on the strip every morning. A lot of the dealers would be content to chill and let their money come to them, but Maine-Maine had to watch every penny of his get made. While most cats, seeing the kind of paper he was folding, spent all day riding around smoking weed and fucking with bitches, Maine-Maine spent every day on his grizzly. He owned two cars, a '94 Camry, a pretty-plain vehicle, and a '92

Fleetwood Cadillac, but he rarely ever went anywhere of importance. At the age of twenty-two, with no children and living in his mother's basement, he didn't have any bills of his own. His real passion was collecting basketball jerseys.

I'mma hurt the club at Charlene's this Saturday, Maine-Maine thought to himself. There was a big party at the Apostles' social club this weekend celebrating the life and death of Domino, a deceased Apostle, and he planned on shining that night. He couldn't help smiling as he thought about how fly he would look in his jersey, leaning on the bar buying shots of Rémy. Happily, he puffed on his Black & Mild. He didn't even notice a dope fiend walk up to the bottom steps of the stoop.

"A, homie, is Nod Squad working?" the dope fiend hissed, breaking Maine-Maine's early morning daydream.

Maine-Maine looked down from his perch on the stoop at the dope fiend. The addict looked to be about in his late twenties. On his head was a filthy North Carolina blue bucket hat covering most of his brown facial features. "Yeah, Nod Squad got a bomb, A. Just follow the light."

The dope fiend turned and looked across the street at the line of addicts. He turned back to Maine-Maine and rasped, "Family, I want some diesel, but I ain't got no cabbage."

"Well, you need to get the fuck on," Maine-Maine stated cruelly. He wondered what was wrong with the dope fiend's mouth.

"Don't get me wrong, baby boy. I ain't dry-hustling or nothing. I got me some shit that I'm trying to sell."

Maine-Maine laughed. "What the fuck you got, A? Oh, I know. You probably got some bootleg DVDs or CDs. Or better yet—you probably got some useless shit like a baby blanket or something."

The dope fiend allowed a good-natured but weird laugh to slide from between his lips. Nonchalantly, he said, "Nall, baby boy, it ain't nothing that priceless. It's just a semiautomatic shotgun that I'm trying to get rid of."

The mention of a shotgun managed to get Maine-Maine's

attention. He already owned three hand pistols and he knew that a semiauto shotty could definitely come in handy.

"Where is it, A?" Maine-Maine asked as he climbed down off the stoop and descended to street level. He stood face-to-face with the dope fiend.

"I couldn't carry that motherfucka up here on no dope strip. And how I don't know that you gone try to stick me up for it?"

"Apostles don't steal," Maine-Maine stated proudly as he noticed for the first time that the dope fiend was speaking through clenched lips with wires and broken rubber bands all over his dental landscape.

Insane Wayne said, "In that case I got it in the trunk of my whip."

"Where's that at?" Maine-Maine asked.

"Right in the vacant lot on the next street over from here. I didn't want to park too close to the dope strip."

"What you want for it, A?"

"It's a good gun, family. I want at least a big-face hundred or three twenty-dollar blows and a forty piece in cash."

"That's a lot of scratch for a big-ass shotgun, A," Maine-Maine commented. He was lying though. He knew if the shotgun was in good condition that was a steal. "Let's go check it out, A."

Before leaving, Maine-Maine checked out the block. The early morning dope traffic was moving around as the dope fiends copped and bounced. Security on both ends of the block was on point, and the shorty with the bat was keeping the line straight. Satisfied that his operation was tight, Maine-Maine made up his mind to go and cop the shotgun if it looked good. For a second he hesitated as he started to retrieve his pistol from the mailbox, but he put that idea out of his head. He would already have to take the alleys to make it home with the shotty. Even if the dope fiend gave him a ride, he still didn't want him to know where his mother's house was located. Also it wouldn't do to have a gun on his person in the event they got pulled over by the cops. If he'd already given the dope fiend the money for the shotgun and they got curbed by the twisters that was the addict's problem.

Insane Wayne asked, "You ready to go and have a look at this?"

"No problem," Maine-Maine replied. "Lead the way, A."

"Follow me," Insane Wayne said as he dipped through the gangway beside the abandoned building.

Through the gangway and past the garage leading into the alley Maine-Maine followed Insane Wayne. Across the next street in the vacant lot Maine-Maine could see the rear of the dope fiend's Honda Accord. In a couple of moments they reached the small foreign car parked in the vacant lot full of glass and debris.

"I'mma pop the trunk, family," Insane Wayne announced as he walked to the driver's side of the vehicle and opened the door. "The shotgun is in there under all them clothes and shit. I'll watch out for the po-pos while you take a look at it."

When Maine-Maine heard the trunk's locking mechanism release, he lifted the trunk lid and saw a gang of clothes. Bending over he began digging through them until he reached the bottom of the trunk—no shotgun. Not understanding the absence of the shotgun, Maine-Maine started to straighten his back and said, "A, homie, I don't see it."

Out the corner of his eye, Maine-Maine saw something long, shiny, and sharp glittering in the hand of the dope fiend the second before Insane Wayne plunged the hunting knife into the side of his neck. With an outward ripping motion, Insane Wayne snatched away most of Maine-Maine's throat with the serrated blade of the knife.

Maine-Maine clutched at the space where his throat used to be with a look of utter amazement on his face. He wanted to run but his legs gave way under him as his body catapulted into shock. All Maine-Maine knew at this moment was that he wanted to ask the grinning dope fiend why he had killed him. The white fabric of his Denver Nuggets jersey turned scarlet red in milliseconds as his blood cascaded over his clutching fingers. In slow motion he sat down in the vacant lot. His hands were still trying to form a makeshift bandage as he fell over on his side.

Insane Wayne chuckled as he pulled a Green Bay Packers hat from the trunk and tossed it on the ground beside Maine-Maine. As his victim bled to death, Insane Wayne pulled slowly out of the vacant lot.

25

THIRTY-FIVE FLOORS OF POLISHED GLASS AND STEEL GLEAMED in the night. A midnight blue Chevy Impala glided to a stop in front of the North Shore condo building. Behind the tinted glass of the automobile, Solemn Shawn collected his bag of Bennigan's food as Murderman sat behind the steering wheel and watched him.

"Them some big-ass salads, A," Murderman commented.

"These boys be right too," Solemn Shawn assured him. "Nessa be fucking with the garden salad joint, but I get down with the country fried chicken joint with blue cheese dressing, A."

"A fried chicken salad? I bet a sister thought of that. It sounds like it's good though."

"It is, A. You should try one."

"That's all right, yo. If they make an Italian beef salad or a gyro salad then I'll get down, A. Are you in for the night?"

Solemn Shawn looked up at the building. "Yeah, I'm about to chill, A. I'm going to eat this salad and watch the NBA on TNT. Play-off time. What you about to get yourself into, A?"

"Me and Yo-Yo got a little business to take care of. We found out that bitch Vee and his ho-ass Governors are behind Ghost getting offed. We gone send that bitch a little message, you know what I mean?"

"Be careful," was all Solemn Shawn said as he opened the car door and climbed out.

Murderman waited for the Head Apostle to get safely inside the building's lobby before he zoomed off into the night to handle his business.

In the lobby of the condo building, Solemn Shawn ignored the probing eyes of an elderly white couple as they waited for the elevator. He was used to the cold silences and even colder stares of the building's mostly well-to-do tenants. On the elevator the smell of the fried chicken in the salad wafted from the Bennigan's bag. Solemn Shawn could have sworn he heard the older man's stomach growl. That brought a smile to his lips as he listened to the soft jazz leaking from the elevator's speakers. At the sixteenth floor he left the elevator and walked to his apartment door. He unlocked the door and went inside.

In the foyer, Solemn Shawn kicked his off his shoes and padded into the darkened living room. He set the salads down on the table behind the modern deco sofa and flicked on a lamp. To his surprise, Vanessa was sitting on the couch. Her legs were folded under her and she was hugging a large throw pillow. On her feet were a pair of pink Footees, and she was wearing a pair of loose-fitting pajama bottoms and a pink baby T-shirt. Her multicolored silk scarf was in place over her braids.

"Hey, baby. What you doing sitting here in the dark?"

Vanessa didn't answer.

Solemn Shawn raised his eyebrows as he headed for the kitchen. He pulled two iced teas from the fridge and returned to the living room. He set the drinks on the coffee table and announced, "I stopped at Bennigan's and got you one of the garden salads like you like." He lifted her tray out of the bag and walked around the couch to hand her the garden salad, but Vanessa wouldn't accept it. Unsure what to do, Solemn Shawn stood there for a moment holding the salad. Finally he shrugged his shoulders and set the salad on the coffee table beside her beverage.

"Woman, what's wrong with you?" he asked as he walked back around the couch to get his salad.

Vanessa still didn't answer him.

Quickly Shawn scanned his memory for something he could have done or not done to piss her off. He couldn't think of anything, so he picked up his salad and took a seat on the other end of the sofa from her. He reached for the remote of the forty-two-inch plasma television and powered the set on. Vanessa was still silent, so he started eating his salad and watching a play-off basketball game. Even though it was only the first quarter it was already a heated battle of buckets. It took only a few moments and he was engrossed in the game.

He knew that he wasn't wrong for ignoring Vanessa's funky mood. If he knew her, and it was hard not to know someone you'd been with for eight years, he knew she would let him know what was wrong with her. Through the second quarter and halftime she was silent. At the beginning tip-off of the third quarter, however, she got up off the couch and walked over and switched the television off. She retook her seat.

Shawn looked at her like she had lost her damn mind.

She looked up from her pillow and asked, "How long we gone do this?"

Slightly pissed off, he asked, "Do what, woman?"

"How long we gone act like we live this normal life. Like you work an honest job."

Shawn rolled his eyes to the ceiling. "What brought this on, Nessa?"

Her voice rose a few octaves. "The fact that I felt like cleaning the apartment like a good little woman and I found not one, not two, but three guns. Three pistols. And why you sitting there looking like I'm the one that's crazy; I bet you got a gun on you now."

Bashfully, Shawn grinned. He had forgotten about the mini Intratec 9mm in the back pocket of his jeans. "Would you rather I get caught out there without heat? In case you've forgotten, sometimes I'm around not-so-nice people. I don't even know why you acting like that. The first time you met me I had a pistol on me. That's the kind of life I live, Nessa."

"That's what I'm talking about," she said as a tear ran down her pretty face. "What kind of life is that to live? My grandmother told me anywhere you got to take a gun to go, you don't need to be there. We can't even go out with my friends from work and just have some fun, a few drinks and dancing. You might bump into one of your enemies or someone might step on your shoes or something and your security might have to kill them."

Shawn waved her off. "C'mon, now, Nessa. That is totally absurd. Where is this stuff coming from? I've never heard you talk like this before."

"I'll tell you where it's coming from," Vanessa sobbed. "It's coming from the woman that agreed to marry you and wants to have your children someday."

"Vanessa, what are you talking about—you can't even have kids."

"I can," she muttered, burying her face in the pillow. "I've always been able to."

"What did you say?" Shawn asked.

"I've always been able to have children," Vanessa confessed. "I just told you that so you wouldn't ask. In the beginning I was taking the pill. For the last few years it's been the three-month shot."

Shawn was stunned. Over the years he had relegated himself to being childless as long as he was with Vanessa. He felt a slight feeling of betrayal wash over him. All he could bring himself to say was, "Why?"

His woman was silent.

"Why, Nessa?" Shawn repeated bluntly. "Why would you have me think for all these years that you couldn't have children?"

"I'll tell you why," she said softly. "I watched my friends, cousins, hell, even one of my sisters fall for guys that live like you. Gangsters, thugs, live niggas, whatever you want to call them. I watched these women fall in love with these bad boys. They had babies by these men and planned lives with these men. Everything was gravy as y'all say—for a while anyway. Then they started getting killed and locked up. They started getting high on the shit they was selling and dragging these women into their bullshit. I watched my sister go to the penitentiary because she loved a nigga so much she took a case for him.

"While she was in prison this same man kept hustling and ended up getting killed. I used to drive my mother and my nephew to the joint so this little boy could see the only parent he had left living like a caged animal. I vowed to myself then that I would never have a baby by a man like you. I'm sorry, but I couldn't put a child of mine through that uncertainty. Can you understand that, Shawn?"

Shawn said, "I can overstand that. I can't even be mad at you. It's true, Nessa. A lot of cats don't make it out the game. You know that and I know that. You've always dealt with that fact though. That's what made me sure that I want to make you my wife. Your decision shows that you have convictions, morals, and beliefs that you hold strongly to, but my question has to be, Why is this surfacing now?"

"Because I want my husband to be with me now and forever. I don't want to talk to you through some thick-ass glass. I don't want to be one of those wives who has to visit her husband in the graveyard. I don't want you paralyzed, or in prison for life. I don't want to have to worry about unseen enemies. Or if one night someone will break in here and kill all three of us in our beds."

Shawn allowed her words to marinate in his head. "Well, since I know you never open your mouth about a problem unless you've thought it through, I suggest that you tell me your plan instead of sitting there pouting."

After a pause Vanessa said, "You really think you know me, don't you. First rule of management: Instead of bitching about a problem find a solution, then bitch. You know my cousin and her husband moved to Tacoma, Washington. Renee, the one I went to visit last year. I've been talking to her a lot lately and I have to admit that the place is ripe for investing."

Solemn Shawn interrupted, "What kind of investments?"

"Don't laugh, you promise you won't laugh."

"Woman, tell me."

"Krispy Kreme doughnuts."

He wanted to laugh, but he knew Vanessa was serious. Still he asked, "You want to sell doughnuts? I mean, they are some pretty good doughnuts, but you expect to get rich selling them?"

"You ain't got to say it like that," she sneered. "Yeah, doughnuts. When I was out there I noticed a million Starbucks, but no Krispy Kreme. All I kept thinking was that that good-ass coffee needed a good-ass doughnut to go with it. So I did my homework on purchasing a franchise and starting it up out there. Krispy Kreme is like a new age franchise. If you got the cash they'll send you everything you need and send you to school, plus invest money with your franchise so you can expand. I made a few calls and everything is favorable. With my projections we can be building our second store within a year of opening the doors of our first one. In five years' time we'll be worth millions off of selling doughnuts."

"It's that simple?" he asked.

"Yeah, it's that simple," Vanessa replied sarcastically.

"Let me get this right. You're saying that all we have to do is pick up and move to Tacoma to get rich. So where do you propose we get the seed money?"

Vanessa spread her arms wide. "Look around. This condo is worth two hundred thousand easily. I got about sixty thousand in savings, and no telling what you've got. I'm telling you, Shawn, I didn't work my ass off to get a master's degree in business to be stuck in somebody's bank as a glorified teller. I know the ins and outs of running a business."

Shawn rubbed his clean-shaven jaw. "Sounds good, Nessa."

"What do you mean, 'sounds good'?" she challenged, ready to assail him with more facts and figures.

"I mean I like the way it sounds. Let's do it."

"For real, Shawn?" Vanessa gushed.

"I said yes, woman. I just need a little time to get clear of a few commitments, then we can fold our tents here."

"Thank you, baby," Vanessa said as she reached out to hug her man, but he grabbed both of her wrists, stopping her embrace. "What's wrong, Shawn?"

He looked her in the eyes. "Now I might not have college degrees like you, but I think you know that I'm not slow. I might not know trigonometry or nothing but I think I got the simple math thing down pat. I'm only counting two of us here. A while ago you said 'the three of us.'"

"H-H-Huh?" she stammered.

"Don't start stuttering and muttering now, woman. What exactly did you mean by the *three of us*?"

Vanessa's head dropped as she breathed, "Me, you, and the baby."

Shawn's heart skipped a beat. "The baby? What? I thought that you just told me that you had been getting the shot?"

With her voice barely above a whisper, Vanessa said, "I was supposed to get my shot again a few days after you proposed. I even went so far as to drive to my doctor's office, but I didn't go in. I just couldn't. I missed my period last month and I just thought my cycle was thrown off because I didn't get my shot, but when I missed my period again this month, I decided to take an EPT. Plus if you got up in the morning you would have noticed that for the last week I've been throwing my guts up every morning before I go to work. I bought the pregnancy test about four days ago on my lunch break, but I didn't take it until today. Right before you came in I peed on the little stick and there were two lines. That means I'm pregnant."

He used her wrists to pull her gently onto his lap. "So that's where all this stuff came from. I was wondering what brought this on."

"Are you mad at me?" Vanessa asked in an almost childlike voice.

He wrapped his arms around her waist and kissed her forehead. "Why would I be? This is a blessing."

"So you're not mad?" she asked again.

"I said I wasn't, woman."

A sly smile crept onto her lips. "Okay, well then, move so I can get my salad. I'm starving."

Playfully Shawn slapped her on her behind as she got up to get her salad.

26

Solemn Shawn stopped outside the doors to the chapel. He was no longer a young boy, but an astute observer could tell that he was new to his adolescence. His former scrawniness had been replaced by moderate muscularity, and several inches had been added to his height during his state vacation. Long nights of reading in half-light had ruined his once perfect vision, but he felt the wealth of knowledge lodged in his cranium was well worth it. He squinted up at the caged clock on the wall outside of the chapel, but he couldn't read it from where he was standing. He pulled his state-issued eyeglasses from the shirt pocket of his DOC shirt and put them on his face.

Glasses in place, Solemn Shawn looked back at the two boys who formed his security detail. One was a shrimpy but feisty boy named Low Down, the other was Vee, who had proven himself to be ambitious and cruel. His security detail couldn't tell but there were butterflies in Solemn Shawn's stomach. He knew that behind these chapel doors lay his destiny. In two days he would at last be eighteen years old and finally he would be released from the juvenile joint after almost four years of incarceration.

Four long years for avenging the death of his only real friend. Fate worked in strange ways though. It was in here that he made some friends who he felt would be with him for life. In here he learned how to work the system and survive. In here he learned in the words of his mentor and friend Big Ant, to "play the cards you been dealt." Big Ant, the first friend he'd made in here, was waiting out there in the world for him with a place to stay and a chance to get money. Solemn Shawn had meticulously planned for every scenario so that his transition back to society would be easy and profitable.

Too bad he couldn't go home to his family. Family. That word brought mixed emotions to his heart and mind. It had been four long years since he'd seen his twin sisters, Samantha and Tabitha. Sam and Tabby, jumping rope, smelling like chewing gum, and trying to follow behind him everywhere. He knew that his little sisters still loved him. His mother though was another matter. She had really disowned him. In four calendars she had visited him only once. That visit was just to let him know that when and if he got out it wouldn't be wise for him to darken her doorstep. In a surprise show of matronly love she had actually managed to let a tear eke from her eye as she told him good-bye that last time.

Crestfallen, Solemn Shawn had slunk back to his cell and wept. Big Ant had been there for him then, and now the older man would be there for him again when he got out. With no one else to turn to, Solemn Shawn had asked his friend to give him a place to stay. The big homie readily agreed to let him stay at his girlfriend's house with him and his son. As soon as he was home he would reunite with his best friend and fellow Apostle Dante. Tay had been home for seven months now and under Big Ant's wing he had begun to establish the Apostles on the outside. In his last kite Tay wrote that members were joining left and right. Murderman would be joining them in about eighteen months.

Vee broke Solemn Shawn's daze. "What's up, A? Why we still standing here? You act like you ain't ready to go in there."

Solemn Shawn looked at Vee harshly at first, but he softened up his glare. Impatience was one of the things that would get Vee in trouble one day, he thought. He couldn't deny it though—Vee was right. Here he was acting like a sappy teenager when there was business at hand. No time for apprehension, this was the day he had been waiting and planning for. The fact that it was finally here made his knees want to buckle from nervousness. Swallowing the lump in his throat, he grabbed the chapel door handles and swung the doors open.

With a hint of a smile on his face, Solemn Shawn proudly strode down the aisle. Every pew of the chapel was packed with boys—no, young Apostles. As their leader walked down the aisle, the Apostles rose silently pew by pew. By the time he reached the pulpit every one of them was standing. Solemn Shawn climbed behind the pulpit and his security detail stood on either side of him.

Chaplain Brown was nowhere to be seen. The old priest was in his room. He would usually take an afternoon nip from his flask that ended in a long nap, making it easy for one of the Apostles to swipe the chapel keys.

At the pulpit, Solemn Shawn fingered the huge Bible there as he looked out at roughly 150 Apostles. The butterflies were replaced by the pride of being the head of a young, strong gang full of hardheads and badasses who would go to their deaths for him. "Take your seats," he commanded.

Silently his gang took their seats. The absence of noise was unreal. Whenever this many boys were assembled in one place, especially juvenile convicts, there was usually abundant noise, but not here. Every teenage boy in the room waited for his leader to speak.

Solemn Shawn cleared his throat. "I'm going to the crib," he stated.

There was a tremendous roar of applause as the boys jumped to their feet. For several moments the boys clapped heartily, then Solemn Shawn silenced them with a wave of his hand. They retook their seats.

He continued, "Even though I'm leaving, the Apostles ain't going nowhere. They can't kill all of us and we ain't going nowhere. We are our brothers' keepers. We will feed our brothers, protect our brothers, give our brothers shelter, and give our brothers knowledge. If we live like we have been destined to live as brothers, not strangers but brothers, even places like this will be like home for a weary Apostle. Our enemies shall fall before us because we fear nothing but God and the loss of his tender mercy. Apostles, now is not the time for any disloyalty. We are . . ."

As Solemn Shawn was giving his speech, Vee drifted off. At sixteen years old he felt he deserved to be named the next Head Apostle. He would take the Apostles to new heights. They would need to become more ruthless to survive; Vee could see it coming. As they had banded together, others would do so too. Gangbanging was the future for the streets of Chicago, and it would take him to make them the top gang. All of that preacher shit that Solemn Shawn liked to spew would be the first thing he would get rid of. "Apostles don't steal." What kind of stupid shit was that? Solemn Shawn wasn't fooling nobody. Vee knew that he was just pilfering their rules from the Bible. I'll change all that shit, Vee thought.

A deafening roar brought Vee back to the present. He looked around to see what he had missed and saw Murderman leave his seat and advance toward the pulpit.

As Murderman joined him at the pulpit, Solemn Shawn continued, "Under Murderman's leadership we will continue to grow and be respected. We will give respect foremost and expect it to be returned. As an original Apostle, Murderman understands the true meaning and spirit of this thing we have built."

Vee was stunned. His mind couldn't fathom that he had been passed over for the promotion to Head Apostle. After all the niggas he had stabbed for the cause. All the cats he had stomped for even breathing a bad word about the Apostles and he was repaid by treachery from Solemn Shawn. Silently, Vee fumed.

With a smile on his face, Solemn Shawn left the juvenile prison chapel for the last time.

27

"MAN, IT'S SLOW THAN A MOTHERFUCKER TONIGHT," TONTO mentioned to his identical twin brother, Toobie.

The polished silver ring in Toobie's eyebrow glistened under the streetlight. "Hell yeah. You know the last few days before the first don't shit be moving. Everybody want—"

"—credit," Tonto finished. "Then these funky motherfuckin' cluckers act like they too good to pay double-ups. Like we just supposed to be giving them our shit on credit for the regular price." He looked down at his boots. Offhand, he said, "I need me some new Tims. These boys is scuffed up."

Toobie stopped fiddling with the spiked stud in his tongue and looked down at his brother's boots. "Man, you just bought them there about two weeks ago. You don't need no more new boots."

Tonto said, "How you gone tell me that I don't need no boots. It's hard trying to keep suede looking right. Just 'cause you like to wear yo stomps till they running over like one of them skateboard-riding chumps, that's up on you."

Toobie shot back, "I know you ain't talking when you be trying to run out and buy a pair of shoes every week like one of these fake ballers. Studs don't even be having no cash in they pocket, but they got on some new Jordans and shit. Fuck that! I would rather look broke than be broke."

"I heard that shit," Tonto agreed, seeing his twin's logic. "But, nigga, we ain't nowhere near broke. When the first of the month roll around and we get rid of the last of that shit that we got, we gone have enough to get a half a pie and still have some change left over. Then we—"

Toobie jumped in, "—keep selling bags, bagging up all eighteen of them onions. We cop a half at least two times and flip it, then we'll be on a whole thang. But we ain't gone do like these other studs that make it to a cake and start thinking they balling. We gone keep copping a cake and chopping that shit up. Shit, if we get a six-month run like that, won't nobody be able to tell us shit. That way—"

Tonto picked up his twin's litany. "—niggas won't know how much cash we getting and Vee and them won't be trying to tax a motherfucka. The minute they see a nigga pushing a little weight they start trying to tax you. Once we get this run in, I say that we need to pull up from this set before these thirsty-ass niggas find out what we doing."

"They ain't even got find out," Toobie vented. "Niggas just be guessing. If you make a hundred they think you done made a thousand. If you make a stack, they act like they seen you count ten stacks in front of them. Plus, once we drop these fat-ass bags out here and it get rolling, then niggas gone start getting nosy. Niggas start hanging on the spot trying to get they little shit off and when they can't, they run to the State Department and try to say y'all stopping them from eating. Next thing you know the State Department on some catch-up shit, trying to have us on some Cold War shit."

Just the thought of having Cold War declared on them was enough to make the twins shiver. Over their tenure in the Governors they had watched quite a few boys become victims of the Governors' street version of excommunication, and they had to admit none of the consequences had been very pretty. A large percentage of the incidents that resulted in Cold War on former Governors was sparked by jealousy and envy. The State Department always found some minor rule infraction to hide behind.

The last victim had been Wayne. The twins had personally participated in his conviction and the carrying out of his sentence. They gained financially when Governor Bing gave them Wayne's cocaine and a cut of his money. It had been a bit much for them to beat Wayne and leave him stretched out in their pit bull ring covered with dog feces and blood, but it was required of them.

Trying to get off the subject, Tonto said, "Give me one of them squares."

Toobie pulled a pack of Newports from his pants pocket and handed it to his twin. When his brother extracted one and handed the pack back, Toobie took one out for himself. After Toobie lit Tonto's square, he lit his own. They both held their cigarettes in the same hand and often managed to puff on them in unison.

"You know we can't do this forever," Tonto mused. "We been lucky so far, twin. If we get this run in like we trying to do, then it'll be time to put some space between us and this place."

"I understand that shit, twin," Toobie acknowledged. "You ain't got to drag me away from this place; I want to see other shit anyway. I been kinda thinking why don't we move to the 'Sota and try getting this money."

"Nigga, get the fuck outta here!" Tonto exclaimed. "Minnesota is burnt up! Cats been going there for years hustling. If you get caught getting down dirty up there them people try to lose yo ass. Man, they be giving niggas football jersey numbers if you get popped off. I ain't trying to go get down in some place that Chicago niggas been playing for years. If I go out of town and hustle it got to be somewhere these niggas ain't burnt to the fucking ground. I ain't even trying to go like that, twin."

"I did hear from a friend of mine that it's pumping in Davenport," Toobie offered. "Plus, my man told me that you don't have to consent to a search if you don't want to and the pigs got to leave you the fuck alone."

"Get the fuck out of here!" Tonto scoffed.

"For real, Tonto. My homie's cousin hustle out there. He say that if the police roll up on y'all they got to ask can they search you. If you say nall they got to push on. Plus, he say that there is a gang of little towns that they go hustle in. Them one-cop-in-the-car type of towns. I say we at least check that shit out for ourselves. Then if..."

Tonto flicked his Newport butt in the gutter, a split second before Toobie did the same thing. "Hold on, Toobie. Here come Angie."

A tall, ultraslim, dark-skinned woman approached the twin Governors. She was wearing a dirty, blue-jean skirt that had seen better days and a nasty-looking, gold Champion sweatshirt that was three times her size. Hanging off her head was a tangled, lint-filled phony ponytail that was secured to her own meager, filthy hair by a greasy-looking Scrunchi.

"Hey, twins!" Angie said loudly as she made a beeline for them, trying to switch her thin hips.

Toobie rolled his eyes.

Tonto greeted her warmly. "What's up, Angie."

Walking past Toobie, Angie got as close to Tonto as he would permit her. "Ain't nothing up, Tonto, with yo fine ass. You know that you—I mean both of y'all—is getting so tall and fine I barely recognize y'all. Y'all done turned into some grown-ass men on Angie. Shit, I remember when I used to babysit y'all asses."

Toobie made a face behind Angie's back. "Every time that you ain't got no ends, you come around here trying to bring up them old-ass stories of when you used to watch us for our mama. If anything we used to watch you. Watch you eat up all our mama's food, drink her liquor, and stay on her damn phone."

Angie turned to Toobie. "That's why I ain't never really got along with you, Too-Too. You was always a mean little cuss. Always trying to hurt somebody feelings and shit. When I used to couldn't tell you two apart, I would wait for you to say something and I would know it was you, Too-Too. Tonto was always nice and respectful, but you have always been mean and nasty."

"Thanks for the compliment," Toobie sneered. He added, "And you better quit calling me Too-Too."

"What's wrong, Too-Too?" Angie asked playfully. "Scared one of your gangbanging-ass friends gone find out that yo name is really Little Too-Too?"

"Fuck you, Angie, with yo pipe-smoking ass!" Toobie said. He walked a few feet away from his twin and Angie to sit on the hood of their Cutlass Supreme parked at the curb. "I don't want to hear that shit. Leave me the fuck alone."

Toobie rolled his eyes at Angie and she rolled hers back before turning to Tonto. "Tonto," she cooed, "I ain't got no scratch and I'm trying to get high."

"For real, Angie?" Tonto asked half sarcastically.

"Stop playing, boy. Shit ain't been too good for me lately. Ole Angie ain't been doing so good. I'm about to go in the rehab next month. I'm just trying to enjoy myself for a last few days before I go detox. After I get my check on the first, then I'm gone throw myself a little party and then I'm going to this treatment center downstate for the next six months."

Toobie cut her off. "Damn, Angie. Look how many times you been to the rehab. You need to get the fuck out of here with that bullshit."

"I'm talking to Tonto, Too-Too. This time it's for real. This place I'm going, I heard it really works. It's called the Miracles Farm. A friend of mine just got out of there and she looks good. She used to be smaller than me. Now she fat and greasy-looking like a pig or something. Shit, that girl used to smoke like a broke stove. If they could get her off crack then they really do grow miracles down there.

"I ain't even asking you to believe me, Tonto. This time it's serious to me. I'm telling you. I just got a couple more days to get high, then I'm gone."

Looking into her eyes, Tonto wanted to believe her. He had

always liked Angie, but he knew the power of crack cocaine. It wasn't that it couldn't be beat, someone just had to be serious to conquer an addiction to the Colombian cocktail. He knew that Angie could easily look into his eyes and tell a bald-faced lie; lying was the least of things a crackhead would do to get their hands on some drugs.

Skeptically, Tonto said, "Angie, if you lying you ain't hurting me—you hurting yo'self. Girl, you used to be pretty as hell. Tall and thick. Now look at you. And you smart as hell. I remember how you used to help me with my homework and shit. That hard-ass algebra shit was killing me and you showed me how to do that shit easy."

"Y'all is killing me over here with this stroll-down-memory-lane bullshit," Toobie commented.

Tonto politely showed his brother his middle finger. "I'm saying, Angie, I'll let you hold one of these dubs but that's all I'm gone give you." Over on the hood of the car Toobie let out an exasperated whoosh of air, but Tonto ignored him. "I ain't gone even charge you double. But I'm telling you, don't come back 'less you got some scratch 'cause I ain't finta hit you no more. You need to get yo shit together though. I ain't finta be fucking with you like this no more. I'm for real, Angie."

With a big Kool-Aid smile on her face, Angie gushed, "Thank you, Tonto."

Without answering Tonto stepped into the gangway and reached his hand into a Ruffles potato chip bag on the ground among the debris in the gangway. He pulled a bundle of dimes and twenties of crack out of the bag. Unrolling the plastic bundle, he extracted a fat twenty-dollar bag of crack from the bundle and retied it. He tucked the bundles back into the chip bag and left the gangway. He walked over to Angie and with a smooth motion that came from tons of practice he slid the twenty into her palm.

Still holding on to her hand, Tonto said sternly, "I want my money too, Angie. So don't decide to just smoke yo check up on the first and then try to bounce to the rehab. Come hit me with my paper."

"I'mma bring you yo scratch," Angie assured him. "You ain't even got to worry about that. I got you as soon as I get my check and I'm gone spend some money with you. Bye-bye, Too-Too," she said quickly and scampered down the block, leaving Toobie cursing in her wake.

The string of expletives from his brother made Tonto smile. Laughing, he said, "Angie be having yo ass on the moon when she call you Too-Too."

"That ain't my motherfucking name," Toobie spit. "She be doing that pussy shit on purpose. I be wanting to slap the shit out of yo ass for standing up there grinning and giving away our coke to her ass."

"Man, Angie is cool. She always pay that little money, Toobie. You just don't like her 'cause she ain't never really fucked with yo ass."

"Whatever, Tonto."

The twins fell silent. A few cluckers came and went, making small purchases—nothing spectacular. Finally the small tension passed between the brothers.

Tonto said, "Man, let's go get something to eat."

"I am hungry," Toobie confessed. "I say let's give this about another hour and then go get something to eat."

"Damn, Toobie," Tonto bitched. "I'm hungry as hell right now and you talking about in an hour. Ain't shit really moving out here. We could go get us a couple of plates from Alice's diner and go to the tip."

"You know that once we eat ain't neither one of us gone want to come back out here," Toobie pointed out. "Plus I want to call my little white bitch up. I already told her earlier to come through tonight and bring one of her friends that like dark meat. Once I get some of that homemade meat loaf in me and get me some brains, ain't no way I'm leaving the tip."

"Fuck that meat loaf. I want me a half of that smothered chicken with them buttery-ass whipped potatoes, some of that baked macaroni and cheese with about four of them sweet-ass corn muffins. Ohhwee, I'mma kill that shit!"

"Calm yo ass down, Tonto. Nigga, you sound like yo dick getting hard talking about food."

"Fuck you, nigga. I enjoy food like you enjoy tattoos and getting shit pierced, motherfucker. Shit, you know that since we got our apartment and moved out of Ma's place we been eating bullshit all the damn time. If it wasn't for Alice's diner I don't know what we would do." Tonto looked at his watch. "Let's do it like this. We can call in an order. It'll take about twenty, thirty minutes. You go pick up the food and I'll stay here and work. When you get back with the meals we can be up. What do you say about that? Even you can't argue with that."

"Fuck you," Toobie retorted. "You make the call. Make sure that you get me cabbage and mashed potatoes with gravy. Get me a couple of them banana puddings and a peach cobbler too."

Pulling his small cellular telephone from the holster on his belt, Tonto quipped, "Will that be all, sir?"

As he dialed the diner and began placing their order, two customers pulled up in a Ford Taurus station wagon. The passenger rolled down the window. "Y'all working, twins?"

"Dimes and twenties. Park," Toobie stated, as he headed for the gangway.

When Apostle Yo-Yo parked the vehicle, Murderman climbed out. He was dressed in tattered jeans and a ratty black sweatshirt.

In the gangway, Toobie was already removing the bundles from their stash spot as Murderman focused on the gangway. Yo-Yo got out of the car and sat on the hood a few feet away from where Tonto was placing their food order on the phone. He was dressed in a similar tattered costume.

"Get us a fat one, baby!" Yo-Yo called to Murderman. "You know that's our only dough till we get hold of some merch!"

Tonto turned and looked Yo-Yo up and down. Bells and whistles were going off in his head. The hype sitting on the hood of the car didn't really feel like a clucker to him. This guy wasn't humble at all—almost defiant under his gaze. The waitress on the telephone finished taking his order and Tonto returned his cell phone to its holster. A few minutes passed and Toobie or the crackhead still hadn't come out of the gangway.

"A, homie, watch for the law," Tonto said apprehensively. "I'mma see what's taking so long. My brother probably need some change or something."

"It's cool, baby," Yo-Yo remarked, as he smiled, revealing perfectly even, sparkling-white teeth.

Tonto strode into the gangway, but he didn't see his brother or the clucker. "What the fuck?" He started to continue through the gangway to the rear of the building, but he sensed that something was wrong and turned to go back to their car and retrieve the handgun under the passenger seat. As he turned, Tonto saw the other hype behind him, smiling and holding a sinister-looking pair of aluminum .38 revolvers.

"Keep walking, vic," Yo-Yo declared.

I knew something wasn't right with these studs, Tonto thought. He followed the man's instructions and headed for the rear of the building. As soon as he cleared the gangway Tonto could see the other hype holding a pair of the same revolvers on his twin as the man behind him. With a terrified look on his face Toobie had his back against the wall.

"Get over here with yo twin," Murderman sneered.

Tonto was thinking, though. "A, homies. If this is a stickup y'all can have that shit, family. We ain't tripping."

Murderman and Yo-Yo looked at each other and broke out in laughter.

"Apostles don't steal," Murderman stated coldly, when the laughter subsided.

"But we do kill," Yo-Yo added.

Both Apostles trained their handguns on Tonto and Toobie. Murderman nodded his head and they began firing at point-blank range. Twenty shots rang out as the hollow points in all four weapons found their mark. Even as the echoing of the miniexplosions were still reverberating through the neighborhood, Murderman and Yo-Yo were making their way to the Ford Taurus. The dying twin brothers behind them in the rear of the building meant nothing to them.

"It's a shame we gone have to get rid of these heaters," Yo-Yo said casually as they entered the car. "These little motherfuckers is mad nice. They feel like toys or something. Plus you ain't got to worry about no stray fingerprints you might have accidentally got on a shell."

"Yeah, they is well-balanced and light," Murderman agreed. "My gun connect got me sounding like his redneck ass. 'This here one is well-balanced and light, you nigras will like it for doing drive-bys,'" he joked in a hillbilly voice.

"Well, tell ole Billy Bob I want about ten of them motherfuckers," Yo-yo said as he pulled away from the curb.

"Bet," Murderman said.

28

ODELL WAS TIRED AND WET. HE SAT ON THE STEPS OF THE first open yard he came across. He took a seat on the porch steps and was about to pull out his little pouch with his crack-smoking utensils when he heard an unmistakably hostile voice.

"Motherfucker, you better get yo hype ass off my gotdamn porch before I put a bullet in yo ass!" the voice shouted.

Heavy steps on the wooden porch above him reached his ears and Odell got up and fled. He cut through a couple of gangways until he found another suitable-looking porch. This time he took care to make sure the doors to the apartments above and below were closed. Again he took a soggy seat and pulled out his tools.

Since early that morning he had been washing cars at the car-detailing shop on 43rd Street. It was a known fact the car wash was owned by the Apostles, but Odell didn't care. The pay was reasonable and you got to keep your own tips—none of that splitting your loot with the other lazy bums. At the A+ Car Wash you had to hustle to get money.

Odell selected a fresh pipe—really a five-inch length of antenna—and sprinkled a little crack from his secret stash onto the steel wool in the business end of the straight shooter. He flicked his lighter to melt the crack down a bit, then he held the minitorch up to the end while he took a nice hit. The sound of the crack sizzling was music to his ears. He let the smoke wrap around his brain before exhaling. There were only a few crumbs left in the miniature

Ziploc bag, so he dumped those on the pipe, too, and smoked them. He sat for a few minutes to allow his racing heart to calm down a little, then he packed up his good-times kit and made his way to the street.

He was soaked to the bone, but it was well worth it. Today he had received a twenty-dollar tip from Solemn Shawn himself for washing the gang leader's pickup truck. He'd made the chrome rims on that boy shine like they were fresh out the store. The twenty bucks from Solemn Shawn, plus another forty-three he'd made from other customers, had made it hard for him to stay the entire eight hours. Somehow he'd made it to quitting time; now it was party time.

All he had to do was make it over to the projects on 39th Street. A friend of his had taken him down there to cop a few bags last weekend, and Odell had been stupefied by the product in the projects. The crack cocaine was average, but the bags were so damn big it didn't make no sense. He and his friend had went half on a dub and when his buddy hopped back in the car with the swollen twenty-dollar bag, Odell would have sworn that it was garbage. His friend had explained that in the projects the dealers had to make their bags big because there was so much competition. When he tasted the crack for the first time, Odell had to admit that it wasn't the best he'd ever had, but it was nowhere near the worst either— it was about a seven or eight on a scale of one to ten.

Though he wasn't in a particularly sharing mood, Odell hated to go to the jets by himself. That would mean he would have to walk or use public transportation, and he wasn't particularly fond of either. On the other hand maybe he could get Pharrell to make this run with him and only hit him with about a nickel bag or so. That wouldn't be so bad. Pharrell lived only about two short blocks away, so Odell turned his feet in that direction. As was his custom, Odell's eyes roamed the ground as he walked to his friend's house.

A block before, when Odell had walked out of the backyard, Bull and Grove had spotted him and swung around the block to park and get out. As Odell turned the corner in front of them, the two detectives bolted to catch up with him. They hit the corner a few steps after Odell. Bull reached out and grabbed his collar and slammed Odell against the wall of the building behind him.

Looking over Bull's shoulder, Grove smiled. "If it ain't our old buddy Odell. Thought we had forgot about you, didn't you?"

Odell had almost pissed his already wet pants when he was grabbed from behind. He knew it was the police though. "I haven't done anything, sir. I was just going to visit my friend."

"That's the problem," Grove said. "You haven't done nothing. What did we tell yo hype ass the last time we saw you? Thought we wasn't gone bump into yo dumb ass again?"

"It's not that, sir," Odell replied innocently. "It's just that I've been working and trying to get my life in order, sir."

"Stop lying, you crackhead motherfucka," Bull growled as he punched Odell hard in the kidneys. His solid punch caused Odell to crumple to his knees and grip his aching side.

"I ain't even done nothing," Odell whimpered as the pain coursed through his side.

Grove moved past Bull. With his hand on the butt of his gun, he stooped until he was eye level with Odell. "I'm not mad at the fact that we haven't heard from you. My partner is, but I'm not. I'm willing to forgive you. In church Sunday the pastor was talking about forgiving past transgressors. See, we need your help right now, and that will clean up your debt with us."

A ray of sun began to shine through the clouds on Odell's horizon. Maybe, just maybe, if he could bullshit the detectives again, he could get free. There was no question he would shit on them again if they let him go. "I'll do whatever y'all want, sir."

Grove laughed. "I already know that. This time, though, we gone hold on to yo hype ass. Cuff this bitch, Bull."

The ray of sunshine disappeared as the burly detective slapped the iron bracelets on Odell's wrists. "We need a transport, Grove," Bull grunted. "This motherfucka is wet as hell."

The sound of Grove's knee bones cracking could be heard as he stood and pulled out his walkie-talkie. The detectives were assured of a ride for their captive in a few minutes as Bull deposited Odell on the curb.

Grove leaned down in Odell's face. "We just need a little bit of info," he told Odell. "If you give me what we need, you can be back on the street in a matter of minutes. If you bullshit me, best believe I've got a fresh bundle of dope for yo ass. I've had it for a few days, so it done probably fell off, but I can get you three years on look-alike substance, easily."

Odell started to protest, but Bull silenced him by slapping him in the back of his head with one of his humongous hands. "Shut the fuck up, motherfucka. This is real. If you don't tell us what we need to know you going to jail. Now don't talk, just sit there and let this shit marinate."

With his head down, Odell sat there on the curb and pondered his fate. He definitely was not looking forward to a stay in the county jail, and after that on to prison—no way. It was rather easy for him to determine that he would tell these two dicks whatever they wanted to know; he would even make up some shit if he had to in order to buy himself some time.

A paddy wagon turned the corner and pulled up in front of the two detectives and their captive. In the cabin of the paddy wagon were two officers. Looking extremely disinterested, the overweight driver said, "Put him in the back."

As the detectives pulled him to his feet, Odell whined, "Look, man, I'll tell y'all anything that y'all want to know. Just give me a chance."

Without answering, Bull and Grove walked him to the rear of the paddy wagon. Grove opened the door while Bull prepared to hoist Odell up into it.

"Wait, wait!" Odell pleaded. "Tell me what y'all want and I'll do it. I ain't no good to y'all if I'm locked up! Please!"

The detectives stopped; Grove looked over at his partner. "What you think, Bull? Should we give this asshole a chance or do you think he still feel like playing us like we some vics?"

Bull grabbed Odell roughly and began to shove him in the paddy wagon. "Fuck him," Bull grunted. "This motherfucka don't know nothing about Solemn Shawn—he a motherfuckin' crackhead."

"Hold on!" Odell protested. "I do know Solemn Shawn! I just seen him today! I know where he at right now!"

Again Bull stopped. This was too easy—they had been playing this game for so long, they always knew the outcome. Even some of the so-called hardest thugs would start spilling their guts when threatened with jail.

"Where is that?" Grove asked.

Odell gulped. He knew that he was too far gone to turn back now. "He up at the A+ Car Wash up on Fifty-first Street. I just left there and he was there."

"This bet' not be no bullshit," Grove stated.

Odell said a silent prayer to himself. "That's the real, man," Odell assured him. "He should still be there. He got his truck washed and he was fucking around wit a few of his boys and shit. I'm serious, man."

"You believe this shithead, Bull?"

Bull shrugged. "Maybe."

"All right, Bull. Bring this asshole and we gone go check out his story. If he telling the truth he on the way to wherever he was headed. If not, he on his way to the station." Grove slammed the wagon's door and walked to the officer in the driver's seat. "You guys can take off, it's cool."

The officer behind the wheel didn't ask for any explanations as he rolled his eyes and pulled away from the curb.

In the alley a block away from the car wash, Grove turned in his seat to look at Odell. "Motherfucker, it's simple. Just walk to the fucking car wash and see if he still there. Don't do shit stupid 'cause we gone be real close on yo ass. If he there and you see him don't make no eye contact with him. Just play the shit off and leave. You got that?"

Odell nodded.

"And don't try no bullshit. We got yo ID and yo money, Odell. Now get the fuck out and do yo job, snitch!"

Odell vacated the backseat of the Gang Crimes Unit and half ran, half walked to the car wash. He sighed in relief when he saw that Solemn Shawn's pickup truck was still parked on the street in front of the car wash. He even took a short second to admire the sparkle he had brought out of the paint job. It almost looked like he had buffed the beautiful eggshell-colored pickup truck—he could really see himself in the polished chrome of the twenty-four-inch rims. Sighing, he kept walking because there was no sign of Solemn Shawn in the front of A+. He walked around the back to the alley. Inside the unlocked fence behind the large garage that housed the car wash, Odell could see a group of ten or so men in a circle.

Some of the men were down on their knees and haunches, so Odell knew they had to be gambling. As he walked past the fence, Odell cut his eyes to make sure it was Solemn Shawn—it was. Right beside the gamblers, Solemn Shawn was eating out of a Styrofoam tray. Odell was all smiles as he jogged the block back to the Crown Victoria and slipped into the backseat.

"He still there," Odell announced. "Just like I said. They in the back of the joint inside the fence gambling. All y'all got to do is come up the alley and walk right inside the gate. He right there watching them other rich-ass niggas gambling. Can I go now?"

Grove looked Odell in his eyes with a menacing glare. "You bet' not be lying."

"I'm not," Odell insisted. "Can I have my stuff?"

"I'm gone give you yo money, but I'm gone keep yo ID. Just in case I have to get hold of yo ass again."

"Damn," Odell mumbled. "Y'all be on some straight-up bullshit."

"What was that?" Grove challenged.

"Nothing, sir." Odell acquiesced as he collected his money. "Nothing at all, sir."

Grove laughed—an evil sound. "I didn't think so. Hit the bricks, bitch."

Mumbling and grumbling like an empty stomach, Odell left the detectives' car.

The dice game was rowdy—good rowdy. The gamblers were talking cash money shit as they took their chances with the dice.

Mumps was sitting on a overturned milk crate in the ring of gamblers. He had a handful of money and even more cash on the ground bet against the current shooter. Big Ant stood to Mumps's left. His hand held a sheaf of bills in large denominations and he was craftily placing side bets.

On the fringes of the game, Solemn Shawn stood watching the game and eating an order of freshly fried chicken wings drenched in hot sauce. He was obviously enjoying the fat-mouthing of the gamblers, Mumps in particular.

Mumps was animated. "You motherfuckers going home broke tonight! I told y'all I do this shit for my bread and meat! If I don't break motherfuckers then I don't eat! Don't get scared now! If you scared, go to church or the police station! You niggas is gone realize before I'm done that I'm bad for your economy like George Bush and his son!"

One of the gamblers, a prematurely balding twentysomething by the name of Snake, was shooting the dice. He hadn't had anything but bad luck on the dice the entire afternoon.

"Mumps, you be talking big shit," Snake stated as he shook the dice extra hard. "I'm tired of hearing yo damn mouth."

Mumps smiled. "Snake, what's the problem, A. This is America. I got the right to talk as much as I want to. The constitution says that it's my inalienable right to talk shit and trim pigeons like you."

Snake shook the dice furiously. "You talking that shit now, but when I pass, A, let's see if you still talking shit." He spun the dice out of his hand and snapped his fingers. "Dough, dice!" he yelled at the white-and-black blurs as they hit the concrete.

The dice whirled and twirled across the pavement. One stopped on four, the other kept spinning until it hit a small pebble, then skipped and landed on the number three—seven out; Snake lost.

"Oh yeah!" Mumps exalted, as he began to scoop up a large pile of money. "Like Kool-Aid, baby! You niggas is sweet!"

Snake was livid. He hopped to his feet. "Hold the fuck up, A! The dice hit that motherfucking rock right there!"

Mumps looked up at him like Snake had lost his mind. "What you gone do, shoot 'em and catch 'em too? I catch what I don't like, A. And I liked that so I didn't catch it."

"That's some bullshit!" Snake shouted as he kicked the dice. "Fuck that!"

"You better calm yo ass down, A," Big Ant rumbled. "Nigga, you know that everything in the circle is good."

Big Ant's voice was all that was needed to bring Snake back down to earth. He left the game and jumped into his sparkling-clean, maroon Chevy Tahoe. All the men could hear was the muffled roar of the throaty exhaust pipes as Snake gunned out of the car wash lot.

By then Mumps had retrieved the dice. He was shaking them in one hand as he dropped big faces on the ground. "I need a fader, not a friend. Hundred I shoot, hundred I hit. What's up? Don't get scared now."

All of a sudden a gray Crown Victoria whipped into the lot. The headlights flickered repeatedly as Bull and Grove jumped out the car with their guns in their hands.

Several of the gamblers bolted, while the rest of them rose and looked at the detectives. Grove's face was a determined mask as he made a beeline for Solemn Shawn. Bull knocked his chicken dinner to the ground and grabbed the surprised gang leader's arm.

"What the fuck is up?" Solemn Shawn asked.

"We taking you in for questioning," Grove replied smugly. "We can do this shit the hard way or the easy way. The hard way mean you gone have to stop off at the county hospital before going to the station."

Solemn Shawn asked, "You got a warrant? Because this is private property."

"You think you smart, don't you," Grove snarled. "That's pretty good. I love it when a criminal knows the law. It would have worked, but the only problem is we caught you engaging in an illegal activity. That way we don't need a warrant."

"What illegal activity? Eating a wing dinner?"

"Gambling, asshole," Grove replied. "Bull, cuff him."

The large detective holstered his weapon and pulled out his handcuffs. "Go ahead and resist, punk."

Out of the corner of his eye, Solemn Shawn noticed that Big Ant and another Apostle named Hot Rod were inching closer to the unsuspecting detectives. With a nearly undetectable shake of his head, he stopped their movements. Big Ant's eyes questioned him, but again Solemn Shawn gave his nigh imperceptible head shake.

Bull secured the cuffs on Solemn Shawn's wrists behind the gang leader's back and pushed him in the direction of their car.

As they walked toward the car, Grove noticed the two big face bills on the ground. He smiled and walked over and picked up the two hundred dollars. "Whose money is this?" he asked innocently.

No one answered.

"Well, I guess this is our lucky day, Bull," Grove announced as he pocketed one of the bills and handed the other to his partner.

Just as Bull was about to put Solemn Shawn in the car, he said, "Hold up. Let me leave something with my buddies."

"What is it?" Bull asked testily.

"Go in my shirt pocket."

Bull reached into the pocket of Solemn Shawn's printed Enyce shirt and pulled out a midnight blue velvet ring box. He tossed it to Grove.

Grove opened the box and closely inspected the engagement ring it contained. He whistled. "Gotdamn, boy. You got some good taste and she must got some good-ass pussy 'cause this here is one nice piece of ice. What's this—one and a half carats?"

"Three," Solemn Shawn answered.

"Well, I don't want to be responsible for something like this," Grove said as he closed the box and tossed it to one of the Apostles, who in turn handed it to Big Ant.

Big Ant accepted the ring box as he stared at the dicks with a look that could have melted the diamond mounted in the white gold engagement ring.

As the detectives tucked Solemn Shawn in the rear of the car, he called out, "Take that to Bezo and tell him to hold that down for me, A."

Bristling with anger, Big Ant nodded his head.

THE INTERROGATION ROOM WAS BARE EXCEPT FOR A TEN-inch-wide steel bench that ran the length of the room—deluxe accommodations for the accused. One of the homicide and violent crimes detectives' most successful procedures for extracting statements from suspects was to leave them alone in a room like this for a few hours, and let them sweat it out. After a couple of hours had passed the detectives would enter the room and apply pressure to the suspect. They typically had seventy-two hours in which they could hold a man without charging him with anything, and they tended to use this tactic to their advantage. This simple formula had weakened hardened criminals, causing them to make incriminating statements and even confessions.

Detectives Lonihan and Casey were letting Solemn Shawn sweat it out right now—or so they thought. They spent three hours doing miscellaneous things—eating lunch, doing paperwork, and joking around with the other detectives in the squad room.

Detective Casey looked across her desk at her partner. Lonihan was reading about the Chicago Bulls' latest misadventure in the flesh market commonly referred to as the NBA draft. "Lonihan, let's go check and see if the teakettle is ready to whistle. He's been on the fire long enough."

Without looking up from the newspaper, disgustedly Lonihan said, "This fucking Jerry Krause is such a butt ass. This asshole is responsible for single-handedly dismantling the best team in the history of the Chicago Bulls. He allows the greatest players the game has ever seen to walk away. And who does he replace the six-time world champions with?"

Casey took the bait. She knew that even if she didn't show the slightest bit of interest in professional sports, her partner would still somehow manage to make it the subject of conversation.

"I don't know. Who did Krause replace them with?" she asked dryly.

"With fuckin' babies! This fuckin' genius replaces world-class athletes with fuckin' drooling, whining babies! After every loss he talks about how we're in the rebuilding phase. It took less time to build Rome. This fucking guy drives me nuts. When is Reinsdorf gonna get rid of this stupid son of a bitch? I swear I could—"

"Let's go dig into this guy," Casey said, breaking into Lonihan's sports tirade as she stood. She grabbed her pad from the desktop and headed for the interrogation room.

After folding up his newspaper, Lonihan struggled out of his chair and followed her. When they opened the door of the interrogation room, Solemn Shawn was sitting on the bench with his head against the wall. He appeared to be asleep.

Lonihan walked over and kicked his foot. "Wake up!"

"I'm awake," Solemn Shawn announced. "And keep your damn feet off me."

The chunky Irish detective glared down at Solemn Shawn. "What did you say?"

"You heard me. I said keep your damn feet off me."

Instantly Lonihan's beefy cheeks reddened. He glanced over at his partner with a look of disbelief.

Casey decided to cut him off at the pass. She didn't believe that Solemn Shawn had stewed long enough for any heavy tactics to work yet. She put her hand on the rolled-up sleeve on Lonihan's arm. "Why don't you grab us a few chairs," she told him.

Mumbling under his breath, Lonihan went to fetch two chairs.

When he returned to the room he positioned the chairs a few feet in front of their suspect and eased his bulk into one.

Casey took the other. She held out her hand to Solemn Shawn. "I'm Detective Casey and this is Detective Lonihan."

Solemn Shawn looked at her hand like it was covered in anthrax spores.

She withdrew her hand and flipped open her notepad.

"Why am I here?" Solemn Shawn queried.

"Slow down, punk," Lonihan snapped. "We're asking the fucking questions."

Casey silenced her partner by raising her hand. To Solemn Shawn, she said, "I see that you want to dispense with the amenities. That's cool. I like to get down to business. Do you know James Bingham?"

"No."

"What about a guy named Bing?"

"Never heard of him."

Casey paused. She leaned back in her chair and crossed her legs, careful not to crease her pants. "Want a smoke, Shawn?"

"Don't smoke."

"How about a soda? A cold Pepsi or something?"

"No thanks."

Detective Lonihan couldn't take it anymore. He pointed his fat, pink finger in Solemn Shawn's face. "Listen here, punk! My partner is trying to be nice to you and you're acting like a real jerk wad! Out there on the streets you might be a big man, but not in here, asshole!"

With a chilling smile on his face, Solemn Shawn removed his Gucci eyeglasses. "I don't mind the news, cop, but you can keep the weather," he said as he wiped Lonihan's spittle from his face.

Lonihan's face screwed into a beet-red mask. "You arrogant, little shit bird! You think this is a fucking game! I've put punks like you away for the rest of their natural lives!"

Casey had seen and heard enough. She grabbed Lonihan's arm and pulled him from the chair and whisked him out the room. She slammed the door behind them, cognizant all the while of Solemn Shawn's laughter in the background.

"You're letting this guy make you lose your fucking cool, Lonihan! If you lose your fucking head, you lose your fucking edge! What are you thinking? This guy is smart. Too fucking smart. He made you look like a green shield in there, Detective. Is any of this getting through your thick Irish skull?"

Some of the red had begun to drain from Lonihan's fleshy cheeks, but he was still huffing and puffing. "You heard that fucking jerk-off in there, Casey. Who does he think he is?"

"The leader of the largest, most organized street gang in Chicago," Casey stated matter-of-factly. "And you're in there trying to heavy-hand him like he's some sixteen-year-old triggerman in a drive-by. A Big Mac and a slap aren't going to get this guy talking. We've got to use his arrogance against him. This is not the type of guy that we can tune up to get him to make a statement or incriminate himself. If anything that'll make him shut down."

Lonihan didn't totally agree. "I'm telling you, Casey. This guy is a smart ass and we've got to treat him accordingly. You know how these guys are. I'm not gonna tiptoe around this guy. Fuck him. We're trying to put together a case. A case that the captain has a strong interest in getting squared away."

The two homicide detectives were so busy arguing that they didn't notice Detectives Hargrove and Thensen enter the violent crime division. The two GCU detectives stood and watched them argue for a few moments before Grove interrupted them.

"You two should get married," Grove quipped, causing Lonihan and Casey to become aware of their presence.

"We don't have time for you guys right now," Lonihan snapped.

"You see this, Bull? Look at how we get treated. We bring them their prime suspect and now they don't have time for us. Well, I just had a small convo with the captain and he said that we could have a crack at our illustrious friend in there if you couldn't get anywhere with him. And judging from your little lovers' quarrel, you guys aren't getting anywhere, so we'll give it a go-round. Any objections?"

Lonihan had to stifle a curse. The last time Captain Hartibrig had chewed him out about not wanting to accept help from the GCU was still in the back of his mind. Not wanting to see the look of satisfaction on Grove's face, Lonihan looked down at his shoes.

Casey pointed to the interrogation room. Behind Grove's and Bull's backs she shook her head at her partner. She would never understand how Lonihan had made detective. In her opinion, he was totally inept. She could never get away with half the things he did.

"C'mon, Bull, let's show these homicide dicks how to do this," Grove said confidently as he marched to the interrogation room.

The gang crimes detectives trooped into the room. Grove grabbed Lonihan's former chair and turned it backward before sitting in it. Bull chose to stand. He leaned against the closest wall with a bored look on his face.

There was no change in Solemn Shawn's expression.

Cheerily, Grove asked, "What's up, A? What's cracking, A?"

Not taking the bait, Solemn Shawn remained silent.

"Hey, motherfucka. I'm talking to you."

"I hear you," Solemn Shawn said.

"Well, next time I ask you a fucking question you better answer, nigga. I ain't a stupid, fat Irish pig. I know who the fuck you are and what you and your Assholes are capable of doing, A."

Impatiently, Solemn Shawn glanced at his Kenneth Cole wristwatch.

Grove had to smile. To his partner he said, "You see this motherfucker, Bull? He up in here acting like we inconveniencing his punk ass."

"Humph," was Bull's reply.

To Solemn Shawn, Grove said, "I'm sorry for the inconvenience, Mr. Big-time Gang Leader, but do you mind if we ask you a couple of questions?"

"Shoot," Solemn Shawn said simply.

"We know that Bing was a Governor. We know that Apostles and Governors don't get along. The question is, why did you kill him?"

"I didn't. Didn't know any Bing. Never heard of him. Had no reason to kill someone that I didn't even know."

"You hear this shit, Bull?"

"I heard," Bull answered.

"Well, Bull. Riddle me this. If this asshole didn't kill Bing, then why were his fingerprints found at the scene?"

Grove looked into Solemn Shawn's face, hoping that his announcement would have had some effect on him—it didn't. "So tell me, why were your prints found at the scene of a homicide investigation of a person that you didn't know and didn't kill?"

"I don't know. Why don't you tell me?" Solemn Shawn said sarcastically.

Nodding his head in approval, Grove said, "You're pretty good. It almost sounds as if you really don't know. Nice act. 'Cept for that one mistake, you could have gotten clean away with this one. It was good work too. No shell casings. No witnesses. If you wouldn't have been drinking, you probably would have never gotten sloppy. Tell me though. Why'd you do it? I mean, this guy Bing wasn't a heavyweight. He was a young dude. For you to personally off this dude, he musta really done something. It doesn't even sound like business. It feels personal. What'd he do? Fuck one of your hoodrats? C'mon, you can tell me."

Still Solemn Shawn maintained his silence.

Grove decided to turn the heat up a little. "I'm tired of this bullshit. You know what? I hate you motherfucking, gangbanging-ass niggas! You bitches ain't nothing but parasites! You sick mother-fuckers get y'all hooks into these kids and promise them the fuckin' world, but all you deliver is a fuckin' body bag! Tough guys! I been fighting you bitches all my damn life!"

With cold fires burning behind the lenses of his designer glasses, Solemn Shawn said, "I smell that."

"You smell what?" Grove asked.

"I smell fear on you," Solemn Shawn said. "I've always been able to smell it. I don't smell it on your partner, but it's all over you. You reek of it. You talk about fucking over these kids. The same moth-erfucker that puts packs on these young'uns. Sending them to the joint just so you can fill your quota. Yeah, you scared. That's why you became a cop. So you wouldn't have to be scared no more. You joined the biggest gang. You motherfuckers are the real parasites, using your fear to sell wholesale fear to the masses. Making a liv-ing pretending that you're serving and protecting while you're really living out your sick fantasies of having control and power."

"Get the fuck out of here," Grove scoffed. "You niggas ain't noth-ing but pussies. That's why y'all stick together. You punks don't go nowhere unless y'all deep and got heat."

"Sounds familiar, don't it," Solemn Shawn commented. "I read about dudes like you in psychology books. Cats with inferiority complexes. In order not to feel inferior they overcompensate. I've known little punks like you all my life. Bully motherfuckers that's really bitches."

Grove guffawed. He turned to his partner. "Do you hear this motherfucka? I don't believe this shit. This motherfucka is trying to psychoanalyze me. He got to be losing his fucking mind." To Solemn Shawn, he said, "That psychobabble bullshit may work on those uneducated assholes that you run with, but I don't know who the fuck you think you dealing with. I ain't one of those fuck-ing schmucks you got killing and dying for you. If you so fucking smart—"

The door to the interrogation room was flung open and a short, balding white man carrying a black briefcase burst into the room. Detectives Casey and Lonihan were on his heels.

"Let's go, Shawn," the small man commanded.

"Who the fuck is this?" Grove queried, jerking his thumb at the small man.

"Benjamin Stein, and Mr. Terson is my client. I have been informed by the homicide detectives that my client has not been charged with any crime, therefore I am invoking his Miranda rights and this interview stops now. If you want to talk to Mr. Terson about this matter again, I suggest that you get an arrest warrant."

Grove was stupefied. To Casey and Lonihan, he said, "You just gonna let this motherfucka walk 'cause some fancy-pants mouth-piece comes in here talking slick? I don't believe this shit."

"We don't like it any more than you," Casey said apologetically, "but it's not our call. The captain says to cut him loose."

Grove hopped up and kicked his chair over. "This is bullshit!"

"C'mon, Shawn, let's go," Stein repeated.

A light came on in Grove's head. "Hold on there. He ain't going nowhere. He is under arrest."

"What are you talking about?" Stein asked. "My client hasn't been charged with any crime."

With a sly grin on his face, triumphantly Grove countered, "Yes, he has. Illegal gambling. Your client was picked up at a street dice game."

"Is that true, Shawn?" Stein asked.

"Yeah, but I wasn't gambling. I was eating some chicken."

"Tell it to the judge," Grove grunted, as he pulled his handcuffs from the pouch on his belt.

As his client was being cuffed, Stein said, "This is a misde-meanor, Detective. I expect to see my client free in a maximum of eight hours. If I don't hear from him by then, I'll be back with a court order for his release and a restraining order for you two. Shawn, don't answer any of their questions. Kick your heels up for a few hours. When you get out you make sure you give me a call. I'll post your bond at the front desk before I leave so they can't shit you about waiting on an I-bond."

Ben Stein headed for the door, while Bull and Grove prepared to take Solemn Shawn to the lockup.

30

Shawn Terson stared at the pictures on the walls of Captain Bellows's office. The framed photographs were accompanied by a short shelf that housed several bowling and softball trophies of different shapes and sizes. Alongside the trophy shelf were awards, plaques, and certificates.

With a small smile, Shawn realized that this small collection of personal accolades summed up the captain's existence. If the captain was lucky, maybe one or two more trophies would find their way onto the shelf. Maybe a plaque or two more might adorn the wall, but that was all he had to look forward to—and that wasn't enough for Shawn.

Shawn felt a warm feeling of happiness as he allowed himself his second smile in as many minutes. Today he was leaving. Leaving the place that had been his home for almost four years. He had big plans. He didn't feel bad about his stay. He had been inspired inside of these walls. At the age of eighteen he was already the head of a criminal organization. It was like being the CEO of a company.

Though an outside observer couldn't tell, Solemn Shawn was secretly looking forward to the money and power his position afforded him. He hadn't planned on becoming a leader, but it had happened and he was going to roll with it. It felt good being the alpha wolf.

The office door opened and Captain Bellows entered. There was no ceremony surrounding his entrance, he just appeared and took his seat behind the desk.

Before today, Solemn Shawn had never noticed how small and weak he looked. Bellows always seemed so big and powerful in the past, especially when he was threatening the boys he was charged with keeping in line.

Captain Bellows locked eyes with Solemn Shawn, then looked away. His eyes wandered to the window, which was frosted and barred. He sighed. "Mr. Terson, what did you learn during your stay here?"

Solemn Shawn's mind whirred through the useful information, legal and otherwise, stored in his memory banks, but to Bellows he said, "I don't know."

Captain Bellows sighed again. "I didn't think you would admit that you learned anything worthwhile. I've watched you since the day you walked through the door. I took a peek at your school grades. I could see that they were about average. Too average. That's when I noticed the pattern. You only did enough to get by, never enough to stand out. I always knew there was something about you, so I had one of your instructors slip you an IQ test. Something that you couldn't purposely manipulate. Your score confirmed my suspicions. Do you want to know what you scored?"

"I don't care," Solemn Shawn said with a shrug of his shoulders.

"Borderline genius," Captain Bellows continued. "Test scared me. It made me take a good look at your file. I looked at your case. The judge stuck it to you. You should have gotten off with a slap on the wrist for extenuating circumstances. You shouldn't have had to grow up in here. As smart as you are you had a real chance, but all they did was create a monster. A monster that I have to return to the world.

"Yeah, I called you a monster. I know what you've started. I know some of the things that you've been responsible for doing behind these walls, but try as I might, I couldn't catch you. You were too smart for me. I took the same IQ test as you. My score said I had average intelligence. I took it over and over again. Same score: average intelligence. Funny thing, not being as smart as a boy. The only comfort I drew from that is that I'm not a monster."

Captain Bellows fingered the release forms in front of him. He chuckled as he pulled a gold pen from his crisp white shirt. "Now I've got to sign this shit. Don't have a choice. I have to let you out of here so you can get started on your adult life of crime. Believe me, I know what you're going to do. You're going to be a criminal until someone kills you or you go to prison for life."

Gold pen flashing, Captain Bellows began to scribble his name on the necessary lines on the release forms. Without looking up at the young man, he said, "This is supposed to be your exit interview, Solemn Shawn."

Shawn's eyebrows raised at the captain's use of his nickname.

The captain saw the look on his face. "I know you're Solemn Shawn. This is supposed to be an exit interview, but it feels more like I'm giving birth when I should be getting an abortion. But that's what we do here. We warehouse baby killers, baby thieves, and baby drug dealers until they get old enough to get out and ply their trades as adults."

Captain Bellows finished signing the release forms. He removed a rubber stamp and ink pad from his desk drawer and stamped a big red "Reformed Release" on the top sheet. He smiled at the irony of the stamp, then his smile faded as he pushed the release forms into Solemn Shawn's file. "That's all, Solemn Shawn Terson. I guess I'll see you in hell."

An unemotional smile graced Solemn Shawn's lips as he got up and prepared to exit the office. At the door he stopped and turned. "No you won't, Captain," he said coolly.

Captain Bellows looked up. "No I won't what?"

"You won't see me in hell," the young man said confidently. "I'm an Apostle, I'm going to Heaven."

Softly, Solemn Shawn closed the office door behind him.

31

With her nose buried in a thick textbook, Sakawa sat on her sofa. Frustrated, she tossed her book to the side and got up to go and brew herself some tea. As she was about to cross the threshold of her living room, she heard the telephone ring. She learned across the couch and looked at the caller ID before lifting the receiver. The number on the caller ID wasn't one that she immediately recognized, but she knew it had to be China Doll. Her friend was always trying to call her up from some mysterious number and act like she had been on something heavy. She picked up the headset.

"China Doll, bitch, where you at now?" she said.

Instead of China's voice, Insane Wayne rasped, "Now is that any way to answer the telephone, bitch."

Sakawa shuddered at the sound of Wayne's voice.

Insane Wayne laughed—which chilled her even more. "You don't sound like you happy to hear from yo man, Saki. I thought you loved me."

"I don't love yo ass no more, Wayne," she spit acidly.

"Insane Wayne," he corrected her.

Anger replaced Sakawa's fear. "Yeah, motherfucka, you is crazy if you think I love yo ass after the shit you did to me! You hurt me and I ain't never done shit to you!"

"C'mon, now, boo. I know you ain't mad about me getting a little shit on my dick," Insane Wayne scoffed.

"You know what, Wayne! I hate yo trifling ass! Fuck you!"

"Nall, bitch, fuck wit me," he slurred.

"Listen to you. You sound like you got a mouthful of shit. You need to get them fucking wires and shit out yo mouth. I know yo damn jaw been healed. That shit ain't cool, motherfucka."

"You wasn't tripping on the wires and shit in my mouth when I was sucking yo fat hairy-ass pussy," Insane Wayne replied. "It tasted nice and sweet like old times too."

The thought of that night made Sakawa shiver. Her head swimming in anger, she shouted, "Nigga, fuck you! I hate yo motherfucking ass!" She could hear the laughter stream out of his twisted mouth as he guffawed at her outburst. "Nigga, that shit is funny, huh? You think that shit is funny? Let's see how funny it is when I marry Vee!"

Abruptly Insane Wayne stopped laughing. "Saki, don't play with me, girl! You ain't finta marry that nigga!"

Enjoying his obvious discomfort, Sakawa taunted, "What if I do, nigga? What yo punk ass gone do?"

"I-I-I'll kill both of you bitches!" Insane Wayne sputtered. "Fuck that! Bitch, I don't know who the fuck you think I am! You better respect my shit, ho! Bitch, and you better not keep fucking with that nigga either! I ain't playing wit yo ass!"

It was Sakawa's turn to laugh. "Listen to the big, tough, booty-hole bandit. Fuck you. You had your chance. Nigga, you the one that left me after them niggas robbed you and beat yo ass. I woulda helped you get back on yo feet. I loved you. Woulda went through anything with you, but you left me. Then when you finally come back, you tie me up and rape me. What type of sick shit is that? That's some sick-ass shit. I bet you ain't done nothing to the niggas that done that shit to you, but you feel good about fucking me in my ass. Well, you got the name right. You really is insane. You's a sick bitch."

Insane Wayne's voice was like a bitter-cold Chicago winter wind as it whistled through the telephone. He seethed, "Bitch, I got you! I got you and that nigga, bitch! I got some business to take care of, then I'll be to see you, ho! I'mma kill you and that bitch-ass nigga Vee! Ho, I hope you got yo papers in order 'cause you dead, bitch! You and—"

Softly Sakawa replaced the telephone receiver into its cradle. She sat on the sofa thinking for a few moments before rising and going into her neat but small kitchen. She collected all four of her butcher knives and began to place them in strategic hiding places throughout the apartment. In a few seconds she was done and returned to the sofa and plunked down on the cushions. The placement of her weapons, coupled with the fact that the landlord had changed the door locks, gave her a small sense of security.

The telephone chimed. Casually she leaned over to pick it up with a string of curses ready to go if it was Wayne again. "Hello," she said warily into the telephone receiver.

Vee's voice came through the headset. "What's up, ma? I need you to come downstairs for a minute."

Sakawa moaned, "I really don't feel like it right now, Vee. I'm getting ready to study for a test I've got to take in two days at work to get a good evaluation, so I can get a gotdamn raise."

Vee wasn't trying to hear that. "Girl, bring yo butt down the damn stairs. I got something I want to show you."

"What is it?"

"Just come down."

"All right," Sakawa conceded. "But I ain't going nowhere with you. I ain't even dressed and I got to study for this fucking data entry test."

She slipped her feet into a pair of white Classic Reeboks and grabbed her door key. She thought about the silk scarf wrapped on her short hairdo, but she decided against removing it. *Fuck Vee,* she thought as she went out the door. *I know I still look better than every other bitch that he probably fuck with even when I ain't fixed up.*

In front of Sakawa's building, Vee was leaning against his truck with a big-ass grin on his face. "Damn, girl, you look like a hot mess," he wisecracked as she stepped onto the porch.

"Fuck you, boy," Sakawa retorted. "I was in the crib chilling. Now what is it that so damn important that you got to show me now?"

"Girl, you better watch yo tone of voice," Vee threatened playfully.

She wished that he would wipe that stupid grin off his face. "Quit playing, Vee. I told you I ain't got time for this shit. I told you that I'm studying and that shit is hard as hell."

"Bring yo evil ass here," Vee commanded.

As she walked down the stairs and over to him, Sakawa grumbled, "My one totally free day that I got to study and you come over here playing and shit." She stood in front of him with her arms crossed and a slightly aggravated look on her face.

Vee found her attitude amusing. He laughed and handed her a thin sheaf of hundred-dollar bills. "I want you to take this stack and go shopping."

Sakawa didn't soften as she accepted the money. "Is you finta take me shopping?"

Vee shook his head. "Uh-uh, I got a funeral to go to. I'm on my way to my tip, so I can take a shower and change clothes."

"I ain't finta get on the bus. I get enough of the fucking CTA riding that motherfucka every day to work and shit. China Doll used to be trying to come get me, but that bitch had me late two days in a row."

"Who said you got to get on the bus?" Vee asked with his smile widening even more.

"You ain't gone take me. How the hell else is I supposed to get to the mall?"

"In that," Vee announced like a game show host as he pointed to the midnight blue Chrysler Sebring coupe parked in front of his Excursion.

Sakawa's hands flew up to her heart and mouth. "Stop playing, Vee. Vee, stop playing."

He dangled the car's keys in front of her. Looking pleased, Vee bragged, "Girl, that ain't shit. I told you if you was my girl you would be straight."

With her face totally covered in awe, Sakawa snatched the keys and walked over to the car, then she hesitated.

"Gone get in the motherfucka, girl. It's yours. It ain't brand-new, but it got low mileage and it's paid for. The bill of sale is in the glove compartment and it's in yo name."

At the driver's-side door, Sakawa hesitated again and turned to Vee. "I can't take this from you. This is real nice, but I can't take it."

The look on her face said the total opposite, but Vee could tell she was just refusing because in her head refusing such an extravagant gift was the thing to do. "Girl, you better take that whip and ride it. I don't need the motherfucka and I know you got to be tired of riding the fucking bus and shit. Gone sit in the motherfucka."

The locks popped smoothly with a barely audible click as she hit the button on the alarm remote. She slid into the well-kept leather interior and looked around. Even though it was a used car the interior looked new. Vee walked to her side and closed the door. He made a twisting signal with his fingers, telling her to fire it up. She stuck the key in the ignition and the small coupe instantly came to life. With the touch of a button the window rolled down.

Vee leaned onto the car door. "Gone to the mall, girl."

She looked up at Vee. "Thank you," she breathed. "I really needed a car. You just don't know how much."

The note of sincerity in Sakawa's voice touched Vee. "Don't even trip, ma. I know it got to be a bitch trying to get up and do your thang on the bus and shit. The last bus I was on I was going to the penitentiary. That shit made me swear I wasn't never going to get on another bus again in my life. Now gone go shopping, ma."

"All right," she said softly.

As Vee stood up and stepped back, she checked her mirrors,

then pulled out of the parking space. In her rearview mirror she could see Vee watching her drive away. She stopped and put the car in reverse. It responded nicely as she carefully backed up until she was level with Vee again.

"What's wrong?" he asked.

Huskily, she said, "I was just thinking. When I'm at the mall I could stop in Victoria's Secret and pick out something nice for you to see me in. Then later on you can come over here and I can show you what you been missing out on all these years."

Expressions of amazement, then happiness, then disbelief alternately crossed Vee's face. "Stop playing, Sakawa. You ain't never let me in yo crib."

"Oh, then that's okay," she said, reaching down to put the gearshift back into drive.

"Hold on, hold on," Vee said hurriedly. "You for real?"

"Call me tonight around eight or nine to see if I'm playing. And a small hint. I love fresh pineapple slices and Moët champagne," she said before zooming off. She had to laugh at the look on Vee's face as she sped down the block. At the stop sign on the corner, she turned the radio up and opened the sunroof before pointing the car's nose toward the nearest mall. She looked around the interior of the Sebring again.

"Wait till I tell China Doll this shit," she said aloud.

The funeral home chapel was packed with family, friends, Governors, and curious onlookers. It wasn't often that a set of twins were laid to rest at the same time. The two pale blue coffins were placed end to end. Toobie and Tonto looked peaceful laid out in the silver interior of the caskets. For once they were dressed alike in Governors' colors: green-and-yellow Akademiks jogging suits with matching Green Bay Packers fitted caps lying on their chests.

"... and the end that befell these two young brethren shall befall all who walk their path!" the fat-faced Baptist preacher bellowed from the pulpit overlooking the coffins. "Young men caught up and don't know when the Lord comes He don't care about what set you claim! The Father don't care about what gang signs you throw up! Lord Jesus don't care about yo money, cash, hos! Almighty Jesus only cares about your soul!" Pastor Beacher could see that his sermon was making many of the young gang members in the crowd uncomfortable, but he kept shouting. "How have you been treating your brothers, that's all Jesus care about. Here's your chance now to get right with God! Here's yo chance to join God's gang! On behalf of the church, we extend our hands to you, young brothers! Join the church and get yourself saved now! The way you boys be riding, you need to get right with God! You can't pay off God! You can't scare God! You ain't gone be able to jump on God! You ain't gone be able to shoot at the Lord! You ain't gone be able to intimidate God! The only thing you can do is accept his son Jesus Christ as your Lord and Savior!"

The thirty or so family members of the twins and those who were not Governors in the chapel amened and applauded loudly.

Pastor Beacher mopped his sweaty forehead with a hand cloth. "And now while we receive a selection from Sister Brenda Bohanon, anyone who wants to see their souls saved so they won't have to burn in everlasting fire needs to come forth!"

The thin, old, wrinkled Black man sitting at the organ hit a few notes as a huge Black woman in a choir robe began to belt out the opening notes to "Keep Your Eye on the Sparrow." The funeral-goers began to cry and wail, and most of the gang members in the chapel, headed by Vee and the Governors' State Department, excused themselves and took up posts outside in front of the funeral-parlor.

Outside the funeral parlor the sun shone down on the group of men and boys. Vee was looking dapper in a pearl gray suit with a black satin shirt and tie. His feet were encased in a pair of black ostrich-skin square-toe shoes. A black Dobbs hat with a small gray feather in the hatband sat on his head. Some of the other Governors had on dress clothes, but the majority of them had on their street costumes: blue jeans with football and basketball jerseys, jogging suits, boots, and gym shoes.

The members of the State Department gathered closely around Vee, while the foot soldiers ringed them.

Governor O spoke first. "Vee, I'm telling you, Gov, we got to fuck these motherfuckas up for this bullshit. If we don't catch a few bodies behind this shit, niggas gone start thinking we pussy or something."

Vee looked at O like he had lost his mind. "Don't you think I know that shit? Nigga, don't say no stupid shit to me on the day I got to put two of my Governors in the motherfucking ground! I know what the fuck we got to do! Them Assholes took two of ours! For that we got to do something special."

Looking uncomfortable in an ill-fitting dark blue pin-striped suit, Governor Teddy mentioned, "I know where that nigga Solemn Shawn bitch stay." All of the State Department's attention was on him—something he loved. "I seen that stud at the mall with his little bitch. He thought he was dipped 'cause we was out at the Orland Square Mall. When the nigga left the mall I followed him back to the city. From there I followed that stud over to a crib on 96th and Loomis. He dropped the broad off and bounced. He did some crazy U-turn and I lost him, but I still know exactly where his little runner stay."

Finishing his statement, Teddy waited for Vee to praise him.

Instead, Vee snapped, "Nigga, why the fuck this the first time that I'm hearing 'bout this shit? Why the fuck you ain't been mentioned this shit?"

That good feeling was gone; now Teddy wished he didn't have the State Department's full attention. "It was a while ago," Teddy mumbled. "We wadn't really into it with them Assholes like that then."

Vee didn't want to hear it. "Poo, hit that nigga in his eye," he commanded.

Poo, a short, skinny Governor with large front teeth, promptly whacked Teddy in the eye. Teddy staggered back and covered his eye. After a few moments he regained his composure and rejoined the small group. He took his hand down from his eye. It hadn't begun to swell yet, but it was red and a single tear escaped out of it.

"The next time any one of y'all see one of our enemies and don't take care of that business, it's gone be Cold War on yo ass," Vee announced. "Now, you niggas know what the fuck got to be done. Who gone handle this shit?"

Looking salty, Teddy promised, "I'll handle this shit personally."

Heading back inside the funeral parlor, Vee warned, "Don't make me wait to hear about it neither. I want them putting dirt on that bitch inside of the next week. Now everybody get fuck back inside, that fat choir bitch should be through singing."

"DAMN, MAMBO, YO FUCKING CROSS 'BOUT TO BLIND ME!" Big Ant said as the sun bounced off the window of A-Land and reflected off the chunky diamond-and-gold cross hanging on a polished gold chain around Mumps's neck.

"That's right, A," Mumps said, giving his cross a swing. "This here is five carats of that stuff that Bugs Bunny won't touch. No cracks, no flaws, baby."

Murderman stood in the doorway of the game room, holding a twenty-ounce Pepsi and scanning the street and sidewalk as was his custom. "Yeah, that motherfucking cross is right, A. What that boy run?"

Shaking a pair of blue dice in his right hand, Mumps said, "This piece cost some unlucky stud about ten stacks, but since I copped it from the pawnshop I only gave them studs thirty-five hundred for it. Sweet as bear meat. I got tired of wearing that heavy-ass platinum shit. I just wanted me some good old gold."

"You came up, A," an Apostle named Greg said. He was leaning against the wall beside Murderman. "That motherfucka is tight. I want me some phat earrings though. At least a carat apiece—princess cut. What pawnshop you was at, Mumps?"

"The one across the street from the fed jail downtown. They got some shit in there too. Half the niggas in the jail across the street got jewelry up in there."

"That's fucked up," another Apostle named Baby Day sang out.

"Them niggas be peeking out them little-ass windows watching niggas copping they J out the pawnshop."

A small boy came running up the block. The boy's untied shoestrings slapped against the pavement as he ran until he stopped directly in front of Murderman. His small chest rose and fell behind his dingy, stained T-shirt as he gasped for breath. When he was finally able to get some wind back in his small lungs, he said, "Murder, Tanya said to tell you to come on if you still want to get yo hair braided. She said . . . she said you got to bring some grease too, 'cause she ain't got no more grease. She said to bring some of them 'Cardi Breezeys to drink too."

The grown-ups laughed at the little boy's delivery. Fishing into his pocket, Murderman pulled out a knot of money. He peeled off a five-dollar bill and handed it to the boy. He said, "Don't spend all yo money on Flaming Hots with cheese either. And tie up yo doggone shoes."

"Thanks, Murder," the little boy spouted gratefully. He stooped and tucked his strings inside of his shoes and then he bolted.

Murderman watched the young'un run away with a half smile on his face as he stepped down out of the doorway. "I'm 'bout to go get my hair braided if anyone looking for me."

"Go get pretty, ma," Big Ant said.

In response to Big Ant, Murderman held up a middle finger over his shoulder and kept walking. As he turned the corner of the block, Snake's Chevy Tahoe was coming up the street. He pulled over at the curb in front of A-Land. With a determined look on his face, Snake jumped out the truck—his hand was in the front pocket of his jeans.

Challengingly, Snake said, "Mumps, what's up now, A?"

Raising his eyebrow, Mumps asked, "What's up, A?"

"This what's up!" Snake said as he pulled a gigantic wad of money from his pocket. "Nigga, fitty I shoot, fitty I hit!"

With a hint of relief in his voice, Mumps said to the others, "Oh this nigga came to gamble."

The Apostles began to gather around and form a circle. Some of them to gamble, others to just watch the insane amounts of money that would be wagered in the street dice game. A few minutes later the dice game was in full swing in front of the game room.

Bezo came to the door and stuck his graying head out of the door. At the same time a silver Honda Accord pulled up across the street and parked.

"Mumps, you motherfuckers know better than that!" Bezo yelled. "You motherfuckers out here shooting dice like y'all done lost y'all damn mind! That's all the fuck the po-pos need to see to start sniffing they faggot ass around here! Move that shit in the back or something! I don't know what the fuck—"

The gamblers looked up at Bezo, who had a wide-eyed expression on his face as he gazed past them. One by one the gamblers followed Bezo's eyes. His stare led them to a silver Honda Accord parked across the street. The arm of the driver was hanging out of the foreign sedan. The hand on the arm was holding a pistol. The driver holding the pistol smiled and without warning began shooting at the gamblers.

Bezo dove back inside the game room, but not before he caught a bullet in his left arm. In front of A-Land there was a mad scramble by the Apostles to get cover. Several of the gamblers and spectators, including Big Ant, Baby Day, and Snake, dove behind Snake's Tahoe. The shooter tried to follow their movements with hot lead. He came close when one of the bullets ricocheted off the curb and hit Big Ant in the foot. Mumps was a blur as he dove behind a garbage Dumpster sitting a few feet away from the curb. Greg and two of the youngsters who had been watching the dice game sprinted off down the street.

Shots continued to ring out as the gunman kept trying to hit the pinned-down gang members. Suddenly the crouching Apostles heard more gunfire. The sound of this gun was different—more of a booming instead of the cough-spitting of the pistol the lone gunman in the car was using.

Mumps peeked from behind the Dumpster to see Murderman walking and blasting a .45 at the Honda Accord. One arm
was across Murderman's face, but Mumps could tell that he was
grinning—he knew that Murder loved shit like this. The gunman
in the car directed his last few shots at Murderman, but the
deadly pellets flying at him didn't stop him from continuing to
advance.

Both guns fell silent. The driver of the Honda pulled his gun
into the car and peeled off.

His gun was empty, so Murderman had to let him go. He ran to
Big Ant. The big man was pulling off his left boot to get a good look
at the bullet wound in his foot. He looked up at Murderman.

"Good looking, A," Big Ant said as he winced in pain. "That
motherfucka came out of nowhere. 'Fore we knew it that nigga was
chopping at our ass. Where the fuck you come from? I thought you
was gone to get yo hair braided."

Looking at his friend's bloody foot, Murderman said, "I was
about to go buy some hair grease, then I remembered I had some
African Pride grease in the back room here. When I got to the corner I heard that nigga clapping at y'all."

Snake jumped to his feet and brushed off his jeans and T-shirt.
"That motherfucka was letting that bitch breathe. All I know is I
looked up and saw that blowpipe. Dude was trying to get rid of our
ass. I don't even know who the fuck that was. Did any of y'all get a
good look at the motherfucka?"

"I did but I ain't never seen that motherfucka before in my
damn life. I usually like to know who it is trying to kill me. Did you
know that nigga, A?" Mumps asked from behind Murderman.

"I think I seen that nigga before," Murderman said as he
assisted Snake with helping Big Ant to a standing position. His face
scrunched up in determination, but whether it was from lifting Big
Ant's bulk or trying to conjure up the identity of the lone gunman
wasn't easily discernible. "I know that motherfucka from somewhere."

Leaving his bloody boot with a bullet hole in it on the curb, Big Ant put his arms around Snake's and Murderman's necks and they helped him into Snake's truck. Snake ran around to the driver's side and hopped in.

Murderman stayed on the curb. "I'm going to fill my heater back up and then get my damn hair braided, A. Hit me on the hip when you get out the emergency room and I'll scoop you and take you to the tip."

From the driver's seat, Snake said, "Mumps don't get little, nigga. As soon as I drop off Big Ant I'll be back to get in yo pockets, A. Yo point is still four, too."

"Pull off, A!" Big Ant rumbled. "I got a hole in my fucking foot and you Gamblers Anonymous motherfuckers is still talking about shooting dice!"

Snake was negotiating his way out of the parking spot when Bezo came out of the game room with a bloody towel wrapped around the biceps muscle of his left arm.

"Hold the fuck up; I'm going to the hospital too!" Bezo shouted as he locked the game room door.

33

"WHAT'S WRONG WIT YOU?" VANESSA ASKED AS SHE STOOD over the bed looking down at Shawn.

Without opening his eyes, Shawn told her, "I'm just waiting for my damn allergy medicine to kick in good. Fucking flying-ass pollen from them cotton trees about to kill my ass."

Vanessa walked over to her closet and kicked off her New Balance running shoes and the sweat socks she was wearing over her stockings. She was wearing a business suit, but since her pregnancy she had taken to wearing her running shoes as much as possible. She hung her suit jacket on a hanger and wriggled out the skirt. She left on her satin blouse, but removed her bra. Grunting slightly she removed her panty hose, leaving her panties on and then flopping onto the bed.

"Baby, I'm hungry," she pouted as she grabbed the television remote and flicked on the television set. "This little monster of ours have me eating so much it's a shame. I ate two big-ass bagels with strawberry cream cheese at a meeting this morning. Then I turned around and ate one of them gigantic corned beef sandwiches from A&P Deli at lunch. I don't even like corned beef, but I tore that sandwich up. Then around three I had a soup-and-salad combo from the little restaurant across the street from the bank. Hey, you're not even listening to me."

She gave him a slight shove that caused him to open his eyes.

He said, "Girl, what's wrong wit you? I am listening to yo hungry ass. What you want to eat?"

"I don't know," Vanessa whined as she rubbed her slightly lumpy tummy. "I want something sweet and cold, but not no ice cream. You think of something."

He stretched and swung his feet off the bed. "Girl, you getting on my nerves already. By the time you seven, eight months you gone be a hot mess."

"Forget you," Vanessa said as she threw a bed pillow at Shawn's back.

As he pushed his feet into his slippers, he playfully warned her, "Girl, don't think 'cause you pregnant I won't beat that ass. I can chastise you without hurting my seed."

Jokingly she dismissed Shawn. "Nigga, quit wolfing and get me something to eat. And you better hurry up before I take a bite out you."

Shaking his head all the way, Shawn padded toward the kitchen. He had to admit to himself, even though Vanessa was gaining weight from her pregnancy, she was looking sexier than ever. The image of her lying across the bed with her big thighs, that round booty in her sheer black panties, and her ripening breasts partially revealed in her satin blouse sent blood rushing to his nether region. By the time he reached the black double-door refrigerator he had a chubby in his boxer shorts. He pulled open the fridge and began to look for a sweet and cold snack.

A smile leaped onto Shawn's face when he spotted a large glass bowl of fresh strawberries. A slight rummage through the shelves yielded a tub of Cool Whip. Clutching the bowl of huge red berries and dessert topping, he retraced his steps to the bedroom.

"Take that shirt off," he commanded.

Vanessa obeyed. "Now, Shawn, you know I'm hungry."

"I know and I'm gone feed you," he said. He kicked off his slippers and climbed onto the bed. Opening the Cool Whip, Shawn dipped a particularly large strawberry into the frosty whiteness and held it an inch over her lips.

Vanessa leaned up and took a magnificent bite of the tempting berry. Scarlet fruit juice dripped onto her chin. Shawn relieved her chin of its sticky sweetness with his tongue. He fed her four berries in the same fashion, making sure to lick away any drips of fruit juice from her lips and chin. Using his finger, he put a dollop of Cool Whip on each of her breasts. Next he bit into a plump strawberry and squeezed the juice onto her Cool Whip—topped mounds. Using his tongue, Shawn slowly and luxuriously licked away the cool sweetness covering her nipples.

Moaning softly, Vanessa crossed and uncrossed her legs as Shawn continued licking between, around, and under her breasts. He stopped sucking long enough to feed her another couple of strawberries, then he lifted her hips and removed her panties. They were moist as he discarded them on the floor. As always the sight of her wild, unshaven pubic hair and the fat, pouting lips of her vagina made his penis stretch to its physical limit.

With a feathery touch, Shawn traced lines of Cool Whip from her throat, in between the valley of her breasts, past her belly button, to the top of her bush. Lavishly he planted kisses up and down her torso as he erased the trail of Cool Whip. He got down between her legs and gently rubbed a strawberry on her moist slit. Up and down, around and around her clitoris he swirled the juicy fruit. Vanessa's legs trembled as she bent her knees and spread her thighs as wide as possible. In seconds the strawberry was covered in her gooey sweetness. Seductively Shawn bit the strawberry and allowed the juice to drip onto her pussy.

"Ohhhh shit, Shawn," she purred.

With his fingers gently pulling and rolling her clit, Shawn asked, "Can I have some real cream to go with my strawberries, ma?"

"Hell yeah, daddy!" Vanessa exclaimed. She gripped the comforter to hold on for what she was sure would be a wild ride.

She wasn't disappointed as her man began to delicately lick and suck on her clit. "Yeah, daddy. Up and down like that. Oh, daddy, right there! Yeah! Right there, daddy! Keep going around and 'round like that, daddy! Yes! Oh lord, oh lord, oh lord! I'm coming, daddy! Oh shit! I'm coming!"

When at last she stopped jerking, Shawn kissed and licked his way back up to her breasts and neck. With a firm tug she pulled his boxers down and helped him kick them off onto the floor. He mounted her and slid home into her tight wetness.

"Damn, ma, you super wet," he whispered in her ear.

"You like my pussy wet, don't you, daddy?" she breathed.

"Hell yeah," Shawn mumbled as he tenderly pumped in and out of her.

They made love for a while, then Vanessa said, "Daddy, you acting like you scared of this pussy. You ain't gone hurt the baby. I want you to fuck me. Grab my ass and bang yo pussy!"

She didn't have to tell Shawn twice. He reached under her and grabbed two handfuls of her big, soft ass and began to thrust deep and hard into her.

"That's it, daddy!" she screamed. "Fuck yo pussy! I feel you in my stomach! Fuck yo bitch, daddy! Tear this pussy up! Ahhhh!"

The bedsprings began to protest as Shawn dug in and jackhammered his member into her soft wetness. Faster and harder he pumped until sweat began to bathe them both.

"Don't come yet, daddy!" Vanessa screamed. "Please don't come! Let me turn on my stomach!"

A little reluctantly Shawn dislodged himself so Vanessa could flip over on her stomach. Before mounting her from the back he took a brief second to enjoy the sight of his incredibly voluptuous woman lying on her stomach, with nectar dripping from between her thighs. As he slid into her pussy from the back she clenched the muscles between her legs.

"Damn, ma," Shawn moaned. "You know I can't last behind you when you do that shit. You gone make me come too fast."

"All right, all right." She sulked, but she loosened her grip. "Grab my titties, daddy."

Shawn reached under her and grabbed a handful of her breasts and began to stroke her deeply from the back.

"Harder!" Vanessa commanded and lifted up her hips to meet him.

Shawn pinched her nipples as he pounded into her. Suddenly she began clenching and unclenching him from inside. The added sensation was more than he could handle. He exploded into her.

Spent, Shawn lay on Vanessa's back for a few extra moments, making no other movements than licking her neck and nibbling her ears. Finally he untangled himself and fell on the bed beside her. Unfazed by their encounter, Vanessa reached for a strawberry and bit it in half.

Watching her eat, Shawn felt something that seemed to pervade every fiber of his being so strongly that it scared him. His heart started beating fast and his stomach did a couple of flips. Shawn had to catch his breath. Bewildered, he looked around the room. Then he realized what the feeling was—it was happiness, a thing that seemed to have escaped him most of his life. He looked over at Vanessa; she hadn't noticed a thing. She was too busy stuffing her face with strawberries.

Shawn sat up. "Nessa, I'm almost through with the stuff I had to take care of. I'm almost ready to go."

With a mouthful of strawberry, Vanessa asked, "What you saying, Shawn?"

"I'm saying call the travel agent. In a few weeks I'll be ready to go check out Tacoma. I'm ready to get started on this move. Plus, I don't want my kid to be born here."

"Oh, Shawn!" she gushed, as she got on her knees to hug him. "I love you so much, daddy! You make me so happy!"

"Okay, okay. I love you too, Nessa, but yo chubby ass is getting strawberry slob in my doggone ear."

34

"M1, WHAT'S UP, A?" SOLEMN SHAWN ASKED AS HE STROLLED toward the candy counter in A-Land.

Murderman's head swiveled around from the video game he was playing. "I'll be right wit you, SS. Soon as I get killed."

"Take your time. Beez, what's up, Unc? How's the arm?"

Looking down at his arm sling like he'd just noticed he was wearing it, Bezo said, "I'm living, nephew, so I ain't gone complain. You want something?"

"Give me a Snickers and one of the fruit punch juices."

Bezo pulled a cold can from the fridge and took a candy bar from the counter and handed them to his nephew. Solemn Shawn pointed to a newspaper on the counter.

"That today's, Unc?"

"Yeah," Bezo said sourly as he picked up the television remote and began flicking through the channels. He settled on the Maury Povich show. The subject was women trying to find out who exactly their baby's daddy was by having several subjects take DNA tests. Seemingly, it was the only topic on Maury's show of late. About the newspaper, Bezo stated, "Yeah, that depressing-ass smut rag is today's paper. But I must forewarn you that it is smothered with propaganda, a side order of lies, and a tall glass of media-induced paranoia."

"Uh-oh," Solemn Shawn said as he picked up the newspaper. "You been hanging out with your ex–Black Panther Party friends again. You been fucked up since they let all them Westside old-timers out the joint. I'll be in the back."

"Fuck you, nephew. You need to hear this shit. That's what's wrong with you motherfuckers these days. Since the beginning of time, you coons believe that anything a motherfucker with a pen writes is the God honest truth. From the cats that translated the Bible on back—any motherfucker can write some shit and you stupid motherfuckers read it and believe it. I say that over seventy-five percent of the shit you read today is written by pseudoreligious, warmongering homos.

"Take a look in that there paper. They got a big-ass article about how all these pedophile-ass priests be fucking up these kids' lives and they act like they condone that bullshit. Trying to downplay that trifling-ass sick shit. Homosexuality—that ain't nothing new. That shit been going on since them doggone Greeks decided to play butt hockey with one another. I ain't even mad at that. What two consenting adults do to one another is they thing, long as they don't get none of it on my new shoes. My problem ain't the homos. It's the goddamn, motherfucking, nasty, perverted-ass pedophiles. We used to call them shorteyes back in the day. In those days we wouldn't stand for no bastard to be touching and sucking on the kids. We would kill one of them motherfuckers for that shit.

"Now this motherfucking newspaper writing about this shit like it's damn near the norm in today's society. If one of them kids that was touched and had they whole life fucked up grows up and blows one of them cocksuckers' brains out they damn head, then he wrong. And the Catholic church. Don't let me get started on the archdiocese. Besides the fact them motherfuckers been changing God laws since the beginning of time. Now with these fucking dirty-ass priests they don't want to throw them bums out in the fucking streets where they belong. The fucking archdiocese would rather eat shit than let the world see them trying to clean it up. So, nephew of mine, you take that newspaper and enjoy, because I wouldn't wipe my ass with it. But hey, what do I know, I'm just a shopkeeper."

"Okaaaay, Beez," Solemn Shawn said as he eased through the door to the storeroom. He agreed with his uncle on certain issues, but he really didn't feel like standing still for him to rail for the rest of the afternoon. Spreading the paper out on the table in front of him, Solemn Shawn got comfortable and began to brush up on recent events as he snacked.

He had finished his candy bar and most of his juice by the time Murderman entered the room. He continued to look through the newspaper as he waited for his friend to state his business.

"Sorry I took so long, A. I can't kill them zombies on the fourth level for shit in the world."

"You love them shooting games," Solemn Shawn commented.

"Be trying to keep my aim right. Plus, video games is the only place you could gone on a zombie killing spree. I wish some old mutated-ass shit happened like that in real life right here in the Chi. I would be giving it to them zombie fucks until they tore me apart. All head shots. Like what?"

Without looking up from the newspaper, Solemn Shawn said, "I personally wouldn't want to see no shit like that. And I know you called me down here for something other than discussing video games."

"Aw-ight, A. I know that's your polite way of saying get to the point. You know the shit we been on with the Goofies. I think I know who kicked it off. I recognized the cat that shot Bezo and Big Ant the other day. It was the dude that came to holler at us at Charlene's a while back. That pussy that was calling hisself Insane Wayne. The best I can figure it, I think that motherfucker is behind our recent run-ins."

The mention of Insane Wayne piqued Solemn Shawn's interest. "You talking about the guy whose mouth was wired up. You threw a couple at the dude that night and you said it didn't bother him." Solemn Shawn jumped to his feet. "Hold the fuck up! Remember that motherfucker left with our champagne bottle. The cops said they found my prints at the scene of this guy Bing's murder. It must have been on that damn bottle. That motherfucker planted that shit!"

"Right," Murderman added. "Bing is the reason they fucked him up in the first place. That's the nigga he told on. Think about it. This nigga been pulling stunts on both ends and got us going at each other. All he do is pop up and fuck somebody on either side around, then we go at each other while he chilling."

Solemn Shawn took his seat again. "What do you propose we do about this?"

"I know it might sound crazy, but I thought it out. I think we should have a sit-down with the Goofies and let Vee know the business. If both parties agree we can have a peace treaty while we catch this nigga."

Solemn Shawn chuckled. "For a minute there you almost sounded like our old friend Vee would listen to reason. Don't forget he just buried two of his guys."

"Yeah, well, I think he will listen. I know that he got to be tired of burying his guys. Plus, while we doing each other this stud Wayne is cooling out with his heels kicked up, waiting for another opportunity to catch more bodies. Both the Governors and the Apostles need to be hunting this stud like a fucking dog. I think Vee will listen if we tell him the business straight up. What you say, SS?"

"You're the Apostle of War, I'll go with your decision. If you want to meet, set it up."

"I already did, the meet is tomorrow night."

Solemn Shawn drank the rest of his fruit punch. He closed the newspaper and folded it up. He looked Murderman in the eye. "Just for the record, Vee ain't the sharpest knife in the kitchen drawer, so I don't think he gone believe this shit."

"We'll see," Murderman said.

"That'll be twenty-seven dollars, sir," the cashier at the concession stand told Big Ant.

"Gotdamn!" Big Ant exclaimed as he counted out the required

amount. "This is why I stay my ass at home and watch the sorry-ass Bulls. Twenty-seven bucks for two bratwursts, two slices of pizza, and two watery-ass beers. Then they got the nerve to have crackhead-sized portions. Murder, get yo pizza, yo. I shoulda made you pay for yo own shit since you picked this motherfucking place to meet. I hate the United Center."

"Enjoy the game, sir," the cashier said with a note of conde-scension in her voice.

"Yeah, whatever, honey," Big Ant shot back at her. "Where our seats, Murder? And please don't tell me they in the nosebleed sec-tion."

"Just bring yo ass on and quit complaining. It ain't like we coulda sat at half court and had this meet, A. You sure you good, SS?"

"I'm cool. Just enjoying the brilliance of your picking this place to meet."

"Genius, ain't it," Murderman bragged. "See, SS, you ain't the only one with the brains God gave a billy goat. I didn't want to do that old TV show—ass shit. You know, the meeting in the alley in trench coats—type shit. And this was the only place that me and Vee's people could agree on. It was easy to go online and find a sec-tion where nobody had really bought no tickets for."

"High-ass place," Big Ant grumbled. "The United Center be killing me. They got prices like Jordan still playing here."

"Aw quit whining, A, and come yo ass on. Our seats right through here," Murderman said as he looked at their ticket stubs.

Big Ant groaned when he saw how far away from the floor they were seated. "Damn, nigga, did you get us the farthest seats they had in this motherfucka? I wish I woulda bought some binoculars."

In their seats they began to enjoy the game. A few minutes into the second quarter, Vee, followed by Teddy and O, made their way to their seats in the same row. Vee sat to Solemn Shawn's right with an empty seat between them. Teddy and O sat to Vee's right.

"Vaton," Solemn Shawn said.

"Shawn," Vee returned. "Nice place you niggas picked. We can meet without worrying about walking into a setup."

"Yeah, I was just mentioning that to Murder."

Nodding in the Apostles' direction, Vee said, "I see you got ole Michael Moore and Big Ant here. Niggas still wit you, huh? I thought by now somebody woulda done murdered Murder."

Not letting the slight pass, Solemn Shawn observed, "And I see you still got Thirsty Teddy with you as well. You must have gave back all that time on that rape."

"DNA tests is a motherfucka," Teddy said. "Same way I beat that murder rap."

"Well, enough of the motherfucking small talk," Vee interrupted. "I didn't come here for that shit. I didn't really want to come, but I didn't want it said that Vee didn't want to at least hear a motherfucka out when it comes to peace."

Murder snickered. "Yeah right. But anyway, look, Vee. I know who kicked off this latest shit between us. A while back this nigga that used to be wit y'all named Insane Wayne tried to link up with us. We denied him, told him we don't fuck wit pancakes, and the nigga left with rocks in his jaws."

"What the fuck do Wayne got to do with anything? That nigga was a bitch-ass trick and he got what he deserved. Y'all shoulda took that fag in."

Murderman chose to ignore Vee's smart comment. "Well, I checked some shit out and found out that the kid he tricked on was the first nigga that got got. Behind the wheel of the car he took from Insane Wayne. Don't that sound like too much of a coincidence?"

Vee snapped, "First of all, quit calling that pussy-ass nigga Insane Wayne. That nigga's name is Wayne. Ain't shit insane 'bout his bitch ass. And I know for a fact that bitch-ass nigga ain't killt no Governor. You motherfuckas got some nerve killing a Governor and sitting up here acting like it wasn't y'all that started all this shit. Y'all must think I'm some kind of fucking lame. Y'all trying to pin this shit on some ho-ass nigga we got rid of. What the fuck do I look like?"

"Hold on, Vee," Solemn Shawn said. "You think we doing this for the sake of doing it? If Murder says that's what happened then that's what happened. We didn't even have a reason to get at your guys."

"You motherfuckas is lying!" Vee fumed. "I don't know who the fuck you think we is! Now you motherfuckas is up in here talking about peace after killing some of mine! You got to be crazy!" Vee stood up, prompting Teddy and O to do so. "You niggas is damn lucky that we up in the United Center. We out this bitch."

Never leaving his seat, Solemn Shawn called after Vee. "Just like the old days, Vaton. You never could see the forest for the trees."

"Yeah, and you always thought you was so motherfucking smart when you really was dumb as hell," Vee retaliated. "Ain't gone be no peace treaty. The only peace there gone be is when you Assholes is resting in it."

Murderman surged forward, but Solemn Shawn blocked his path. To Vee, he said, "Okay, Vee. We tried to talk sense to your stubborn ass. We had a chance to put this shit behind us, but you never could listen to anybody. That's a real character flaw."

"Yeah, well, fuck you. You niggas is dead," Vee threatened as he headed for the exit curtain.

"Don't no bitch-ass Goofy threaten no Apostles!" Murderman raged. "SS, let me go! You know the only reason this nigga talking shit is because we up in here!"

Noticing the four other fans in their section were paying more attention to them than the game, Solemn Shawn tightened his grip on Murderman's arm. "Chill that wild shit, M1! Fuck Vee! I already knew that stupid nigga wasn't going to believe you. Now calm yo ass down before one of these cats go get the security. Or did you forget you got a damn MP5 down outside in the car?"

Mumbling all the while, Murderman regained some semblance

of calm. Big Ant tried to hand him a cup of beer, which Murder-man smacked to the floor.

"Now why the fuck you do that?" Big Ant groused. "That funky cup of beer was five fucking dollars. If you ain't want the mother-fucker I woulda drunk it."

"Shut up, Big Ant," Solemn Shawn said.

35

"SORRY I DON'T HAVE TIME TO HELP YOU LOAD UP, TABBY," Samantha said as she dumped the remainder of her cup of coffee down the kitchen sink drain. "If you woulda got yo butt up I woulda had the time."

Tabitha yawned and stretched over by the toaster where she was waiting for her Pop-Tarts to pop up. "It's cool, Sam. I got it. I ain't gone even lie. Wadn't no way I was gone get up this morning and do nothing. That's why I spent all day packing yesterday before I went out to celebrate last night."

Samantha leaned against the counter. "So how was the party last night? You know I wanted to go, but I had to finish up some stuff for work, and the only babysitter I could get was Ma. And you know she doesn't really watch Lil Shawn—it's more like he watches her get drunk."

"Girl, the party was off the meat racks. Shawn had it set up so drinks for me and my friends was free all night. Whatever we wanted. Charlene's is tight as hell. Since most of them niggas that was there is down with our brother wadn't nobody really trying to holler too tough, but you could tell they wanted to. Then I was chilling up in VIP with Shawn and them. That Big Ant is a fool. He damn near had me throwing up, he had me laughing so hard. For a minute I thought Shawn was gone get on that big-brother shit with me, but he let me party without bothering me. That was real cool of him. Man, Sam, their world is so much like ours and at the same time it's different as hell, you know. I'mma miss that brother of ours when I'm away."

"Looking forward to summer school?" Samantha asked as she grabbed her car keys off the countertop.

Tabitha placed her slightly charred Pop-Tarts on a saucer and grabbed her glass of orange juice. "Not really. Who wants to be in boring-ass Ohio for the summer. But I am looking forward to the big money a sister gone be making when I graduate with my master's."

"I know that's right," Samantha said as she walked over and gave her twin a kiss on the jaw. "I gotta bounce 'fore I miss my Metro train. Make sure you set the alarm system and lock the door. You be safe, and call me when you get to school."

"I will, Sam. Holla back." Tabitha took her saucer and OJ into the living room and got comfortable on the couch. She turned on the morning news and ate her breakfast. She chased the news with some Oprah and ended up napping halfway through the program. Two hours later, she awoke and looked at her watch.

"Shit!" she said aloud. "I gotta get outta here."

Upstairs in her room, Tabitha changed into a pair of jeans and a Kent State T-shirt and matching billed hat. She pulled a pair of wheat Timberland boots on her feet and put her small gold-and-diamond cross around her neck. Next she began to move her totes and luggage downstairs and eventually out onto the front porch. From the porch she began to pack her things in the rear of her Montero Sport.

As Tabitha was carrying a particularly heavy tote to her truck a tall, thin man walked up. He was smiling and plainly dressed in a black T-shirt, blue jeans, and black shoes. On his hands he wore thin baseball batting gloves. A black fitted cap partially hid his eyes, but his smile was pleasant enough despite his brown teeth.

Teddy asked, "Can I help you with that, sister?"

Tabitha started to refuse his help, but the tote was heavy. She smiled back. "Yeah, I could use a hand. I ain't one of them independent-ass girls. I'll let a man help me."

He laughed at her joke. "Let me get the end of that with you."

Together they carried the tote to the truck and pushed it inside.

Wiping her forehead, Tabitha said, "I've got a few more things on the porch you can help me with, then I'll hit you wit a few bucks."

Cheerfully, Teddy said, "Sounds good to me. A brother could use a few bucks to get him something cool to drink."

They made quick work of loading up the last of her things. As Teddy was carrying the last piece of luggage to her truck, Tabitha stepped inside the foyer and set the burglar alarm. When she stepped back onto the porch, Teddy was at the bottom of the steps waiting.

With her back turned as she locked the door, she asked, "Okay, my brother, what you charging me for using your muscles?"

"Your life," Teddy answered, as he pulled a .380 from the back pocket of his jeans.

Not sure that she'd heard him correctly, Tabitha turned slowly. "What?"

"You heard me, bitch!" Teddy said nastily. "I said yo life! You can keep yo couple of dollars to pay yo way into hell, bitch!"

Tabitha's eyes bucked at the sight of the gun in her former helper's hand.

"Bitch, yo man is sure hard to catch, but you ain't!" Teddy spit.

"Wh-What man? I ain't got no man."

Teddy scoffed, "Bitch, get off that bullshit. I know that Solemn Shawn is yo man."

A tiny ray of hope broke through the clouds. Slightly disillusioned, she allowed herself to believe that if she could convince this man that Shawn wasn't her boyfriend, but her brother, he would put his gun up and walk away.

"You got it wrong!" she pleaded. "Shawn ain't my man, he's my brother!"

The gloating look on Teddy's face disappeared for a second, but it returned just as fast. "That's even better, bitch," he said as he pulled the trigger.

Tabitha saw the muzzle flash, then a millisecond later she heard the first bang as a slug struck her in the chest and flung her backward into the door. She heard more loud bangs—seven more, to be exact, as more projectiles tunneled into her flesh. Looking down at her Kent State shirt she realized that it had been ruined by the blood and bullet holes.

Damn, she thought, *I liked this shirt.* She slumped against the door and watched her blood mingle with the broken glass on the porch as she died.

Teddy stuffed his .380 in his back pocket and jogged away down the street.

36

"ROCKS RIGHT HERE, MELLOW," GROVE SAID FROM THE SIDE-walk to the customer in his late-model Buick that pulled to the curb. "You gotta park that car and get out though, fam. We don't serve no cars."

The middle-aged man was definitely interested. "I hope it ain't no weak shit or that B12 shit. It's like a baby drought out here. I been driving around this motherfucka all morning. What y'all working with?"

Grove turned his A's hat to the back—a prearranged signal. "We got dimes look like dubs and it's butter, fam. Park that whip and go through the gangway."

"Cool," the customer said excitedly. He threw his car into park and climbed out.

In the gangway, Bull was standing with a Ziploc freezer bag half-full of dime bags of crack. "How many?" he rumbled.

"Give me two fat ones," the customer said gleefully. "I wish I had more cash on me, but my fat-ass stingy wife wouldn't cut loose of the cash station card."

Bull snatched the twenty dollars from the customer and shoved two dimes into his outstretched hand.

Satisfied with the appearance of his purchase, the customer turned to leave the gangway, but suddenly GCU detectives sprang from all directions.

"Get your fucking hands up!" they shouted as they rushed the frightened man.

The customer promptly popped the two dime bags into his mouth and tried to swallow them. Several GCU detectives responded by choking and pummeling the man until he spit the two bags onto the ground.

Swiftly, they arrested the customer for possession of a controlled substance; his car was towed and he was on his way to jail in a matter of minutes.

As quick and precise as his unit was, Grove still wasn't satisfied. He complained, "Al, you, Torres, and the rest of you motherfuckas better hurry up on the next one. Y'all gone let the whole fucking world know that we here. Shit."

In a few moments the stage was set again——Grove was trying to catch customers while Bull held the bundle. The other GCU dicks were secreted around the perimeter waiting for another addict to take the bait in their reverse sting.

Several more arrests went off without a hitch before a silver Honda Accord glided to the curb in front of Grove and the passenger-side window rolled down. As Grove stepped closer he felt a blast of cool air from the air conditioner.

"Rocks, homie?" Grove asked.

"Y'all got Apostles' work, dog?" the driver asked.

Grove stooped down to get a look at the driver, but he couldn't get a real good look at his face from his vantage point. "Yeah. Apostles' coke. The best shit on the Southside, fam. We got that sizzle for yo missile. Park yo car, we in the gangway."

Insane Wayne put the car in park. Simultaneously Grove turned his A's hat to the back, signaling his unit that they had another one on the line. As Insane Wayne slipped from the car, he held his pistol alongside his leg. He walked to the curb and pointed his pistol at Grove's back.

"Gun! Gun!" Torres shouted as the GCU sprang into action.

"What the fuck?" Grove said as he wheeled around to face Insane Wayne.

There was a malevolent grin on Insane Wayne's face as he pulled the trigger on his pistol. Two slugs sped quickly into Grove's chest, knocking him backward over a short chain-link fence.

Eduardo Torres and Al Severs responded to their comrade's distress by proceeding to fill Insane Wayne full of holes. As Wayne lay on the ground twitching, Grove could see broken rubber bands and twisted wires in his bloody mouth.

Bull came running from the gangway with his gun drawn. He looked down at his partner. "You all right?"

"Help me up," Grove said, holding out his hand.

Bull pulled him to his feet.

"Awwwww!" Grove yelled. "Easy, easy. That shit hurt. That motherfucker tried to shoot my damn heart out. He wasn't playing no games either. Whoever this bastard is, he must really hate these Apostle fucks." Grove unbuttoned his California Angels baseball jersey, revealing his body armor. "Fucking piece of shit ruined my gotdamn jersey. I just bought this motherfucker. Crazy-ass, gang-banging-ass nigga."

"Hey, Grove!" Detective Al Severs called out. "How 'bout a thanks for saving yo punk ass. You ungrateful asshole."

Grove held up his middle finger. "'Bout time you fucks did something right. Now I'll leave you guys to mop up. I'm going to the hospital. I think this dickhead broke a couple of my damn ribs. C'mon, Bull."

37

"You gone be straight, A?" Dante asked from the front seat.

Solemn Shawn didn't reply. Sitting in front of the funeral home, in the backseat of Mumps's Cadillac CTS with Vanessa, he was stunned senseless.

"SS, you straight?" Dante repeated.

"Yeah, I'm cool, A. Let's just get this over with." Solemn Shawn opened the car door and stepped out into an unseasonable rain shower. Raindrops splattered his shaded eyeglasses before he had a chance to open his umbrella. With a touch of a button on the handle, the large, black rain shield popped open and he held it over Vanessa's head as she climbed out of the Cadillac. Mumps and Dante joined them on the curb.

Absentmindedly Solemn Shawn said, "Where's Murderman? Nigga must be running late or something."

"He's here, A," Mumps assured him. "You might not see him but he definitely here. He's heading up the security team personally."

"Oh," Solemn Shawn said, like he'd asked a stupid question.

Uncomfortably Dante shifted his weight from foot to foot. He felt helpless seeing his oldest and dearest friend in this condition. Even if Solemn Shawn had been wildly grieving it would have been better than this—this nothingness.

"Baby, c'mon, let's get out of the rain," Vanessa said softly.

Solemn Shawn looked around like he had forgotten it was raining. "I love the rain," he commented. "Tabby was just like me—she loved the rain. We both loved rainy days. I used to have to chase her into the house when it was raining when she was little. Now, Sam, that girl couldn't stand to get wet. One raindrop and she was headed for the crib."

"It's okay, baby," Vanessa said as she slipped her arm through his.

Solemn Shawn continued, "I heard somewhere that rain is the tears of angels. I guess that's why it always seems to be raining on the day you bury a good person."

None of them knew what to say to that so Mumps tried to lighten the somber mood. "A, let's gone 'head and get inside, SS. You got ole Mambo standing outside in the rain in a pair of four-hundred–dollar gators, baby."

"My fault," Solemn Shawn said. He looked around one more time. "Let's go on inside, y'all."

They walked through the funeral home doors into the cavernous chapel and down the middle of the aisle. The casket was still open for viewing; no less than twenty funeral wreaths surrounded the coffin. Solemn Shawn tried to detour into a pew, but Vanessa pulled him along to his baby sister's coffin. Looking down at Tabitha for the first time, he sobbed as he stood there.

Tears stained Solemn Shawn's cheeks, and he quickly wiped them away. Still holding on to his arm, Vanessa could feel his body tremble. After standing there for a few minutes, he was crying freely.

"Tabby Cat," he sobbed. "Tabby Cat, I'm so sorry that I wasn't there when you needed me. Forgive me, Tabby. I love you. I'm so sorry. . . ."

"You sorry all right, motherfucka!" Lillian Terson-Liston screamed. "You got my baby killed, you bitch!"

Solemn Shawn turned to see his mother being physically restrained by his stepfather and Samantha.

He called out to his sister's living image. "Sammy, I'm sorry I wasn't there to help her! I loved her, Sammy!"

Samantha locked eyes with her brother, then looked away. To their mother, she said, "C'mon now, Mama. We don't need to do this right here, right now. Leave Shawn alone. You know that he didn't hurt Tabby or mean for her to get hurt."

"That motherfucka killed my baby just as sure as if he woulda pulled the trigger himself!" Lillian screeched. "He ain't no child of mine! I hate you! I knew your murderous ways would bring hurt on this family one day! I hate you! I shoulda had an abortion when I found out that I was pregnant with your demonic ass!"

"Mama, I didn't do anything," Solemn Shawn pleaded. "I don't even know what happened."

"You had everything to do with it! I been telling Tabitha for years to cut yo ass loose and stop running up behind you, but she wouldn't listen to me! My own child wouldn't listen to me and look what it got her! My baby's life is over because of you! I don't want you here! If this motherfucka stay then I'm leaving!"

Lillian broke away from her husband and snatched the largest funeral wreath off its stand and threw it at Solemn Shawn. The banner that read "From Your Loving Brother," fluttered to the floor. The wreath missed him even though Solemn Shawn made no attempt to dodge it. His mother flung herself at him before anyone could stop her.

"I hate you!" she screamed in Solemn Shawn's face as she slapped him viciously. The slap sent his eyeglasses flying. She would have slapped him again, but Samantha, her husband, and other family members managed to pry her off of Shawn. "Get out of here, you blasphemous dog! I won't allow you to desecrate my child's memory! I'll kill you first! Get the fuck out of here!"

Speechless, Solemn Shawn stood there with tears slipping from his eyes. For lack of anything else to do, Mumps picked up his eyeglasses and handed them to Vanessa.

Vanessa gave Solemn Shawn his glasses and tugged at his arm. "Let's go, baby. Staying here will only cause more confusion. You can't really blame your mother—she's lost her child. She has the right to be angry even if her anger is misplaced. Right now she feels the need to express and direct that anger. Let's just go home. You've paid your respects to your sister. There's nothing else you can do here but be the scapegoat."

Dante put his hand on Solemn Shawn's shoulder. "Vanessa's right, A. Staying here with yo mama ain't gone do no good. Kiss yo sister and let's go."

Just then Big Ant hobbled up the aisle on a set of crutches. "SS, they right, baby boy. Yo mama ain't finta act rationally right now—she too hurt. Don't worry, Tabby knows you love her, A. Gone get out of here."

Wiping the tears from his face first, Solemn Shawn returned his glasses to his face and walked over to Tabitha's coffin. Again he stared down at his beloved little sister. He leaned down and kissed her cold cheek.

"I love you, Tabby Cat," he whispered. "Don't ever forget that I love you. Please forgive me if something I did got you killed, sweetie. I would have given my life for yours without hesitation. I . . ."

He touched her cold hands as he felt himself breaking down again. This time, though, Mumps and Dante collected him from the casket and steered him up the aisle and out of the chapel. Vanessa paused long enough to hug Samantha and then she followed her distraught man.

They were in Mumps's Cadillac about to pull off when Samantha dashed out into the rain and knocked on the car window. "Shawn!" she said.

Solemn Shawn opened the car door and stood up. He hugged his remaining sister tightly. She hugged him back just as tightly. Finally she broke his embrace and looked up into his face. Raindrops continued to fall, threatening to drench them both.

Sadly, Solemn Shawn said, "You better get back inside before you be soaked to the skin. You know you don't like rain, Sammy Bear."

"Yeah, you know I hate rain," Samantha replied with a forced smile. "I just had to let you know that we all don't feel the same as Ma. You know she dramatic as hell, especially when she drunk. We know you weren't responsible for this and we don't blame you. Your lifestyle, yes, but not you."

"Sammy Bear, I—"

"Shh, big brother, let me talk while I can. I know how much you loved Tabby. Sometimes I thought you loved her more than me. At first I was jealous, then I realized you didn't love her more, you just knew that she needed someone to love. Me, I have my husband and Little Shawn, but who did Tabby have? Only you. That's why I can stand here today and forgive you for any of your actions, directly or indirectly, that caused me to lose my twin sister. I love you, Big Brother. Now go try and get you some rest. I'll make sure that Tabby is laid to rest properly."

Samantha stood on her tiptoes and kissed him on the cheek. Hugging herself, she went back inside the funeral parlor.

Solemn Shawn stood on the curb looking after her until Vanessa rolled the window down and coaxed him into the car.

38

Dante yawned as the bleached-blond waitress with the snaggletoothed grin set his plate of steak, eggs, and grits in front of him. She placed a cream cheese Danish in front of Solemn Shawn.

"I forgot your toast, sugar," she said sweetly. "Is that white or wheat?"

"Make it wheat and bring me four slices."

"No problem, sugar," she said as she hurried off to get the toast.

"Look at you macking down the waitress," Solemn Shawn cracked.

"Get the fuck out of here, A," Dante said as he began cutting his steak and pouring A1 sauce on it. "You know she just playing us up for a fat tip. That's all you gone eat, yo?"

"I ain't really hungry," Solemn Shawn said as he looked out the window of the truck stop at his F-150 and Dante's Maxima. "I really ain't had no appetite for the last couple of weeks. That's all right though, Nessa eat enough for both of us. I woke up the other night and she was chewing on my damn arm."

"What time your flight leave?" Dante asked as he dug into his plate.

The grinning waitress returned and Solemn Shawn waited for her to leave before he answered. "This afternoon, but you know we got to get to the airport at least two hours early to go through all that security shit. I know the last week or so I been missing in action, but

I ain't felt like doing nothing. I was gone wait around for the ground-breaking ceremony on the center, but I just want to move around for a minute. What's our friendly state representative talking about?"

After a sip of orange juice, Dante said, "We just dropped three hundred fifty stacks on that chump. He bet' not be talking about nothing, but doing what he s'posed to do with that scratch. The move we making with that hydro shit was so sweet, once we got to three fifty, we just went ahead and made one more move to flip our money. Even after paying everybody we still had a little over three fifty left for the Head Apostles. We split that shit up equally, but each one of the Heads hit you up with a little something so yo share come out to two hundred thousand."

"That's cool, Tay. I 'preciate that. I could sure use a few extra bucks to get this stuff off the ground in Tacoma."

"So you really gone make that move, huh?" Dante asked as he spread strawberry preserves on a slice of wheat toast.

Solemn Shawn sighed. "Yeah. I been thinking about it for a while now. I got to do something different, A. I mean, I got a kid on the way. I might as well try some new shit while I still got my life and my freedom. Plus, Vanessa and me are going to be married soon. I got her a ring. I might as well get married while we in Tacoma."

Solemn Shawn waved the waitress over to freshen his cup of coffee. She was still grinning.

"Are y'all staying out there?" Dante inquired.

"Nall, just checking it out and looking at a few houses and shit. Other than that I plan to be chilling for the next two weeks. Kick my feet up or take some long walks. If this place is as sweet as Nessa say it is I'm definitely going to move there."

"I heard it rain up there all the time," Dante observed.

After dumping nondairy creamer and sugar in his coffee cup, Solemn Shawn said, "Yeah, I heard that too. You know me though. I love those rainy days, A. I'm kind of looking forward to that. I think I've had my fill of Chicago."

"You said it, SS. Some days I be so sick of this crazy-ass city and crazy-ass weather I could scream sometimes, A. I think it be the weather that have these motherfuckas going crazy and shit. Hot as hell one day, freezing the next. Lake effect snows, unseasonably cold, cooler by the lake, and ozone action days. All that shit be driving cats out of their damn minds."

Solemn Shawn laughed—a dry, hollow sound. "I never thought about it that way. I know it got to be something 'cause cats in Chicago is crazy. Wipe your chin, A."

Dante used a napkin to wipe a jelly smudge off his chin. "Thanks, A. Don't worry 'bout shit while you're gone, A. We got it."

Solemn Shawn watched the parking lot for a few moments while Dante continued to make short work of his steak and eggs. Without looking at Dante, he asked, "Any word on who killed my sister?"

Dante's fork paused. "Not exactly. Murderman and his crew of killers been torturing motherfuckas, kneecapping cats—all that type of shit and still no word. Basically we nailed it down to the Governors. We saying that because of those twins of theirs that got merc'd."

"You really think it was Vee and 'em?"

"Yeah, near as we can guess. The Heads didn't want to bother you so we got together and hollered. Everybody said it seemed likely. Murderman been on his ass for two days now. We looking for him to drop real soon. As soon the opportunity presents itself we gone make sure Vee becomes one of the living challenged. We done allowed this nigga to breathe for too damn long anyway."

"What about his peoples, Tay? If y'all gone make such a major move you got to get rid of the next in line too. Art of war, A. If you get the emperor, you got to get his general too."

Appreciating Solemn Shawn's wisdom, Dante said, "We got that covered too. There's only two studs besides Vee that need to get it too. A chump named Teddy and one they call O. These niggas is supposed to be heavy hitters for the Governors. They ain't no problem though. We assigning death squads on they ass. They ain't ready for this shit. The problem is we been letting these cats live for so long they think we sweet. When it goes bad for these studs it might make things hot for a while, but you'll already be out of town so you'll be cool."

"Sounds like y'all got everything worked out," Solemn Shawn said as he took another sip of his coffee. He reached into his pocket and pulled out some money. He tossed two twenties on the table and stood up. "I'm 'bout to make a few runs. Probably go check out my nephew and my sister before I got to go and get ready to leave."

Dante stood up and hugged his friend. After breaking his embrace, he asked, "What about yo scratch? It's in certified cashier's checks. You feel like getting it now?"

Solemn Shawn glanced at his wristwatch. "Nall, I ain't got time now. I got to drop Nessa off the doctor. Drop the checks off at A-Land and I'll scoop them up before I go out of town. Leave them with Bezo and tell him I said to put it up for me. Hit me if you need me, A."

Dante sat down and ate his last spoonful of eggs as he watched Solemn Shawn zoom away in his pickup truck.

39

"WHERE ARE YOU, SHAWN?" VANESSA ASKED WITH A NOTE OF irritation in her voice. "The airport shuttle is downstairs."

"Fuck! Sorry, baby. I was halfway home before I realized that I'd left something that's pretty important."

"You better not make us miss our flight, Shawn," Vanessa said. She was walking around the condo as she talked to him, making sure that she hadn't forgotten anything. The doorman had already taken their luggage down to the shuttle van. She reminded him, "You know that we've got to get there early to go through all them doggone security checks."

"I know, I know. I'll be there. Just check the luggage and wait for me in the first-class lounge. Get you something to eat so you won't be cranky. See you soon."

Solemn Shawn closed the flap on his cell phone and tossed it on the seat. Like an Indy 500 driver, he steered his truck through afternoon traffic. The throaty roar of the chrome-tipped Harley-Davidson exhaust pipes sounded like a small fighter jet as he gunned his way through every available opening in traffic.

"Damn!" he said aloud. "I got to really make good time to not miss this flight. I'm gone have to park at the airport too. Playing with Lil Shawn and that doggone go-cart."

He had unintentionally let the time slip away as he played with his nephew. Now he still had to make it to A-Land and from there to Midway Airport in forty-five minutes. He wasn't worried about getting his money from the game room, he was more concerned about retrieving Vanessa's engagement ring. It would make their trip less than perfect if he couldn't present her with it during their stay in Tacoma. Just the thought of her reaction brought a smile to his face.

"Sometime today, lady," he said to the driver of a Suzuki Tracker who seemed to have fallen asleep at the red light. "C'mon, c'mon."

Deftly he maneuvered around the Tracker and pulled a series of harrowing passing moves that allowed him to make it to A-Land in less than ten minutes.

All of the parking spaces on the block were taken, so Solemn Shawn decided to double-park in front of the game room. He was putting on his hazard lights when he saw a police cruiser coming up the block. The cruiser pulled alongside his truck.

"You can't park here," the officer on the passenger side announced.

"I'm just running in the door for a moment," Solemn Shawn countered.

"If you leave it, we'll ticket it."

"I'll just be a moment, Officer," Solemn Shawn promised.

"I don't care. If you leave it, I'm ticketing you."

"Fuck me!" Solemn Shawn said as he threw the truck into gear. He whipped around the corner, into the alley, and pulled up in the rear of the game room. Careful not to block the alley, lest the haters try to write him a ticket, he parked and got out. A quick search of his key ring yielded the key to the back door of the game room. He inserted the key into the lock and tried to turn it. When it resisted he remembered this lock always stuck a little, so he jiggled the key until the tumblers gave way.

"Bezo!" he called as he stepped inside the rear room of A-Land. As he closed the door behind himself, a black Oldsmobile Aurora with tinted windows stopped to check him out.

Behind the wheel of the Aurora, Vee said, "I knew that was that nigga's truck, Cave. Did you see that? That was Solemn Shawn."

"Who?" Cave asked nervously.

Vee was plainly excited as he reversed and pulled into the alley. "Nigga, Solemn Shawn. That's the number one Apostle. We done caught this nigga slipping. He by hisself and parked in a alley. You got yo heat, little nigga?"

"Yeah, I got my pistol," Cave answered.

"Good," Vee said as he pulled alongside the building beside A-Land. He parked so he could watch Solemn Shawn's truck. "Little nigga, when that stud come out the door hit his ass up before he get in that truck. I mean empty that blowpipe, nigga. You a killer, right?"

"Hell yeah, I'm a killer," Cave said with way more confidence than he felt.

"Well, you better bake that nigga then or we gone Cold War yo ass. You got me, little nigga?"

"Don't even trip," Cave said as he left the car. He was glad that he got out of the car before Vee could see his knees shaking. Quickly and quietly he ducked by the rear bumper of Solemn Shawn's pickup truck with his pistol in his hand.

Inside the game room Solemn Shawn walked up to the candy counter. Bezo was sitting on a stool, juggling quarters in his hand while he watched an episode of *Springer* on a thirteen-inch color television atop the refrigerator. His arm was still in a sling.

"Bezo, you didn't hear me calling you?" Solemn Shawn asked.

"Nall, nigga," Bezo said. "If I woulda heard you, I woulda answered you."

"You must be drunk," Solemn Shawn observed.

"Ain't nobody drunk, Shawn. The minute I don't jump to it here you go saying that I gotta be drunk or something."

"Have you been drinking?" Solemn Shawn asked plainly.

"What that got to do with anything?"

"Have you been drinking?"

"Nigga, yeah I been drinking, but I ain't drunk," Bezo protested. "There's a difference between drinking and being drunk. If I was drunk, so what. I handles my business like I handles my liquor. Like old dude Eric the Entertainer say, 'I'm a grown-ass man.' I'm yo elder. Fuck you mean, have I been drinking. Nigga, this a video game arcade not corporate America. So fuck it. I been drinking. Hell yeah, and I'm gone continue to drink, gotdamnit."

"All right, Beez. I ain't got time for this. I'm on my way to catch a flight and I'm running late. I came to get that ring and Dante left something here for me."

Bezo swayed to his feet. He pulled up the mat at his feet and used the edge of a spatula to pry up one of the floorboards. He pulled a white envelope and Vanessa's ring box from the hole in the floor and handed them both to Solemn Shawn.

"Thanks, Beez. I gotta run."

"Hold on, boy. You ain't got to be nowhere that damn important that you can't give yo peoples a hug before you leave, nigga. Shit, with the way things going these days this might be the last time I see yo ass."

Bezo lurched over to Solemn Shawn and draped his arms around him. He planted a sloppy kiss on Solemn Shawn's jaw.

"All right, Bezo," Solemn Shawn said as he untangled himself from the drunken game room proprietor. "I gotta go, man."

"You take care, nigga. I love you!" Bezo called after him.

Hurriedly, Solemn Shawn went through the back room and slid out the door. He stopped to lock the door and then popped the locks on his truck.

The chirp of the pickup truck's alarm made Cave stand up and step from behind it. He leveled his pistol at Solemn Shawn's chest.

Preoccupied with his time dilemma, Solemn Shawn didn't look up until he had walked all the way into the trap. He saw the gun in the hand of the young zit-faced boy too late. Time stood still as the young boy pointed the gun at him. He seemed to be waiting.

"Pop that nigga!" Vee yelled from the car.

Cave squinched his eyes and pulled the trigger.

Blam!

Blam!
Blam!
Blam!
Blam!
Blam!
Blam!
Blam!

Solemn Shawn watched the gun leap and jerk in the boy's hand. Instantly he felt the most intense pain of his thirty-something years. Smoking holes, five in all, appeared as if by magic in his shirt. It hurt to breathe and at the same time he was gasping for breath. His stomach felt like it was on fire as his intestines began to bleed in on themselves. He sagged to the ground. The envelope and ring box he was holding fell from his hand as he clutched his stomach and chest. He rolled over on his side and balled up.

Blam!
Blam!

Cave shot him in the back two more times, but he was past feeling pain now.

"Little nigga, bring yo ass on!" Vee shouted from the car.

Cave ran and jumped in the car. Vee pulled from behind the building. He stopped alongside Solemn Shawn's body and opened his car door to look down at his old nemesis. Solemn Shawn wasn't moving. Vee started to pull off, but he saw the ring box, and envelope on the ground. Ignoring the envelope, he scooped up the ring box and opened it. The dazzling brilliance of the diamond engagement ring almost blinded him.

"Gotdamn," Vee said. "Shit, he just saved me the trouble of buying Sakawa an engagement ring."

"Let's get out of here, Vee," Cave said shakily.

"Yeah, you right," Vee acknowledged as he burned rubber out of the alley.

Solemn Shawn lay there as his blood began to pool around him on the alley floor. His body was hurting so badly he wanted to cry out, but he couldn't remember how to make his voice work. *Vanessa is gone act a fool if I miss that flight,* he thought. *I bet when she see her ring she won't be tripping too hard,* he said to himself as he passed out.

As Vee's car passed the garbage Dumpster near the end of the alley, Odell ducked down as far as possible, praying that the men in the car wouldn't notice him. He had seen everything. Although he didn't know the shooter, he most definitely knew who Vee was. Once he was sure the coast was clear, he got from behind the Dumpster and approached the body on the alley floor. He had thought it was, but now that he was closer, he could see it was Solemn Shawn the boy had just executed.

"Damn!" Odell said. He turned to make himself scarce before someone else happened upon the body, but something slapped against his leg. The envelope that Solemn Shawn had carried had been blown against his leg by the wind. Curious, Odell bent and picked up the envelope. As he turned it over he saw the corner of a check. Peering into the envelope he saw numerous checks with very large dollar amounts on them. Without hesitation he broke into a dead run. He didn't stop until he was six blocks and four streets away.

Once he was absolutely sure he hadn't been followed or noticed, Odell riffled through the contents of the envelope. He actually pissed on himself when he realized that he had in his possession certified cashier's checks in the amount of two hundred thousand dollars. The urine stain didn't matter, he was already wet from washing cars all day. Instantly he became paranoid. It was time to go home— his woman would know what to do with the checks. Wearing perhaps the biggest smile of his life, Odell started home.

He'd walked a block when his smile disappeared. He stopped and dug through his pockets. Finally he found what he was looking for. Out of his pocket he pulled a mangled, soggy business card—Detective Hargrove's. The least he could do was drop the police a tip on who'd killed Solemn Shawn—that was the least he could do for two hundred stacks. He decided if he had to he would even go into the police station to pick the shorty out of the mug books. No, he was bullshitting himself. Wadn't no way he was going anywhere near the police station. Whatever he did would have to wait until tomorrow though; he had forty-seven dollars in tips he had to spend first.

This time as he walked swiftly, Odell's head was held high.

40

THE EMT LEANED OVER AND CHECKED SOLEMN SHAWN'S pulse again in the rear of the ambulance. It was very faint—almost nonexistent. Skillfully he used his scissors to cut open the wounded man's shirt. He had to gasp and shake his head at the still leaking bullet wounds.

To his partner driving the ambulance, the EMT said, "No need to rush, Dave. This guy ain't gonna make it. Just another gang-banger going to hell."

Without opening his eyes, Solemn Shawn coughed blood onto the gurney and the ambulance floor. Struggling, he croaked out, "A-A-Apostles don't g-g-go to h-hell. We g-go t-t-to heaven."

The EMT let his training take over as he began to try to stabilize Solemn Shawn's vital signs. As he broke out an IV, he shouted, "Dave, get a move on, this guy might still have a chance!"

The ambulance driver switched on the lights and sirens and mashed the gas pedal to the floor.

But there was no need for sirens or speed as Solemn Shawn quietly slipped away to wherever dead Apostles go when they die.

O TURNED THE STEREO IN HIS CAR DOWN. "IT'S BEEN CLOSE to six months since dude been gone and these niggas is still pushing," he said. He hoped too much fear wasn't evident in his voice.

Obviously there was because Vee barked, "Get yo panties out yo ass, nigga. You sound like a bitch right now. What you thought them niggas was gone do when somebody got rid of dude?"

"I'm just saying, Vee, them Assholes ain't playing since dude got offed. We thought them studs was gone fold up, but they been wiling out. Shid, look at Teddy. That nigga in a wheelchair for the rest of his life and he got to wear a shitbag. They fucked him up."

Vee chuckled coldly. "Nigga, you up in here whining like you the one in the chair. Shid, that nigga is lucky. At least he still alive. I swear, you been acting like a real lady lately. Fuck them Assholes. All them niggas is gone be dead before I get through. I'm surrounded by soft-ass niggas. Just like that nigga Cave. Niggas be swearing they killers and shit, then when the pressure on they fold up. You know what, O?"

"What?" O asked as he gripped the steering wheel tighter. He just wanted to drop Vee off wherever he wanted to go and make it back to the safety of his apartment.

"If I ever hear you talking all soft and girly like this again I'm gone Cold War yo ass and feed you to the Apostles. You understand that shit?"

O didn't respond as he pulled up to a stoplight.

"Nigga, do you understand what the fuck I'm tellin' yo ass? I swear, sometimes you act like you slow or something."

"Yeah, Vee. I hear what you saying," O answered evenly.

"Good then, nigga. Don't let this shit come up again. If it do you gone see that I ain't playing wit yo motherfuckin' ass. Now take me to Sakawa's crib."

As O turned the music back up, Vee reclined his seat even more and hoped that he had sounded more confident than he felt. Really he was only feeding off O's fear to make himself feel better. Inwardly he was frightened. After Solemn Shawn's death, the Apostles had decreed all-out war against his Governors. They had even sent a message that it wouldn't end until he, Teddy, and O were dead. They had almost delivered on their promise by catching Teddy and shooting him down like a dog. He survived only because he was wearing a bulletproof vest and was high off of raw cocaine.

On top of all that, someone saw Cave gun down Solemn Shawn; there was an eyewitness. Whoever it was had fingered Cave, causing Bull and Grove to quickly run him down. In a stroke of luck, they even managed to catch him with the murder weapon. He had told that goofy-ass shorty to get rid of that heater. Almost immediately Cave gave him up to the people, telling them he ordered Cave to kill Solemn Shawn or he would have him killed. He had been dodging the police for a while now, but they were getting closer. They had been to his house and all of his family's houses. He rationalized that his best bet was to turn himself in and get a bond, which his lawyer guaranteed he would be able to afford.

Lately he had been staying with Sakawa. In fact he found himself leaning on her more and more. Ever since he gave her the ring Solemn Shawn was carrying, he had pretty much gotten rid of the last of her inhibitions about fucking with him exclusively. If the ring didn't do it, when he brought the bulk of his wealth to her house,

140,000 dollars, that did. Sakawa was a motherfucker. She definitely had faded every woman he'd ever messed with.

"Gotdamn," Vee breathed aloud as he thought about the way she had invited him into her mouth last night.

O leaned forward and turned the stereo down. "What?"

Slightly embarrassed, Vee scowled. "Nothing, nigga. Quit driving like an old woman and get me to my girl's house with yo punk ass. And take me around the back."

O turned the radio back up. *I got yo punk ass,* he thought. *Yeah I got you. Stupid-ass nigga, you gone get us all killt. I got something for yo ass.*

Vee broke through O's thoughts. "Nigga, watch where the fuck you going. The alley right there."

"My fault."

"I know it's your fault, nigga. And turn that gotdamn music down. I don't want every motherfucker and they mama looking out the window 'cause of that loud shit when you dropping me off. I swear you get stupider and stupider every day."

O said nothing as he turned the stereo off. He pulled up to the back gate of Sakawa's apartment building.

Before Vee got out, he said, "Make sure you have yo ass here at ten. I got to go see my lawyer. That means I got to be downtown by ten thirty at the latest. You got that?"

O stared straight ahead down the alley. "Yeah, I got it, Governor. I'll be here at ten on the dot."

Vee got out and O drove away. A few blocks away he parked and pulled out his cell phone. He dialed a number and pushed the Send button. His party picked up.

"This is O. I want to talk," O said on his end.

"What the fuck we got to talk about?" the voice on the other end rasped.

"Peace."

"Nigga, I know you ain't say peace. When we tried to talk about peace, you motherfuckas ain't wanna listen."

"That wadn't my decision. I wouldn'ta set up the meet if I didn't want to talk. That's why I'm calling you now to see if we can do something about this situation."

"Why the fuck should we give you Goofies peace? Our man is dead, nigga."

"What if I gave you Vee?"

"What, nigga? Stop playing fucking games wit me."

Looking into the rearview mirror at his eyes, O repeated, "If I give you Vee will this shit be over?"

There was a pause. After a moment, the voice asked, "Let's just say that Vee was out the way. Who would fill his shoes?"

"Me. But I ain't on that beefing shit. I just want to get this money until my time comes, you know. A real leader doesn't lead his men to their slaughter."

On the other end, the voice laughed. "You got that right, nigga. Long as you keep it like that, there can be peace. That is if what seems to be both of our problem is out the way. So when can we get at dude?"

"Tomorrow morning at ten o'clock. No bullshit. Old dude will be naked. No bullshitting. Is it a go?"

"Yeah, it's good. Remember our deal though, 'cause I will," the voice warned before disconnecting the call.

"Vee! Get up! It's time for you to go," Sakawa said roughly.

"I'm up, I'm up," Vee rumbled.

"No you ain't. You said you had to leave at ten and it's nine fifty."

Rolling out of bed, Vee complained, "Why you just now waking me up?"

Sakawa pulled his pillows over onto her face. "Nigga, you lucky I did. I just got up my damn self."

In the bathroom, Vee slammed the toilet seat up to relieve his bladder. He flushed and moved over to the face bowl. Grabbing a face towel from the rack he wiped his face. A quick toothbrush full of toothpaste later and he was back in the bedroom pulling on his clothes.

He sat on the bed to pull on his shoes. "What you doing today, girl?"

"I got one class this afternoon, then after that nothing," Sakawa said from under her mound of pillows.

"Well, I got some running around to do, then I'll be free later on. Maybe we can grab a bite to eat and check out a movie or something."

Sakawa's response was a muffled grunt.

Vee's cell phone hummed as he stood up and picked up his fitted hat off the dresser. He flipped it open. It was O. "You had better been on time, nigga. Here I come."

He slapped his phone closed. Before he headed out the back door, he pulled a banana from the bunch on the counter. Once he was out the back door and down the two flights of steps, he made for the back gate alongside the apartment building's garage. He stepped into the alley—no O.

"Where the fuck this nigga at?" Vee said aloud. "I'mma have this nigga fucked up if he make me late for my appointment."

"O ain't coming," Murderman announced as he rose up out of the open garbage Dumpster to Vee's left.

Without a word, Vee dropped the half-eaten banana and took off back the way he came. A few seconds later he came back walking with his hands in the air. Dante was following him, pointing a pistol at Vee's back.

Murderman hopped down out of the Dumpster.

"I didn't do it," Vee began. "It wasn't—"

"Nigga, shut up!" Murderman commanded as he aimed his .45 at Vee's head and shot out the back of his skull.

Dante let his .40-caliber loose. Both large weapons punched neat, death-bringing holes into Vee's head and torso. Tires screeched as a large, old-school Bonneville shot down the alley. The driver squealed to a stop at the scene of the massacre.

"Get in, A," Big Ant said from under the steering wheel. "That nigga dead."

Dante ran and hopped in the front seat of the sedan that was in mint condition. Murderman knelt and glared into Vee's face, watching him die. He crossed himself with his gun hand.

"That was for you, SS," he said to the sky. "Now you can rest in peace."

"Bring yo ass on!" Dante roared. "You know the whole neighborhood heard this shit!"

Like he didn't have a care in the world, Murderman strolled to the car and climbed in.

Inside her apartment, Sakawa heard the shots and sat up in bed. She looked down at Vanessa's enormous engagement ring on her finger and thought about the money Vee had stashed in her apartment. "Hotlanta, here I come," she said as she got up and began to dress.

Letter from the Author

The street life is like a gun,
you don't pick it up if you have a choice.
It may look inviting like a woman whose vagina is moist,
but in the end a bullet or cell will silence your voice.

—FROM THE POEM "LIFE'S LESSONS,"

BY Y. BLAK MOORE

In any large, urban setting, street organizations or gangs exist inside the boundaries of so-called civilized society. The violence they inspire touches many people and leaves the otherwise ordinary lives of some citizens in shambles. Gangs are viewed as blights on our urban landscape and in most instances this adjudication is warranted. Gang activities such as intimidation, assault, sale of illegal narcotics, and murder have reached tremendous proportions in the ghettos and housing projects of cities such as Chicago. If you live in a major city in these United States of America, you cannot deny that you've heard or seen the headlines, "Child Slain in Gang Cross Fire."

As a former gang member myself, I "overstand" how easy it is to get caught up in the street lifestyle. As a battle-scarred veteran of this culture I know that it has no positive aspects; if it does they are far outweighed by the negatives. The feeling of comaraderie and loyalty that many members seek never materializes or it is often counterfeit. I can honestly remember that we spent more time beating up or giving "punkinheads" to our own members for rule infractions than attacking our supposed enemies. Our enemies, real or imagined, usually are of the same ethnicity (Black, Latino, or Asian) as we are and live in the same impoverished circumstances.

Millions of dollars and countless man-hours can be and have been spent researching this phenomenon. City, state, and federal laws are being drafted to make sure participants in this way of life are severely punished for crimes against their fellow man. All this legislation serves to do is to treat the symptoms, or put a Band-Aid on a bullet wound as I like to call it.

The answer to this problem? I wish I knew. Maybe one doesn't exist, especially not while the preexisting urban environmental conditions continue to plague our society. Maybe it's a form of tribalism as ancient as man himself. Often the only form of realization that this lifestyle and culture is wrong comes when it is too late (e.g., when you get yourself killed or when those cell doors slam shut). Minority men, Black and Latino, are traditionally the staunchest supporters of this lifestyle, and we must consciously make a decision that our brethren are not the enemy. Translation: Y'ALL STOP KILLING EACH OTHER OUT THERE OVER NOTHING.

Peace,

—Y. Blak Moore

To all the gods out there, know this:
The time we're spending hustle-hating and fighting
is time we could be spending getting paid and uniting,
but I ain't mad at y'all.
I know that enlightenment is a journey not a destination.
—FROM THE POEM "CHECK MY RÉSUMÉ,"
BY Y. BLAK MOORE

Acknowledgments

First and foremost I have to thank and acknowledge the Creator. Fortunately I haven't fallen from Your grace. Though life is uncertain, the Creator's love is not.

Really and truly I have to acknowledge all of the souls who have passed from this physical plane as a direct or indirect result of street organizations and their activities. As impossible as it may sound, I hope that one day a turned hat, hand signs, or colors won't be an excuse to harm someone or to end their life.

And I know that some of you will ask what gang in Chicago is this really. My answer: *none of them.* The street organizations or gangs that exist in Chicago, especially the large Black ones, are the products of the minds of certain men (David Barksdale, Larry Hoover, Jeff Fort, Mickey Cogwell, etc.). Great men in their own right, but most great men are often misunderstood or misinterpreted. The Apostles are a product of my mind. This book isn't a veiled attempt to depict the exploits of any real street organization or its members. *This is purely fiction! No one was killed in the making of this novel.* There are some strange truths to be found here, as any veteran of urban America can attest, but nonetheless, it isn't a true story. After some of the things I've witnessed in the streets, in my opinion it would be a huge disservice to those who have died from this sort of lifestyle, to those indi-

265

viduals who are incarcerated, or to those just surviving day to day on the bricks, to have any reader think this is some type of historical, factual account.

From the cats in the County to the cats who ain't never coming home, I'll make sure you're in my prayers.

Humbly I thank the readers who supported my work (even those who borrowed a friend's copy). Readers truly deserve our homage, for they make us writers relevant. I wish that I could thank each one of you personally. Keep e-mailing and I promise that I'll keep answering. Keep checking for me 'cuz I'mma give you the true grime.

I want to express my deepest and heartfelt thanks to Iceberg Slim and Donald Goines. These two brothers opened the doors for writers like me a long time ago. I've never seen African-American (Black) fiction writers given their just due, but I will. Without Donald, the world would never know Y. Blak Moore. Peace and blessings to both of you.

Melody Guy, BCBE, the editor of my first novel, *Triple Take* (another person applying for sainthood), I'm glad that you have superpowers. Thanks for everything. I'm glad that you took time out of your busy schedule to come down to Philly to give me a face to put with that voice. Don't worry, I'll give you free lessons on slanguage. To Kate Blum, for making everything comfortable for me on my first tour, and to Danielle Durkin.

David Isay and the Sound Portraits family. Dave, you continue to lend me the wealth of your experience and wisdom. I'll make sure that I don't break the chain. To my man Lloyd Newman, I didn't thank you in the first novel for bringing my work to Dave's attention. So here goes: Thank you.

Sara Rimer from the *New York Times*. I'm thankful that you took time out to meet and write about an unknown author from Chicago. You are truly a wonderful and emphatic writer.

Akilah "Killah" Hasan, you remain the major force behind Elemental, Ink. Killah, thanks for all of your help and support. You've truly been that friend in my life that I wish everyone had. Oh yeah, quit trying to renegotiate your contract, fam. It's a wrap, you already the number one draft pick. Good looking out to Poppa Hasan, thanks for all your help.

To my man Zo the Alkhemist (hope I spelled it right), you continue to drop jewels on me when I need them, truly proving knowledge comes before wisdom. You remain one of the elements that keep my uni-verse from crashing in on itself. Thanks for the ELEMENTAL logo too. (It's crazy phat!) Tez, keep on doing your thang. It'll pay off in the end; all hard work does. Khari B., it's time to get your superhero costume out of the layaway. (Now that's a real Black superhero, his costume been in the layaway since *Beat Street* was in theaters.) Chelesea Darling D'Amini (Baby Mama from Hell!), keep coming up with them crazy designs so you can finally pay me some child support. Big Rob, aka Big Business, keep doing your thang. To the spoken-word/poetry community, keep writing and spitting the real. Sloppy, carbon copies save that shit! Love to all the poets.

Devan Moore, keep on trying to reach for your goals. Our sun will truly appreciate your quest for excellence. Oh yeah, we got to get that boy an agent. Peace to Moms, Grimy Mike, Auntie Mary, and 'em.

My sister Ytteb (Tebby), and my nephews Dwight, Devin, and Darius. Teb, you're doing a bang-up job. Keep it moving. It'll turn out all right. Smile. Please stop sighing!

Love to the Low End and the Wells. Extensions forever! Peace to you all—man, woman, and child. To all the gods from the Darkside: 511, 514, 527, 510, 534, the original Gams. Too many of you cats to name. Love to my man K, Nolan Ryan, Ghost, Godvilla. Thanks for holding me down whether it was a few bucks, a few words of encouragement, or the willingness to get in some hatah's ass on my behalf.

Thanks again to all the beauty shop people.

To Shelia Owens, it was truly a blessing and a privilege to work with you. Here's to our future.

I'm still the same Blak. Love you whether I mentioned you or not. If that ain't good enough, K.M.A.

Oh yeah, to any and all hatahs of *Triple Take* and anything else I write. F.Y.I. (Sorry, Melody, but I wouldn't be me if I didn't say how I felt.)

PEACE!

the **Apostles**

A READING GROUP GUIDE

STRIVERS
ROW

Y. BLAK MOORE

QUESTIONS FOR DISCUSSION

THE QUESTIONS AND DISCUSSION TOPICS THAT FOLLOW are intended to enhance your group's reading of Y. Blak Moore's *The Apostles*. We hope they will provide new insights and ways of looking at this fast-paced, insightful novel.

1. Throughout *The Apostles* we see flashbacks to Solemn Shawn's life with his mother and stepfather. Do you think that the abuse Solemn Shawn suffered as a child explains his behavior as an adult? Does it justify his behavior as an adult? Shawn grew up in a juvenile detention center; did the punishment fit his crime?

2. Vee is indignant when Solemn Shawn chooses Murderman instead of him to be the next Head Apostle inside the detention center. Is Vee right to feel outraged by Shawn's decision? Do you think that Shawn made the correct decision?

3. Vee runs the Governors by subjecting its insubordinate members to corporal punishment or "Cold War." Is this an effective way to run an organization? Does fear of punishment make the Governors more or less loyal to Vee? Does Vee seem fair-minded when he orders corporal punishment or Cold War for a Governor?

4. Officers Bull and Grove tread a fine line between legal and illegal behavior when they patrol the streets. Are they "dirty cops," or are they just trying to do their jobs? Should members of the Gang Crimes Unit be allowed to operate under a different set of rules because of the nature of their work? Do officers in other departments respect, or resent Bull and Grove?

5. When Sakawa loses Wayne, she is determined to find a way to make Vee pay. After a few dates, does Sakawa really hate Vee as much as she says? Does Sakawa ever develop feelings for Vee, or is she just after his money? Is Sakawa capable of settling down with just one man?

6. The Governors and the Apostles seem to operate under the principle of "an eye for an eye." Does either gang gain anything when it avenges a murdered member? Does this type of revenge create an endless cycle? Do you think that there can be a legal or ethical justification for murdering someone?

7. Solemn Shawn's sisters accept him as a part of their lives despite his involvement with the Apostles. Should Samantha and Tabitha accept gifts that Shawn buys them with money he earns as an Apostle? Would Shawn care if his sisters told him that they couldn't accept him unless he stopped participating in a gang? Do Shawn's sisters understand the extent of his involvement with the Apostles?

8. Vanessa lies to Solemn Shawn for years about her inability to have a child. Can you understand why Vanessa chose to do this? Should Shawn have been upset that Vanessa lied to him?